PAULUS HO[...]iving in
Vienna. Winner of many literary prizes and commendations, he was
most recently awarded a European Literature Prize in 2009 for *The
Sweetness of Life*.

JAMIE BULLOCH's translations include *Ruth Maier's Diary* and novels
by F. C. Delius, Martin Suter and Daniel Glattauer.

"[...]e standard features of the crime genre are just a framework for the
[...] interesting stuff: not how people die but how they live . . . A truly
[...]ulating find"　　　　　　　　　　　JONATHAN GIBBS, *Independent*

"[...]n extraordinary book, a disquieting psychological shocker set in a
[...]ustrophobic alpine town . . . Hochgatterer presents a kaleidoscope
[...]he town's most unsavoury inhabitants . . . elegantly, subtly told in
[...]ie Bulloch's smooth translation from the original German"
　　　　　　　　　　　　　　　　SUSANNA YAGER, *Sunday Telegraph*

[...]series of case histories, beautifully written, in cool clear prose"
　　　　　　　　　　　　　　　　HAMISH WHITE, *Scotland on Sunday*

[...]ochgatterer is very good"　　　KATRINA GOLDSTONE, *Sunday Tribune*

[...]scrupulous, serious novel, in which crime and detection are
[...]echanisms allowing the author to examine the psychology of his
[...]aracters"　　　　　　　　　　　　JESSICA MANN, *Literary Review*

"Two [with Marek Krajewski] of the most acclaimed talents in the new
wave of international crime writers"　　　　　　　　BARRY FORSHAW

"A brilliant and disturbing exploration of unbalanced minds that
culminates in an explosive climax"　　　　　　　　　　*Shotsmag*

Also by Paulus Hochgatterer in English translation

The Mattress House (2012)

Paulus Hochgatterer

THE SWEETNESS OF LIFE

A KOVACS & HORN INVESTIGATION

Translated from the German by
Jamie Bulloch

MACLEHOSE PRESS
QUERCUS · LONDON

First published in Great Britain in 2008
This paperback edition first published in 2012 by

MacLehose Press
An imprint of Quercus
55 Baker Street
South Block, 7th Floor
London W1U 8EW

Originally published in Germany as *Die Süße des Lebens*
© Deuticke im Paul Zsolnay Verlag, Wien, 2006

English translation copyright © 2008 by Jamie Bulloch

The moral right of Paulus Hochgatterer to be identified as the author
of this work has been asserted in accordance with the
Copyright, Designs and Patents Act, 1988

Jamie Bulloch asserts his moral right to be identified
as the translator of the work

'Father of Night' (pp. 8, 9, 10, 11) by Bob Dylan ©1970 Big Sky Music
'Desolation Row' (pp. 139, 141) by Bob Dylan © 1965;
renewed 1993 Special Rider Music
'Ballad of a Thin Man' (pp. 190, 191, 193) by Bob Dylan © 1965;
renewed 1993 Special Rider Music
'A Hard Rains A-Gonna Fall' (pp. 240, 241 243) by Bob Dylan © 1963;
renewed 1991 Special Rider Music

ISBN 978 1 84724 771 1

10 9 8 7 6 5 4 3 2 1

Designed and typeset by Libanus Press, Marlborough
Printed and bound in Great Britain by Clays Ltd, St Ives plc

"But since the great foundation of fear in children is pain, the way to harden and fortify children against fear and danger is to accustom them to suffer pain."

JOHN LOCKE

ZERO

The child slowly pushes her index finger around the rim of the cup, until the tip touches the liquid's wrinkled surface. She draws a tiny circle, lifts up her finger as soon as she is sure that the skin is going to stick, moves it carefully away from the cup and wipes it off. Although she knows that a lot of people do not like milk skin, she does not mind it herself. The cocoa tastes bitter, just how she likes it, lots of cocoa, not much sugar. When she tilts the cup and stands it upright again, a dark brown mark is left on the inside.

Grandfather is playing Ludo with the child. She got all sorts of new things for Christmas – Lego, books, an animal family and a Game Boy – but ever since she learned how to count he has played Ludo with her. Just because it is Christmas, he told her, there is no reason to do things differently. In the beginning he used to help her count, or he miscounted on purpose to help her win. But he does not need to do that any more.

Three. Square by square, the child moves her pawn. She only ever has one pawn in play at a time and she is always yellow. Five. Grandfather's soldier makes a huge leap over all the squares. The child's pieces are called pawns, the grandfather's are soldiers. It has always been like that. Grandfather's soldiers are blue. Six. The dice rolls to the edge of the tabletop. On the floor doesn't count. That has always been the rule, too. "Again," Grandfather says. "Again," the child says. Two. Shame. Sometimes she rolls two sixes in a row, and then a five afterwards. Grandfather raises his eyebrows. "Eight," the child says. In September she started primary school. She sits next to Anselm with the special glasses for his lazy eye. He has no clue about six or eight. The yellow pawn is now right by home. If Grandfather throws a four then it is dead. Grandfather has knobbly fingers. On the chest of drawers there is a tiny Christmas tree with three silver baubles and a few strands of lametta. "There's no point in me having anything bigger," Grandfather said, and when the child asked him why he had not put any candles on it, he replied, "It would be dangerous if I fell asleep." Four.

The doorbell rings. Grandfather gets up. He glances at the board. His hand grasps the edge of the table for a second. The child cannot see who is at the door. Grandfather is talking. The other person is talking. Grandfather turns round again.

"Four," he says. "Got you!" Then he puts on his jacket and leaves.

The child climbs along the bench to the alcove. She pushes the curtain on the left to one side. It is dark outside. At Christmas time it is always dark very early, but that does not matter if the moon is shining. Opposite, its windows lit up, is the house where she and her parents live, together with her sister, brother, Emmy the dog, Gonzales the jerboa (who belongs to her brother even though he never feeds it), the white dolphin, the reindeer, and the dolly whose name nobody knows. Behind one corner of the house are the black trees which you can walk between. But that bit is not yet the wood. If Emmy is with you it is easy, and you can go from tree to tree as far as the raspberry bush without being frightened. Emmy is a Border Collie; they are the cleverest dogs in the world.

Sometimes the child imagines she lives somewhere completely different, down in the town, in a tiny room at the back of the newsagent's where her mother buys the papers and cigarettes for Grandfather; or on the Mühlau, up where the animals forage, and where the road is not tarmacked any more and leads through two tunnels in the cliffs, because there is no room for it next to the gushing stream. She imagines that the moon is in the sky and that Emmy is there, and that she can eat chestnuts and hay, and that it is a little cold outside and very warm inside, and she imagines that she will go home at some point and Mother will open the door and look very surprised.

Four. The yellow pawn is standing there, having a rest, and it is almost home. The blue soldier is standing there and resting too. Maybe neither of them knows what is in store for them. You could take both of them – one in the left hand, one in the right – climb the hill behind the house and look out over the town. Then you could dig out a cave in the snow with a peephole at the front, and inside you could make tea and eat Christmas biscuits, but only those tiny pastry musical instruments with icing sugar on top.

She will return the pawn and the soldier to their squares: the pawn just by the home column, and the soldier four squares behind, as if nothing had happened. Grandfather will take off his jacket and while he turns away she will put them both back, very quickly and quietly.

The child climbs off the bench, her right hand clutching the pieces, and crosses the room. She takes her new red quilted jacket with the squirrel on it from the stool next to the chest of drawers and puts it on.

It is cold outside. The moon is so bright that the snow between the front door and the wild cherry tree shines like the glass lampshade in the bathroom. The path to the house is well trodden, as usual. Other tracks lead off to the left; these are new. The child steps into the footprints. They are not very far apart, like Grandfather's when he walks in front of her.

A blue horse comes galloping over the hill behind the barn. The yellow pawn sits on the horse and laughs. He reaches out his smooth pawn-arm to the child and pulls her up. They ride over the triangular field, straight ahead to the large juniper bush, past the old stack of spruce wood to the point where the path divides: left into town, and right into the mountains. The snow sprays up. The yellow pawn sat behind the child feels as warm as a radiator.

The tracks run alongside Grandfather's house as far as the box hedge. The child pushes a finger into the snow which sits on top of it. A caterpillar could come along, crawl into the hole and go to sleep. The child sniffs. In winter the box has only a slight smell. She can still taste the cocoa. Good. Where the footprints are replaced by an even track curving to the right, she notices something else. The hum of an engine. The child looks up, convinced that a helicopter is about to rise above the barn. She will wave with both arms, that is what you do. But the helicopter does not come, and the noise goes away again. The child trudges on a few more steps and finds herself standing beside two wheel tracks, from a car or tractor. She steps into the right-hand rut and walks up to the black rectangle of the barn. To one side, the snowchild and snowdog that they built together two days ago are playing in the moonlight. Everything is still there: the cap, the broom, the chestnut which sticks out for a snout. The child goes over to the dog and stretches out her arm as if she were holding a broom too. "Now there's three of us," she says. She spins around and around and feels happy, as if the whole world were watching her. Then she realises that she has got a bit further to go. There is something in front of her, on the ramp which slopes gently up to the barn door. It is not a snowman.

It is lying there like someone making an angel in the snow, its arms spread wide like wings. It is swallowing up the moonlight. The child steps slowly forward. Then she bends over. The black lace-up boots are like Grandfather's. Looking closer she can see that the trousers are dark green. The trousers are turned up a few centimetres at the bottom. The jacket is made out of that coarse light-brown material which never wears out. Almost everything is the same. No gloves. Almost everything. The arms, the shoulders, the collar. But there is no head where it should be. Even a pawn has a head there. The child crouches right down. The head is not missing. Where there should be a round head on the ground, there is something flat instead. The flat thing is squashed into the snow and it is completely black. The child reaches towards it and pokes around in the middle with her finger, where it is a bit silvery. The child shudders in horror. The silver stuff feels wet, but also hard. The child stands up and makes her way back.

First along the car tracks, then the footprints. The snowchild, the chestnut nose, the box hedge. The hole where the caterpillar sleeps. The horse is not coming this time. Things change.

Along the wall, then left to her parents' house.

The moon disappears in the light of the doorway. Her brother stands there and looks at the child's hand. "What have you got there?" he asks. The child opens her fist. A yellow pawn and a blue soldier. She should have put them back, the pawn right by the home column and the soldier four squares behind. The child does not move. "Four," she says. "Four. Got you." The tip of her index finger is red. The pawn still has its head, and so has the soldier.

Now the dog is there. It sniffs the child's legs, then her hand. It crouches, flattens its ears, and lets out a howl. The child steps towards the dog. It creeps backwards and stares at the door as if it has seen a ghost standing there.

ONE

He opens the door. Cold tumbles into the room. At first all is quiet, then he can hear a car starting in the distance. Nothing else is stirring.

On the wall, the poster with the Rule. He can feel himself falling apart. The phrases.

Listen, O my son, to the precepts of thy master.

It begins in the middle. A fault line that he cannot locate. He swallows a couple of pills.

He stands there. His skin is burning. Only the tips of his fingers are free of pain. A rustling sound comes from outside. Probably the fox slinking across the courtyard. The air smells of nothing. The moon set a long time ago. Everything is a delusion. He slowly tenses his thighs. The Rule. Words which he puts together.

Cheerfully execute.

He goes through his routine. Isometric exercises to begin with, one set of muscles after another. Legs, arms, neck, upper body. Contract, relax. Contract, relax. Afterwards, a few stretching exercises. First the hips. Kneebends. Gentle stretch jumps, no straining at all. He swings his arms, then thrusts them upwards.

From the age of forty the risk of tearing muscle fibre increases dramatically. He read that in a weekend supplement, just after his fortieth birthday. One always learns about the scary things in life at precisely the right moment. His torso slowly starts to warm up. He stretches his arms out sideways. That wild clear-sightedness emerges from his temples into his field of vision. The fissure begins to disappear. The fear remains. He knows he cannot do anything about it.

He slips into the grey cotton tracksuit, puts on socks and running shoes. The right shoulder of his sweater is wearing through. He will give it to Irma to mend. She might complain about her elbow pains, but she would rather none of them tried to patch up their own clothes. Her eyes have got worse recently and her sewing is even more atrocious than it used to be, but nobody tells her.

iPod on the waistband, headphones in the ears. It is always the same. Number six. "Father of Night". On a loop.

Along the corridor, no light, twenty-seven paces. Down the steps, left past the offices, through the narrow door and into the back garden. Packed snow beneath his feet, the path has been cleared. By Bernhard, the man who can go for weeks without uttering a word.

He sets off. The night is as black as the inside of a velvet pouch. It spurs him on. Earlier in the evening the stars were bright in the sky. He thought of the small village by the River Salzach with its curious promise. For a while he was unbeatable. Now he has the Devil at his back.

He crosses the open courtyard to the plane tree near the wall, slips through the railing gate which is not quite closed, although it looks as if it has been locked for centuries. He is out.

He knows that they call him "the runner", and that some also call him "Mr Perfect" because of his physique. For several weeks, Ngobu, the visiting student from Nigeria, has just been referring to him as "L.D.R." – "Long Distance Runner". That will catch on, he senses, everyone will call him that. These things always catch on.

He jogs along the north side of the boundary wall. There is no wind, and he reckons it is one or two degrees below zero. He crosses Weyrer Straße and turns into Abt Reginald. Single-storey houses. Wrought-iron fences as old as he is, cream-coloured louvre shutters, box hedging and tall conifers in the front gardens. The tax consultant has a sensor positioned too far away from his house, activating the light by the front door when anybody passes. The plaque, about a metre square, gold lettering behind thick perspex: "Magister Norbert Kossnik, registered tax consultant and accountant". Accountant: a crook who bribes tax officials and blackmails his clients – that is the truth of it. And there he is, standing in his loden body warmer, his heavy silver-plated watch chain across his paunch, three days' stubble, hobnailed shoes, reading glasses on a cord. Hit him, he thinks. Smash his face in.

The kindergarten, the primary school. Pictures in the windows, a snowcastle in the playground, a well-ordered world. Friedegund Mayerhofer, the head of the kindergarten who is soon to retire. Her designated successor: Lea Wirth, whose whole life has been plagued by the fear that one of the children might fall off something. Cut down all the trees and demolish multi-storey buildings! Keep children on the ground! That is what some of the fathers say.

At the end of the street he turns right into the unnamed cul-de-sac which stops behind the council's vehicle depot. Under the shed roof stand two huge, dark-red snow ploughs, with several smaller ones for the side streets. Behind them is a pile of gravel, as tall as a house. Everyone is saying that this winter has been a joke. But it might arrive yet.

The small alleyway which hits the promenade by the river at the point where it enters the wood. The passage that he always sings along to loudly: *Father of night, Father of day, Father, who taketh the darkness away*. Alders and willows with thick trunks. He can hardly see the ground at all. One early October morning he came across a badger here. An enormous torpedo-like animal that bolted into the undergrowth, slurping and hissing loudly.

Now he can really feel the running taking effect; he can feel how, starting with his legs and ears, this frame that supports him is growing. Suddenly there are extensions – small, shiny wire grids – around his nerve tracks. For a time he will forget that the other side exists, the black abyss where Satan sits, the one who annihilates everything. *Father of day, Father of night, Father of black, Father of white.*

He knows every square metre of this area and he closes his eyes for a moment. His step remains as sure as ever. He keeps on imagining that he is driving through the streets in a gigantic snow plough. First he tosses the parked cars aside as if they were toys, then lurching left and right he tears chunks out of the facades of the houses.

He runs on with long strides, the balls of his feet pounding on the ground. And so he starts to fly; he recognises this from some of his dreams. Relax, run straight ahead, and keep pushing off. At some point you lose contact with the ground and hover for ten, twenty metres, then you land again with two or three steps. There are people who do not touch the ground at all. Clemens is one of these permanent hoverers. He glides over steps, gravel and grass as if he were on an air cushion, always a couple of centimetres above the ground, while his face radiates an inner arrogance, a sense of superiority which comes from his position. At some point he is going to hit Clemens. Just like that. Not a brutal punch, but a half-serious slap in the face; more a demonstration of principle than an act of violence. Controlled aggression is a much-neglected strategy when standing up for one's ideological beliefs. It is not about destruction, but occasionally using a bit of muscle to back up one's actions. Those in important positions – head teachers, police, politicians – could do with being slapped about a bit; why not? Clemens, too. With his trimmed goatee, his darned socks and his signet ring.

After a minute in the wood you notice just how many different shades of black there are. Even the edges of the path are distinguishable, as are the bare branches against the sky. At this hour in the park, the crows sleep in the limes and chestnut trees.

Father of cold and Father of heat. He is thinking constantly, no interruption. Hot and cold. All his life. One day, he will fetch them, both of them, and nobody will dare raise an objection. It will be a sunny day, they will arrive by train, and when he collects them they will rush towards him, right into his outstretched arms.

Brightness from lamps. On the left, the wooden bridge which leads to the paths on the north side of the river. The bridge has been lit up at night-time ever since old Schöffberger missed the first step a few years ago and plunged over the bank into the river. Straight ahead the rafting camp, perhaps two hundred metres away. The shallow pitched roof of the shed stands out slightly against the background. He cannot make out the annex with the office and changing rooms.

He wheels to the right. Imhofstraße, named after a former Bürgermeister. The road is clear. At the north-western corner of the cemetery there is a path with a thick layer of gravel. People visit cemeteries throughout the year. *Father of minutes, Father of days.* Winter burials. Weinstabel, the gravedigger, has the red and white mini-digger in his garage back home. He loves digging through layers of frozen earth and he makes notes about how thick they are. A lined notebook with an orangey-red cover. Some people say he makes his lists on the left-hand side, while on the facing page he describes the state of decomposition of the bodies. He is also said to have a huge collection of skulls, but all gravediggers must attract these sorts of rumours.

The plaque beside the door. The Rule. *It is now the hour for us to rise from sleep.* The night runner. What a name that would be.

The key phrase which sinks right in and keeps one alive. At some point it starts to bypass one's consciousness.

He crosses the main road, takes the railway underpass, runs alongside the huge halls of the sawmill, then through an estate of terraced houses. Through two windows he can see the blue glimmer of television sets. A few hundred metres down Grafenaustraße, a car advances towards him, its headlights on full. He raises a hand to his eyes and gives the driver the middle finger when there is no reaction. The engine sounds like a tank's. Looking back at the vehicle, he thinks it might have been a breakdown truck. An old model, a really old model. People break down at night, too, he thinks.

The butcher's, the second-hand shop, the esoteric shop with the yellow-green spiral on the outside. Marlene Hanke's van; she owns the second-hand shop. Two motorbikes – he cannot place their owners. Just before the railway crossing he imagines that the signal lights start to flash, the barriers come down, and a mysterious train rushes past, huge and crusted with ice, like out of one of those films about Siberia or Alaska.

When the crowns of the Rathausplatz lime trees emerge as silhouettes to his left, he feels better – it is always the same.

Father of black, Father of white.

There are few things I'm sure of, he thinks. My name is Joseph Bauer. I live in a complicated world. I made a solemn promise. I recite phrases. I run.

TWO

On those days when the town was shrouded by fog in the morning, life was usually quite peculiar. People were tense, drivers forgot to turn on their headlights, and one had absurd déjà-vu experiences. The air felt colder than it actually was. The tree trunks shone black. There was the lake, but no sounds came off it. It was unsettling, without one noticing it.

Horn was walking to work. Normally he went by bike but Martin Schwarz, his neighbour, had cleared the snow in his plough the day before. The road surface was now like glass. The intention was good, but he doubted Schwarz had given the slightest thought to the grip of bicycle tyres.

Although his winter boots had moulded soles, Horn slipped frequently in the steeper sections. Wherever possible he avoided going off the path. The snow got under his trouser legs. As he was wearing long socks and had tied his boots tightly, this did not bother him. At the point where the road turned to the west, and where the steeples of the abbey poked above a small pine wood, the same thought had occurred to him for the past ten years: why did I move here? Of course, he had come up with hundreds of different answers: for Irene, who had really wanted to because she had twice been rejected by the symphony orchestras; or for the children, because they had imagined it would be a better place to bring them up; or for the air, mountains and the crazy notion that country people were less psychopathic; or, of course, because of the thing with Frege. But he found none of these explanations really satisfactory. Was it your typical escape from the city? An attachment to the idea of an idyll? More variety at work? He did not care. He made a snowball and threw it into the trees.

Horn took the shortcut over the huge field which sloped gently towards the south, and where they grew corn or beets in summer. He met the highway near the junction leading to the wildlife observation centre. He felt warm. He took off his gloves and put them into his coat pockets. The pavement began after the place-name sign. Horn stamped his feet hard a few times to dislodge the worst of the snow from his trouser legs. The entrance into the civilised world, he thought.

Pappelallee, which forked off at an acute angle, turned into Siedlungstraße after a few hundred metres. One 1970s gabled house after another. Illuminated Christmas trees stood in the front gardens. The occasional chimney puffed out smoke. He imagined people inside coming out of their bathrooms and walking past half-empty plates of biscuits.

Irene was probably sitting with her cello, trying out her new bow, Tobias was asleep and Michael had left abruptly with his girlfriend the day before. Yet again he had started to argue with his mother the moment he saw her, and Irene was unable to approach the issue in a different way. But he had taken his presents with him. A dark-grey, woollen Timberland jumper and the new Nick Cave album; Horn could not remember the rest. Gabriele, Michael's girlfriend, was nice. Dark, bristly short hair, slightly heavy build, quiet; no competition for Irene. She had given him a Moleskine notebook. He kept it in his pocket, and was still astonished that she had been so spot on with her present.

Right into Gaiswinklerstraße, as far as the river. The view of the long gravel bank on the other side, of the rough-hewn rocks of the embankment and the fronts of houses beyond. A little way down the river, just before the road bridge, he could see the water gauge on the bank. The last flood had been two and a half years ago, in August, when the Kamp had broken its banks and, a little to the north-east, the Enns had swamped the entire town of Steyr. Here, just a few refrigerators had come a cropper, as had a firm's computer equipment, which stupidly had been installed in the basement. Otherwise nothing had happened. The hospital was on a hill thirty metres above the water level – absolutely safe, they said.

Horn crossed the car park and went in the side entrance as always. Whenever anybody asked him why he did this, he said, "I can't bear the sight of the porter in the morning." But it was probably down to some stupid compulsion.

Behind the doors of the central laboratory the centrifuges whirred, then several people laughed in unison. One of the ceiling lights in the corridor flickered nervously. He climbed the steps to the second floor. By the entrance to the children's wing he met Elfriede, who was on her way to a ward sisters' meeting. She looked as round and red-cheeked as ever and tripped up over her words when she wished him a belated happy Christmas. "Fog's coming down over the town," he said. "The lake won't freeze in the next few days." Over her shoulder she called out something about "skating", and then was gone.

Horn's office was tucked away at the back of K1, the general paediatric ward. This meant that it was on the whole very quiet. Only at visiting time did he hear fretful mothers in the corridor or the whining siblings of patients. From time to time a ball or a tricycle crashed against his door, but this had never bothered him.

Early in the morning he would stand for a while at the window – the view over the river and the reed beds as far as the river's outlet, behind these the lake and the cliff walls. "That's why I moved here," he thought. "Because of that." He hung his jacket up in the cupboard, placed his boots by the heater, and put on his work shoes. His colleagues had smirked when he first turned up in his blue Adidas Records. "They're making a comeback," he had said. "I was sixteen then – it's the only time in your life when you've got that inner certainty that you can make something happen." Some of them had agreed with him, and Sellner, the consultant on I21, had said that he'd been a Puma boy in his time. Thinking about it now, Sellner added, they were due a revival.

There were coffee and biscuits at the morning staff meeting. That was a one-off. Then Leithner, the Primarius, arrived five minutes late. That never happened, either. He muttered an excuse which nobody took any interest in and wished everybody a happy Christmas. Inge Broschek, his secretary, put a plate of Christmas stollen in front of his stomach. A few people laughed. Leithner usually ate standing up and there were all sorts of witty remarks about what meals must be like in the Leithner household.

Cejpek had been the duty consultant. He reported on a young woman who had been admitted with extreme cardiac arrhythmias and kept the team busy all afternoon and half of the night. Then her partner had brought in two empty packets of an old anti-depressant and everything fell into place. One way or another she would have landed up in intensive care. Horn just nodded when Cejpek and Leithner looked over at him. He would deal with the woman as soon as she was in a fit state. There had also been a diabetic who kept on becoming hypoglycaemic because he switched his insulin type; a sixty-year-old woman with a fresh infarction of the posterior wall; and a 130-kilo man with an attack of gout in the right metatarsophalangeal joint – nobody had shown the least sympathy for this one. Two patients had died: a man who had been suffering for a long time from pulmonary oedema; and a ninety-seven-year-old woman. Those with flu had been sent home with aspirins and good wishes, and the wards had been full of Christmas calm.

Some of Horn's patients had come back early from their time out of hospital, including Caroline Weber. A month and a half after her post-natal psychosis she had not yet made a full recovery, and on the evening of 25 December her husband had brought her into hospital because again she had started to believe that her newborn daughter was the Devil. Horn knew about it already as he had been telephoned at home and asked for a prescription for medication. Caroline Weber was twenty-eight years old, her husband was a patient man who drove mechanical diggers, and when asked how many children they would like to have together, he said, "A few more."

She gave him grounds for concern. A few years back her mother had climbed onto a stationary goods wagon and put both her arms over the contact wire. Subsequently they found several sheets of notepaper in her flat on which the woman had scribbled over and over again long penitential prayers. Not long afterwards her husband, Caroline's father, got together with a chubby woman with platinum-blonde hair. Caroline seldom mentioned him. Once she said, "I couldn't give a damn whether I know what my father's up to or not." Mother dead, father also dead in a way, the Devil for a child – people had been dealt better hands.

Horn found himself imagining a little girl cooing in his arms, with Michael and Gabriele, the beaming parents, beside him. Irene remained in the background, muttering something about those men who preferred girls. All of them were quite relaxed. A new element, he thought, introduce a new element and things change. He also wondered if, at forty-eight, he was not a little too young to be a grandfather.

Lili Brunner, the small, round junior doctor, gave Horn a nudge. He jumped. The others were staring at him.

"I'm sorry, I was just thinking about something rather funny," he stuttered.

"A daydream," Cejpek said a little sardonically. Cejpek never tired of maintaining that he was a natural scientist, 100 per cent, and that the psyche was a highly absurd form of organised matter. On the other hand, he referred every other patient to Horn for assessment. "A high-ranking official in the *Land* highways agency," he said. "I was so proud that we'd got to grips with his hypertension, and now he's getting more depressed by the day."

"That happens," Horn said.

"Oh, I'm so pleased," said Cejpek caustically, grabbing a piece of lebkuchen.

Horn grinned. "It's always better when people are suffering from something you know," he said. Brunner frowned. Amongst her medical colleagues she was the standard bearer of seriousness. It seemed appropriate that she had been involved for more than a year with the building of a hospice ward, even though she had not had any traumatic death-related experiences in her childhood, as Horn kept on claiming. But she gave the continual impression that she was subjecting you to moral scrutiny, and sometimes he wondered whether she might not be a member of a secret order.

The rest of the meeting was just trivia: Christmas menu, ungrateful children etc. We got a blue spruce today, and you cannot imagine how quickly a dropped sparkler can make a hole in the carpet. Amongst other things, they tried to get Inge Broschek to say whether or not she had got the fur-lined Prada bag she had been raving about for ages. No success there. In the end she stood up, brushed a few crumbs from her skirt, threw her head back, and left the meeting room with a sphinx-like smile. Horn was pretty sure that Leithner had bought her the bag, but he said nothing.

In the office there was a small heap of referral notices in his pigeon hole. He rolled them up without reading them. Don't rush anything, he thought, one thing at a time, especially at Christmas.

He looked at the river through Broschek's window. The fog was creeping up the hill. "And we're not supposed to get depressed," he said, because he could not think of anything better. Broschek did not react. Horn was happy. Something was missing. He could not think what.

The outpatient waiting room was sparsely populated. A thin woman with obvious breathing problems. An old man who had fallen asleep in his chair. Reisberger, the pharmacist, who clutched the left side of his chest – this was probably another non-heart-attack. A couple sitting either side of a boy whose lower arm looked to be bound in a whole stationery cupboard of rubber bands. A few people who he just glimpsed out of the corner of his eye. Of his usual suspects only Schmidinger was there, red-faced with a film of grease shining on his forehead. No, thought Horn, I'm not going to get depressed.

Linda sat at the reception desk. She was wearing a natural white, merino-wool jumper and brimming with holiday joy. "Nurses shouldn't be allowed to wear jumpers like that," Horn said.

She smiled and offered him her shoulder. "It's Christmas. You can touch it," she said.

"Wouldn't dare, ever."

"Why not?"

"Your Reinhard might come along with his chainsaw."

She laughed. Linda's boyfriend was a manager in the regional forestry agency, and in fact an extremely gentle soul. "He cries every time he gives the nod for a tree to be felled," Reiter, the assistant in casualty surgery, had scathingly observed. Everybody knew that Reiter would have liked to have his way with Linda. But given his black curls and neon-coloured Hugo Boss shirts he did not have a chance. Linda was one of those redheads whose every freckle represented a chunk of self-confidence. Horn thought briefly of Irene. She had been exhausted recently and a little bit distant. Perhaps it was just because of the thing with their son.

Linda pressed three card files into his hand. "Schmidinger, a new one and Heidemarie. She's not here yet, but she rang." Horn was pleased. Heidemarie, the student with the nicest depression in the world.

"I'd always pick her last," he said. "You've got to give yourself a good one to finish with." Linda frowned.

In the outpatient room there was a small table decoration made out of spruce twigs. A dark-red candle with gold stars. This piece of high kitsch was one of the few things that made life bearable. It had taken him a while to admit it. You've got to give yourself a good one, he thought. Always a good one to finish with and, if possible, the shitty ones first. The really shitty ones. He called for Schmidinger.

A hair-raising aftershave with an undertone of sweaty feet. "I tell you, I've had it!" Horn had known something like this was coming. Had it. Rock bottom. Destroyed. Broken. Completely finished. The man was sitting in his chequered jacket with leather patches on the elbows. He had pushed the tips of his fingers below his belt, and was licking his lips incessantly.

"What do you mean you've had it?" Horn asked.

"My wife . . . you already know."

"Is she provoking you again?"

Those eyes, Horn thought, those nasty, small eyes that roll around like two red marbles. The nose, slightly upturned, and the pouting lips repeatedly moistened by the tip of his tongue. There are moments when I can't stand my job, Horn thought.

Norbert Schmidinger had discovered the usefulness of psychiatry some time ago, just after he had thrown the then one-and-a-half-year-old Melanie against a wall for the first time. A neurologist from Linz had provided him with a certificate of temporary mental incapacitation, thereby saving him from prison. From that time on Schmidinger had been a regular visitor to the psychiatrist, always just after his wife or one of his three daughters had contact with casualty or the police. Horn had got to know him during an appeal process against an injunction banning him from the family home. He had not been able to avoid admitting that Schmidinger had shown a certain willingness to receive treatment. Horn had felt dreadful about it for weeks afterwards.

"My wife . . . you already know . . . same as ever."

"I bet she even got to you under the Christmas tree."

"If it's never happened to you . . ."

"With a present she absolutely knew you'd hate?"

"You can't imagine . . ."

"I expect your daughters started up the day before. While decorating the tree."

"I'm trying really hard!"

Who copped it this time, Horn wondered – Renate, his wife, or Birgit, the youngest one again? She had just turned five.

"Who copped it this time?"

The red-veined marbles hung motionless for a second. Then Schmidinger drew breath through his teeth. "You know who it was," he said. 'It was you who wrote that clever thing about my impulse control."

Why are we so bloody afraid of describing them as they are, Horn asked himself. Why don't we write "full-blown psychopath" when there's one sitting opposite and double underline it?

"I've read there are some people who can't stand on one leg, no matter how hard they try," Schmidinger said. "And if you've got a weakness like mine, well, I don't think it's any different."

"Who copped it?" Horn asked. "Who was on the receiving end of your weakness?" Schmidinger did not answer, but kneaded the fat on his stomach and licked his lips.

"You see, I came here. I'm not skiving. I want to be treated," he said and gave a crooked grin.

Horn felt slightly faint. Enough, he thought. That's really enough. Nobody's going to ruin Christmas for me, nobody – least of all someone like that!

"Are you still taking your medication?"

Schmidinger shook his head ruefully. "I got problems with dizziness after the first week."

Eczema, Horn thought, I'd have put money on eczema. In the instruction leaflet it's listed before dizziness as one of the "common side-effects". He had always been repulsed by people who were "provoked" by their nearest and dearest. He prescribed Schmidinger half a tablet of Clozapin twice a day and instructed him to come back for another examination in a week.

"And if you don't come, I won't sign those forms any more," he said.

Schmidinger folded the prescription, put it away and got up. "Thanks," he said. "Thanks a lot." As he left he was still wearing a crooked grin.

Horn wrenched open the window. Outside, an H.G.V. with carrots painted on the side drove past. Schmidinger would probably not come. He had his prescription and would use it to demonstrate his willingness to receive treatment if anybody asked him.

He drives me mad, thought Horn, leaving the room. I try to resist it, but he really drives me mad. "If the police ask about him," he directed Linda, "just for once they can have all the details."

Linda was in total agreement. "For that you can have biscuits afterwards," she said. Just at that moment biscuits were what Horn least desired. I'd like to get my hands on her now, he thought.

The next patient, a new one, was panicky. Maybe thirty years old, pale, and wearing a jacket, shirt and cords that did not match. He would not sit until Horn assured him that nothing would happen. He reminded Horn of somebody. He could not say who.

"Are there any animals in here?" the man asked. "Please tell me whether there are animals in here!"

Horn shook his head. Most of the puzzle fell into place quite quickly.

"How long ago did you stop drinking?" he asked.

The man shrugged his shoulders and then looked Horn in the eyes. He seemed quite relieved. "How did you guess?" he asked.

"When someone reaches a certain level of misery, they always think they're in it alone," Horn said. Then he talked about those young men who take their work stress home with them and cannot let their hair down before they have helped themselves to a few units of alcohol. As soon as the pressure increases in accordance with their position at work, these men resort to the tried and tested remedy during the daytime as well, knocking back a few glasses of schnapps at decently spaced intervals. Then, during the Christmas break, because playing with the children and sleeping with the wife provide some relaxation, they forget about the supply of these few units of alcohol. "And then your brain starts to make you see pink elephants," Horn said. He fetched a small bottle of Diazepam solution from the cupboard and counted out forty-five drops into a small tumbler. "Drink this now and sit in the waiting room for twenty minutes," he said. "Then we'll see what happens." The man gave the impression that he would be prepared to hold his breath for twenty minutes if he was asked to. He was quivering pitifully when he left the room.

"He reminds me of somebody," Horn said, popping an aniseed biscuit into his mouth.

"Pippin," Linda said.

"What?"

"He looks like Pippin, that hobbit from *The Lord of the Rings*. Perhaps a tad taller." A picture formed in Horn's mind. A small man with a rather desperate smile. Linda was absolutely right. He had seen the third part at the cinema with Tobias. At the end of the film Tobias had been much the livelier of the two of them, even though he had sat through the whole ten-hour marathon. Ten hours in one go.

"Does Pippin drink?" he asked.

"Of course," Linda said. "All hobbits drink. Wouldn't you drink if you were a hobbit?" Horn was stuck for an answer. Besides, Heidemarie had just breezed in. She was wearing a fake-fur coat and a dark-red headband. "An Elven princess," Linda muttered. He had no idea whether she was jealous. With her, at any rate, he could spare the line about paternal feelings; that was certain.

Heidemarie looked as if she had been crying. It transpired that she'd had a string of sleepless nights, during which she had spent long periods weighing up the reliability of various methods of suicide. Her parents had given her money for Christmas, a medium-sized sum, in a spotted envelope, with a note saying it was the simplest solution – their expectation was that she would reject the things she was given. "They can't do anything else," she said. "They don't give each other presents." They had agreed on that years earlier. Probably most relationships are based on an arrangement to steer well clear of each other, Horn thought.

They talked about her childhood Christmases, the emptiness of the massive sitting room, and Christmas trees hung with lametta. Music came from the record player, of course, and the food was always ghastly. She had only ever felt understood by one great-aunt, whom the family had tolerated for a few hours on Christmas Eve over a period of about ten or twelve years. When the aunt died in the wake of a cardiomyopathy, her mother said, "Thank God! We'll finally have some peace." Perhaps it was then that the feeling of loneliness had begun; she did not know exactly. I'd like to give her a big hug, Horn thought, and he knew that, deep down, that was the diagnosis. You write "depression", he thought, prescribe some medication, and know that in every case it's about wanting to be hugged.

"Do you know what the worst thing is?" she said after a while. "The worst thing is when you notice yourself getting lost; you see the very thing you think you're made of seeping out of you. At the end, what's left of you is an empty sack, nothing else." Horn had no idea what to reply. As you get older, he thought, there are certain things you no longer know what to say to.

She talked about having passed an exam in administrative law, and he still had no answer as to why this young woman had started studying law and not tunnel engineering, architecture or picture restoration. Or even psychology. Nevertheless, he could imagine her standing at the front of the courtroom and representing abused boys, or little girls who had been thrown against the wall by their fathers. "The worst thing, Your Honour," she would say, "is not that something is planted inside these children, what we might, for example, call violence or trauma. No, the worst is that everything which was once inside these children is beaten out of them or fucked out of them." She would not be afraid to say "fucked", and the judge's eyes would pop out of his head.

"I imagine it's lovely to have a wife who can play the cello at Christmas," Heidemarie said, and looked sad.

Horn hesitated with his reply. "Yes," he then said. "It is lovely." He thought about how Irene had played the largo from Handel's *Xerxes* on Christmas Eve and how, at that moment, he had loved her so much it had hurt. And he reflected on how it was essential for psychiatrists to let people get close to them – he never, for instance, pushed Heidemarie away when she overstepped the boundary to his private sphere. They discussed how life could be unfair and the forthcoming summer semester. He slightly increased her dose of anti-depressants and also prescribed her some sleeping tablets. "When you're back in Vienna you won't need them any more," he said. She nodded and stood up. When he made to shake her hand she took a small packet out of her coat pocket.

"Happy New Year." Dark-blue paper with tiny, brightly coloured stars. It looked like a C.D. Before he could thank her she was gone.

He turned the thing over a few times then put it aside. He would open it when he got home.

Linda was deep in conversation on the phone and waved him away when he bent down to ask her to send Pippin in. "That's unbelievable," she said, ignoring him and twirling a lock of hair with her index finger. Horn went into the waiting area himself.

The man came up to him, beaming. "It's all gone," he said. "Completely disappeared as if it had never happened." Horn gave him half a packet of Diazepam tablets together with precise instructions as to the dose.

"Do you need me to give you the usual warnings?" he asked. The man shook his head.

"I'd like to see you again in a month," Horn said. He knew that this one was not going to come back, either.

Horn made his notes in the patient files. The data-processing system was functioning perfectly. Even the diagnosis key was working. After the disaster caused by the program changeover which had been going on throughout the hospital since the middle of October, this was a pleasant surprise. People expect my generation to be sceptical towards technology, Horn thought. That's really terrible.

Linda was still on the phone when he left the outpatient ward. He blew her a kiss. She lifted her arm and just for a moment he thought she wanted to keep him there. He waited for a few seconds, then went on his way.

In the stairwell Horn looked through the referral notices. He arranged them by floor, from top to bottom as always. Seven cases – three in orthopaedics, the smallest department in the hospital. Köhler had been on duty; that explained everything. Not only was he was a textbook neurotic, he showed too keen an interest in psychiatry. In the beginning Horn used to tease him quite a bit – hammer toe was really a complex psychosomatic phenomenon and stuff like that – but this had led to a large increase in the number of consultant referrals, and so Horn had stopped.

Third floor. In casualty, an old man who had just had a pelvic plating. In a state of disorientation because of the long period under anaesthetic; it would sort itself out, more or less. In obs, an extremely pale, tear-stained nineteen-year-old mother who seemed to be slipping into post-natal depression. As expected, two of the three referrals in orthopaedics were unnecessary: a young man with an aseptic necrosis of the tibial plateau, who had been stupid enough when outlining his medical history to admit that he occasionally smoked cannabis; and a woman who was in pain following an operation on her vertebral discs – it appeared to be the psychiatrist's job to sort this out. Horn scribbled "analgesic deficiency syndrome", even though he knew that Köhler was a rather humourless man. The third referral was justified: a fifteen-year-old gymnast whose right lower leg had been amputated two days before Christmas. An osteosarcoma in the upper third of her tibia. Horn chatted to her about dancing and skiing, and said that a prostheticist liked nothing more than measuring up a pretty girl for a new limb. Before he left Horn gave her the number of Konstanze Witt, a psychotherapist who had her practice above the promenade, just a few minutes' walk from the girl's house. Just in case she felt she could not deal with it all on her own.

Second floor. I22 reeked of burnt milk. It was one of those smells he had hated as a child. Sweaty feet and burnt milk. Perhaps doctors turn to psychiatry, he thought, if they can't bear the smell of sweaty feet. "It stinks in here," he said to Doris, who was just coming from the storeroom with an armful of bedlinen.

She grinned. "That's what happens when a Filipino sister tries to make coffee with frothy milk."

"Josephine?" he asked. Doris nodded and laughed. Josephine was always doing strange things. For Christmas she had decorated every available spot in the ward with colourful origami swans. Most people had thought it a nice touch.

The big cheese from the highways agency Cejpek had told him about was enthroned in his bed, staring at the telly. *Home Alone 2* for the thousandth time. When Horn asked him to switch it off for a moment his face turned red. The patient revealed himself to be a compulsive personality, no hint of depression. Horn jotted down those very words: "no hint of depression". With Cejpek it was always best to be as frank as possible. Amongst other things the man was responsible for awarding a variety of contracts for highway repair. "How often do you get bribed?" Sometimes Horn felt the irrepressible urge to be confrontational. The man went pale. It was probably a good thing as far as his blood pressure was concerned. "By the way, a major American study has shown that television makes you impotent," Horn said before leaving the room. He was sure that the man was one of those people who were impressed by major American studies, just like Cejpek.

I'm hungry, thought Horn as he crossed the hallway. Recently I've been much hungrier than usual. He checked the time. Another unusual thing: half a day had gone past, and all that remained of it was the unpleasant memory of a psychopath like Norbert Schmidinger. Perhaps also just a trace of that feeling that a sad law student had wanted to be hugged.

He went into the kitchen. I23 was one of those wards where it was best to go into the kitchen first, whether you were hungry or not. Twelve psychiatric beds, which were Horn's responsibility, plus seven people on the verge of death, divided between three rooms at the end of the corridor – the start of Brunner's hospice ward. This accumulation of misery needed to be compensated for by satisfying one's basic urges. Horn saw a truffle cake which was missing a small piece, less than a quarter. The partners and children of the hospice patients always brought cakes with them, especially at holiday time, even though they knew that these offerings could not put off death. The relatives of the psychiatric patients brought nothing but anxiety and stale coffee. Christina, the deputy ward sister, came in and put a bag of food on the work surface. "I'll make us something afterwards." She was tall, slightly angular, and she went snowboarding in winter. Even giving birth to a Down's syndrome daughter three and a half years ago had not put a stop to her hobby. The little girl had been going to kindergarten for a few months and was making excellent progress; Lea Wirth, who had been very sceptical at the start, had taken a particular liking to her. The girl's father had done a runner before her first birthday. "Selling sailing boats and a handicapped child – clearly not a good combination," Christina would sometimes say bitterly.

"So that means no cake before my round." Horn pulled a face. Christina laughed and felt his upper arm. "You're still so unbelievably thin."

"Nonsense!" He took a step back, feigning disgust. He had always let Christina get away with everything: criticism, compliments and comments about his physique. It had nothing to do with the fact that her daughter was handicapped.

Benedikt Ley, the eighteen-year-old carpenter's apprentice with the double nose ring. On Christmas Eve he had helped himself to the remains of the (unidentified) chemical hallucinogen that had left him in a pretty ugly state a week earlier. In spite of substantial neuroleptic infusions he was perched on the bed, sweating, his eyes wide open in horror. When Horn asked him why he had taken the stuff he merely ranted unintelligibly. "Perhaps it was just too expensive to throw away," said Raimund, the orderly, who was accompanying them on the round. He must have some experience of these things. Horn had never quizzed him about it.

"His father's still beating him up, even in public," Christina said from outside the room.

"Even though he's grown up?" Horn said.

"A real long-distance driver couldn't give a shit about that," she said. Horn had never met Herr Ley, although he had seen the mother on several occasions. She always wore black-rimmed spectacles and a dark-violet flowery suit. This mum's desperate to look good, Horn thought, but then found this a tasteless observation.

They were standing by Caroline Weber's room and Raimund was explaining how she had dragged him into her delusion as one of Satan's helpers, when Elfriede came down the corridor. "I23 extends Christmas greetings to the paediatric department," Christina said, smiling.

Elfriede ignored her. "They're coming with a seven-year-old girl," she said to Horn. "Completely numb, not saying a word, not even moving. The paramedics say they've never seen anything like it." Horn thought for a second.

"It's not the first time they've brought us one of these." Elfriede waved her hands around in frustration. For a moment she was unable to express herself.

"It must have something to do with the grandfather," she said finally. 'The little girl found him. In the snow. There was something about his face."

THREE

Kovacs took the spruce stakes which Lipp, the young uniformed officer, had brought him from the barn, and, with the face of an axe, drove them into the ground, one after the other – six in total. For the first two or three knocks he could feel the resistance of the frozen earth under the snow. Then he took the roll of yellow police tape and stretched it from stake to stake, around once, twice and three times. He would have preferred not to have stopped at all, but to have continued going round and round in circles until what was in the sealed-off zone vanished. This was the last thing he wanted, no matter what was behind it. He could cope with violent husbands; with the drug dealing that in summer took place on the promenade, and in winter in the back rooms of a particular hotel; with the illegal prostitution on the Walzwerk estate; and with the recent car thefts from locked garages, too. The knives and knuckle-dusters that were occasionally seen glinting at night did not horrify him, and even when a year back Clemens Weitbauer had thrust a shotgun into his half-brother's chest during an argument and pulled the trigger, he had been able to deal with it. But this, on the other hand, he just wanted to wish away, far away; he felt it with the full force of his fifty-three years. It had nothing to do with the Christmas amnesty, which was now well and truly shafted, nor with the fact that he had let the entire team – or at least Bitterle and Demski – take their holiday. Old Strack had been on sick leave since October, but nobody seemed to have missed him.

The small snowman with the hooped cap and the snow-animal with the missing nose were outside the sealed-off area, as if they were looking on. Kovacs went over to them. He gave the police tape to Lipp. They had forgotten the camera.

"What do you think of a detective who hasn't got a camera on him?" he said.

Lipp blushed. "Sorry," he stuttered. "I didn't think of it either."

Lipp was not Demski. Demski was always there and he always thought of everything: cameras, dictaphones, fixing solutions, glass containers, spare batteries, handcuffs etc. Now he was on holiday – diving in Kenya if Kovacs remembered rightly. Demski was swimming with tiger sharks and his wife and child were no doubt lying on the beach.

"Have you even seen anything like this?"

Lipp shook his head. "Don't think so."

"Are you going to be sick?"

"Don't know."

Lipp had only just turned twenty, he was stick thin, and you could see from his hair that he cut it himself. "If you're unsure whether you're going to be sick or not, then take the car and get hold of a camera from somewhere," Kovacs said, "so that our colleagues don't start moaning later on." For a few seconds Lipp stood there not knowing what to do. Kovacs motioned him over to the car. "In the meantime I'll take pictures with my head." As he left, Lipp turned around again.

"He looks like he's been crucified," he said. What bollocks, thought Kovacs.

It was cold. A narrow bank of fog was sitting on the hill behind the buildings. Kovacs had also forgotten his gloves. I forget the camera because Demski's not here, he thought, and I forget my gloves because I don't have a wife any more. He bent down. There was something in the snow, driven into the broad tyre tracks which were all over the place. A small, dark-brown stone, that was all. He put it in his pocket.

Which was the Apostle who was supposed to have been crucified upside-down? Peter or Andrew?

Kovacs forced himself to take a look. The man's body lay on the shallow ramp up to the barn. The legs both pointed to the door; the arms were stretched out to the side. The nape of the neck was exactly at the point where the ramp started, which meant that the head was on the flat. Or what was there in place of the head.

A torch, thought Kovacs as he crouched by the police tape. A torch wouldn't go amiss either. The cameras were back in the equipment store, as were the torches. Forensics would have all sorts of torches, that was sure. Kovacs looked at his watch. Another half an hour, maybe a bit longer because of the fog.

Splinters of bone were visible, a bit of artificial denture, grey hair. One eyeball had remained undamaged; it looked funny. It was underneath the largely intact eyebrow, fairly central but skewed a little to the left. Apart from that, shredded skin and lots of congealed blood.

The head's driven over, thought Kovacs. He slips and someone drives over his head. That person gets out of the car, pulls him up the ramp, and arranges him like that – no, that's got to be crap.

A jacket made out of thick, ochre tweed. A material impossible to find these days. Three of the four buttons were fastened. Moss-green cords, turned up at the bottom. Tall black lace-up boots, probably with a loden lining. Old men loved wearing things like that. No gloves, no cap. He meant to go outside, Kovacs thought, but not for long.

A police car stopped in the distance. Töllmann and Sabine Wieck got out. They looked around and then made their way slowly over to Kovacs. Töllmann kept stopping and laughing loudly. He was wearing the steely-grey, calf-length loden coat that the Furth police had stopped issuing ages ago. Even Kovacs had not got one when he entered the force fourteen years before. He took a few steps over to them. "Schnapps, frozen to death, or both?" Töllmann asked. "Both," Kovacs said, stepping aside. The moment Sabine Wieck's knee touched the police tape, she vomited. Töllmann was standing a few metres further back and was on the whole perhaps a little less sensitive. But his face was an unhealthy colour.

"A dead old man, Lipp said on the phone," he stammered. "That's all he said: a dead old man."

"Who could do a thing like that?" Sabine Wieck retched with the remnants of her gastric juices. "What beasts could do a thing like that?"

Why's she not thinking it might have been an accident? Kovacs wondered. And: why's she thinking of beasts in the plural? Slightly too loudly, as if he just wanted to have something to say, Töllmann asked about forensics and the pathologist. Kovacs said that the man's name was Wilfert, Sebastian Wilfert. He had always lived here, latterly in an outbuilding – a former stable and machine shed which he had converted for his and his wife's retirement. His wife had died over a year previously. Lipp had come up with all this information, but had not been able to find out anything special about the man. "Just an old man," Lipp had said. "An old man like hundreds of others. In mourning for his wife, shovels snow, sits in front of his house, and enjoys spending time with his grandchildren."

Kovacs told Töllmann to wait for Lipp by the sealed-off area and help him take photographs when he returned.

"You come with me," he said to Wieck. "We'll go into the house and see what those people have to say." She smiled weakly.

"Don't worry about it. Everyone has their vomiting-over-the-yellow-tape moment. You're not expecting it, but suddenly there it is." It had happened to him thirty years earlier. A small lorry had lost a piece of aluminium on the Tauern motorway, a single object, not that big – perhaps three, three and a half metres long and five kilos in weight. In the police reconstruction it was reckoned that one end of the metal bar had hit the road, and it had flown up in the air, and come back down in an arc like a spear. It had soared over the two cars behind and pierced the windscreen of the third, bang in the middle. It passed between the husband and wife, who were sitting in front, without touching them. The couple had three children: eleven, eight and four. The two older children had the little one between them in the middle. It had been a white Mitsubishi Lancer, he remembered it vividly.

He said nothing. He felt sorry for her, walking next to him with a yellow face and a uniform which was slightly too big for her. "Look around," he said. "Free up your mind and just look around. Don't concentrate on anything in particular; that way you'll notice the important things." Wieck lifted her head and gave him a look of surprise. He was grinning. When he spoke like that it always sounded a bit Zen Buddhist, even though he could not give two figs about any of that Far-Eastern stuff. He could see that she was actually looking around. The winter sun stood above the house as in a calendar photograph.

The husband and wife standing in the door opposite them seemed shrivelled. It was always like that in these situations. You would go up to people who had just experienced something horrific and they would look as if they had shrunk by several centimetres. The son-in-law and daughter: Ernst and Luise Maywald.

Kovacs always began his chatter in the same way: "The most dreadful things usually turn out to be accidents." He would say it even when he knew for sure that it was utter rubbish. Then he thought of that child and the aluminium bar, and knew that he was at least partly right. They always had to start by assuming it was an accident, he said – although a crime could not be ruled out – and the first impressions and most recent memories were crucial to clear the matter up, so he was obliged to dispense with sympathy and courtesy etc. Everybody understood this; no-one ever made a fuss. On the contrary, people were happy to be allowed to talk.

The hall was large and square, like in most old farmhouses. A yellow slate floor. Along the wall, opposite the front door, a long, narrow patchwork rug with the family's boots lined up.

In the sitting room, a dog growling and baring its teeth, standing in the way. "Emmy!" – the woman. The dog obeyed at once. A larch floor, broad, oiled planks. Kovacs had a thing about floors. He could not explain where it came from. The walls panelled with a light wood: maple or birch. "It's very nice here," Wieck said. "Bright and welcoming." She knows what to say, Kovacs thought. "My husband is a skilled carpenter," the woman said. She was of average height and powerful build. She wore jeans, a wine-red jumper and a headband over her medium-length, dark-blonde hair. Very determined, thought Kovacs, she knows what she wants, and her husband knows how lucky he is to have her.

A large stove with a dome-like design. Three children on the bench surrounding it: a girl of about fourteen, a slightly younger boy, and a little girl in the middle of the two. I don't believe it, Kovacs thought. Then he offered his hand to all of them. I've seen the woman before, he thought, in town, at the supermarket, at the petrol station, somewhere.

"Do you want to talk to all of us together?" the woman said. She has her grief under control, Kovacs thought, and she's trying to imagine what's going to happen now. The man stood a bit further behind, chewing his upper lip, his right hand in his trouser pocket. The children were sitting there in silence; the older sister whispered something over the little girl's head to her brother. It would be alright.

The man fetched four chairs. The children were allowed to stay where they were. The dog lay down at the feet of the little girl. A lot revolves around the children here, Kovacs thought. Wieck got a pen and notepad from her inside jacket pocket. When he got the chance he would ask her whether she would like to transfer to his team.

"How can something like that happen?" the woman asked. "Who on earth could do such a thing?" She rubbed her eyes with her thumbs and index fingers. Kovacs waited for a few seconds. She doesn't believe it was an accident, he thought, and she's not thinking in the plural.

"Who found Grandfather?" he said. The man raised his head and looked at his younger daughter.

"Our grandfather was always careful," the older girl said, gulping deeply. The boy nodded in agreement. Wieck cleared her throat. The woman pointed first at the younger girl, then at the dog.

"Katharina found Grandfather," she said. "And Emmy."

The evening before, Luise Maywald explained, her daughter had been over with Grandfather, as she had been every day recently. All three of the children had a very close relationship with their grandfather. It was just as you would imagine it – going for walks, telling stories, playing Old Maid.

"Ludo," said the older girl – Ursula, if Kovacs remembered rightly.

"Yes of course, Ludo too," the mother said. "Both – sometimes one, sometimes the other." Then suddenly their little daughter had been standing in the hall. At first glance, the mother went on, she looked the same as usual, perhaps a bit frozen, but it had been pretty cold outside over the last few days. The dog had started to behave oddly; it was tense and annoyed, she remembered, as if somebody it did not like was in the room. Kovacs glanced at Wieck. She'll make a note of all these things, he thought, things like: "a bit frozen" and "as if someone was in the room". But that uniform really doesn't suit her.

"Katharina stretched her arm out and opened her fist," the woman said. "Inside were the two Ludo pieces, a blue one and a yellow one. Emmy had flipped her ears back and Katharina said something strange: 'Four, four, got you.' Then we could see that her fingers were covered in blood, and from that moment she hasn't said another word." For a while they had all thought that Katharina had hurt herself somewhere, and because she would not talk, not even a moan or anything like that, the mother – feeling helpless – had taken her daughter to the bathroom. First she had washed her hands and then undressed her. But she did not find a wound.

"Which fingers?" Wieck asked. The woman did not understand at first.

"Which fingers were covered in blood?"

"Thumb, index finger, middle finger," the woman said, extending the index finger of her right hand and crooking her middle finger and thumb underneath. "Like that, as if she'd been poking around somewhere."

"Poking?"

"Yes, but we didn't think of that till much later. Poking – that's what must have happened."

The first thing she had done afterwards was to phone her father, but there was no answer. That was quite normal, she said; his hearing had not been the best. After the third attempt she had then sent Georg, her son, over, because at that stage nobody had thought that something might have happened. Georg had come back five minutes later; Grandfather was not there.

"Did you notice anything about your grandfather's house?" Kovacs asked. The boy shook his head. One of those twelve-year-olds whose hair was starting to show signs of greasiness.

"Was the front door open?"

"No, it was closed." Wide eyes, still no hint of puberty in the voice.

"Any lights on inside?"

"Yes, there were – the light above the table; and on the table was the Ludo board."

"And your grandfather wasn't there?"

"No, he wasn't."

The boy had called out for him and got no answer. He was not in the bedroom, bathroom or loo either.

"And outside?"

The boy shook his head again. "He wasn't outside either."

"I mean, did you call him?"

No, he had not called him – it was cold and dark.

"And so you just looked straight ahead and ran back the quickest way." Wieck had bent forwards a little. She is attentive, Kovacs thought, she asks the right questions and she understands children. The boy nodded.

"And Emmy growled at me," he said. "For no reason."

"What sort of dog is she?"

"A Border Collie." Whenever the older girl said something it always sounded very definite. A little podgy, Kovacs thought, some flab around the middle, pretty glasses. No doubt a fantastic older sister. When she grew up she would become like her mother.

The woman explained that her father used to go out for walks all the time, even at night. He particularly loved the hill behind the barn. There he used to sit on a chopping block next to the pile of spruce logs and would often stare at the mountains for hours, or down at the town.

"So we didn't work it out straight away," the man said. "Although Katharina behaved a bit oddly to begin with, and looked straight through us the whole time, she then sat down in front of the telly and it was all pretty normal."

"It wasn't until I tried to take the Ludo pieces out of her hand when she was going to bed, and she started to yell hysterically, that we wondered whether something had happened after all," the woman said. "Her eyes bulged and she howled like she'd never done before. Then my husband said that perhaps she'd seen an animal – a goat or a fox. A little later he said it might have been a dead animal."

He had put on his jacket, she said, and done a turn of the property, around the two houses. It had not occurred to him to go over to the barn. He had wanted to take the dog with him, but it was lying next to Katharina's bed as if bolted in place.

"It was full moon," Ernst Maywald said, "and the air was totally clear, that was the only remarkable thing. I stood by the hedge and looked down at the town, for thirty seconds perhaps. It was as if you could touch everything, every single lantern on the promenade."

They had then gone to bed without being especially worried. His father-in-law had always been healthy and he set great store by his independence. There had been no indication that anything had happened to him.

"How old was your father?" Wieck asked.

"Eighty-six," Luise Maywald said. "He would have been eighty-seven at the beginning of March."

It was the crows that had attracted his attention, the man said, it had been like in a film. He was on the early shift and so had left the house at half-past five. On his way over to the garage he had noticed two things: first, that the light was on in his father-in-law's house; second, the excited cawing of the crows. "It was coming from the barn," the man said. "So I didn't get into the car, I fetched my torch from the boot."

"And then you saw him?" Wieck asked. Sometimes she can't wait, Kovacs thought – when the tension gets too great.

"Yes," the man said. "I mean, it was strange. First I saw the crows all around, maybe ten or twenty. On the snowman, snowdog, in the snow, as if they were making a circle. They didn't fly away until I got quite close and shone the torch directly at them. There ..." He hesitated. "There weren't any birds on the body itself."

Kovacs did not find it difficult to imagine the scene that he described. The body did not look as if it had been picked at by animals, he was certain of that.

"And then you phoned?" Kovacs said. The man remained silent.

"Then he came back," the woman said. "I was in the bath and saw him in the mirror. My first thought was that someone had stolen our car from the garage."

"The car?"

"Yes, he was so pale and completely at a loss. He was supposed to be driving to work . . ." She has a feeling for those close to her, Kovacs thought, and she knows her husband. Ernst Maywald was tall, rather gaunt, and had huge hands.

He had told her immediately, and before the urge hit her to run outside she had thought of Katharina. Suddenly, they both realised where the bloody fingers had come from the night before, and why their daughter had looked so shocked. "I went up to her bedroom and pulled off the duvet. She was lying there curled up with her fist clenched and the Ludo pieces inside."

They had gone to the barn together. For a moment, everything had gone black and she had to sit down in the snow. It was only then that they had contacted the police from her husband's mobile. The young officer arrived twenty minutes later; the others would follow on, he said, and not much else.

40

Kovacs looked at the little girl. He pointed to her fist. "Have you got the pieces in there?" he asked. The girl stared into space and said nothing.

"He fell over and died," the big sister said. "He was an old man."

"That's what we told them," the mother said.

"Have you seen your grandfather?" Kovacs asked. The boy and the older girl shook their heads. The father threw up his arms in protest.

"For God's sake, no!"

"I think it would be a good idea," Kovacs said. Wieck looked at him, surprised. He leaned over and whispered to her that she should first go outside and make sure that the man's face was covered. She put her notepad away and stood up. She still looked blank.

"Is that really necessary?" Luise Maywald asked. Kovacs ignored her. He slowly stretched his hand out towards the little girl. "It'd be great if you could show me the pieces," he said. The girl looked straight past his right ear.

"I'd be really happy if you'd let me see the pieces – just for a bit."

At the very moment that he touched the child's clenched fist with his fingertips, she began to scream. The mother pressed her hands over her ears. The girl was screaming blue murder. She stared straight through Kovacs. She doesn't give a monkey's whether I'm happy or not, he thought.

As he approached the barn, Kovacs could see that Fat Mauritz from forensics was there. He must have shooed Lipp, Töllmann and Wieck away and was enlarging the sealed-off area. The bank of fog was closing in. The sky above them was greyish-yellow and a few flakes of snow were falling here and there.

Kovacs instructed Ernst Maywald and the two children to stay where they were. Katharina had continued to scream and so had stayed in the house with her mother. "I hope you know what you're doing," the father said. He had put on a quilted body warmer but was still shivering.

Sebastian Wilfert's face was covered by a piece of dark-green plastic sheeting. It was impossible to guess what was underneath. "Perfect," Kovacs said.

"I photographed everything," Lipp said. "But then forensics suddenly turned up. I should also tell you that Gasselik's been released as part of the Christmas amnesty. Because he's so young."

Kovacs shook hands with Mauritz. Sometimes they watched football together.

"What do you think?" he asked.

"The tyre marks," Mauritz said. "Maybe somebody drove over his head. But you know that we don't normally say anything ..."

"Before you ... first, second, third – yes, I know."

Who drives over an old man's head? Kovacs wondered. He motioned to Maywald and his children to come over.

"Is that your grandfather?" he asked. The children nodded.

"What's that green thing there for?" Georg asked, pointing to the piece of plastic.

"Somebody drove over your grandfather's face," Kovacs said. "It doesn't look pretty."

The girl gulped several times.

"What are the legs pointing up for?" the boy asked.

"I don't know," Kovacs said. "He was just lying like that." He means "why?" and asks "what for?" he thought, some people do that.

"He fell over and he's dead," the girl said. "He was an old man." She gulped several more times. Then she started to cry. Her father gave her a hug.

"Is that what you wanted?" he asked. "Did you have to put it so bluntly?" Now he's shaking out of anger, Kovacs thought, and he's got big hands.

Mauritz was on the phone. "And a tent," Kovacs heard him say.

"Do you mean to spend the night here?" he asked. Mauritz tapped the side of his head. Kovacs looked up: the odd snowflake, no more. But still, he knew that precipitation was the natural enemy of forensic science.

Wieck walked over to Kovacs. "I thought I'd take a look inside the garage," she said.

"Why?"

"Perhaps somebody really did steal the car." She laughed.

FOUR

I'm eating mashed potatoes with fried onion rings. Lore cooked it. It tastes alright, especially the onion rings. She's still a Polish whore all the same. I'm drinking lukewarm peppermint tea. Gerstmann is going back and forth across the car park, clearing it with the snow plough. It's pointless as it's going to snow again tomorrow. Gerstmann does pointless work and we pay him for it. Sometimes he just takes one of the cars and goes for a spin. Then he comes up with some excuse such as the car's got to have a run around. Dad says that Gerstmann is the most important man in the company after Reiter, head of sales. Because he knows everything that's going on.

Daniel's back. He's lying down in his room, asleep. He never used to sleep so much. He says he's got to catch up. He says that after four shitty months of being deprived he really needs to catch up.

The dishwasher door is jammed. I leave the plate next to the dishwasher. Lore will clear it away. Daniel says that at home she prays to a picture of a saint who worked miracles, and then she does it with various men. Just like all those Polish whores. They've all got shocking hairstyles, too, mostly platinum blonde.

I help myself to a slice of Christmas stollen from the plate. It's from the cake shop and a week old already. Mum says that there's so much fat in it that it won't go stale. It tastes like it, too. Maybe a touch of vanilla. The second slice tastes of almost nothing but fat.

It's a miracle that I'm not getting porkier. That's what everyone says who's seen me eat. Daniel says that people who are highly strung can eat what they like without getting fat. But that can't be true, as our dad's tummy hangs over his belt and they don't come more highly strung than him.

The door to Daniel's room is closed. I imagine him lying there on the bed, on his stomach, his right arm wrapped around his head. He said that sometime he'd tell me what happened inside. He always says "inside" and he says he'll know when I'm ready. Anyhow, he's been training for the last four and a half months. You only have to look at his arms to see that. "You've grown again," our mum said when he came home. He didn't say a word.

Two things are on my desk: my Game Boy S.P. and this newspaper cutting. In fact it's a copy of a newspaper cutting that Daniel gave me. *Kurier*, page four. "Was It Really an Accident?" in thick black letters, underlined in red felt-tip. Under the headline, the story of an old man who died when someone crushed his head. "The man's head was so badly mutilated as to be unrecognisable," it says. The man's name was Sebastian Wilfert and apparently he lived above the town, towards Mühlau. There's a photo of the man next to the article, but you can't see what he looked like because red circles have been scribbled all over the face. It could have been anybody's face. "The Force is going to take control of you," Daniel said when he gave me the article. To begin with I didn't understand what he meant by that. Then he whacked me. That always helps. It unblocks everything inside me.

The racetrack is beside my bed. A huge figure of eight, with four lanes. My dad said that you need a racetrack at my age. He had one, too. I switch it on and put the yellow car with the blue double stripe into the groove. I take the controller and do a lap, quite slowly. I find it pretty crap, to be honest. A lap of F-Zero G.X., Devil's Dungeon for example, in the Blue Falcon, is way more exciting. If I tell my dad that, he just says: a fortnight's C.B., C.B. meaning computer ban. If I then tell him that a Gamecube is a console not a computer, his eyes go funny and there's a little bit of B.H., B.H. meaning bodily harm. Daniel administers it to me and I don't tell anybody about it.

I zoom off, cut my speed just before the bend and then go full throttle again immediately out of it. If you're not a total spastic you can master it in a few hours.

How can an old man's head get crushed at Christmas time? O.K., old people slip and break their hips, and gardeners reach down into the shredder because a few lilac branches have got stuck, and their hands become instant sludge. But someone's *head*?

Tear into the corner so that the back swings right out but the car stays in the groove – that's the art of it. Of course, to begin with you're always coming off, and they stand there saying: you'll ruin all the cars in no time. And: I should have known it – why should you suddenly behave differently from normal? And you can see that the only reason they don't take it straight back from you is that it's Christmas.

I bet that people go to that house wanting to see the body. Each one of them wants to see the head which isn't a head any more, but everything's been sealed off and the police are not letting anybody in. Someone, no doubt, gets all excited and says some crap like, "The public has a right to know!" while imagining this red pile of sludge with perhaps a false tooth sticking out of it.

I put the blue car with the white star in the third lane and take the controller in my left hand. I'm so hopelessly right-handed that it takes precisely half a lap before the blue car comes flying off. I'm a bit gutted because it's my favourite car. Cars on, full throttle, go! 360 degree flip! Again. And again.

Now Daniel's standing in the doorway. The hood of his grey

top is pulled down over his head. He's started doing that recently. He comes over and whacks me. It's O.K.; I expect I made a heck of a racket.

"Have you read the article?" he asks.

"Yes," I say.

"Have you memorised all of it?"

"I think so."

He hits me again, quite gently this time. "I am your Emperor," he says, "and you are my creation."

I say nothing. I breathe like Darth Vader.

FIVE

Eleven people are sitting in the nave. He can tell that at a glance. It is one of his strengths. Sometimes he has to make an orderly list of his strengths: I can learn things by heart; I can solve quadratic equations in my head; I can tell how many people there are at a glance; I can run the marathon in three hours.

In the second row, Herr and Frau Weinberger; on the other side of the aisle, old Kocic; behind him, Frau Ettl, the office assistant; next to her, Irma. The two of them are friends. At the back on the right is a young lady he does not know. She is wearing a dark coat and a red scarf.

Two days ago an old man died. The name Sebastian Wilfert means nothing to him. The others say they usually saw him around on feast days. At least while his wife was still alive.

Lord, have mercy on us. Christ, have mercy on us. Lord, have mercy on us.

Irma is bellowing as usual. In her case it has nothing to do with that sanctimonious volume which some people use to demonstrate their piety. Irma suffers from a chronic calcification of the middle ear and is virtually deaf. The doctors say that it would be useless to operate again.

A meaningless reading from the Epistle to the Ephesians, warnings aimed at the congregation. Be moderate! How ridiculous – after all, this Apostle Paul was a terrible narcissist himself. What got him going was influence and money. But you cannot say that to some of the brothers. Robert, for example, maintains that Paul was actually more important for Christianity than Jesus himself, and if you challenge him on this he gets offended.

By now the whole town must be talking about the death of the old man. If you die of pneumonia or a heart attack nobody could give a damn, but if someone drives over your head then everyone is talking about you. A sculpture of St Sebastian is fixed onto the second column on the left. Being shot through by arrows would get chins wagging, oh yes.

The forensic pathologist is saying that it happened in the middle of the night. Because of the low temperatures outside, however, she had to allow for some leeway in the calculations.

In the darkness of night the spirit of God appears and crushes the face of the enemy. "Crushes" is the right word.

He tries to remember the moon that night. He cannot. He recalls the massive plaque belonging to Kossnik, the accountant, and his fantasy of driving through the town's streets in a huge, dark-red snow plough. He wishes he had his iPod on him.

Just before the Gospel readings the Weinbergers start to get on his nerves; it is always the same. That expression of conformism, that "please preach something nice to us" look which they fix him with during the week as well, even though they know full well that sermons are not held on weekdays.

Who hath taken his evil thoughts and dashed them. The Rule. I know that I'd like to smash their faces in, he thinks, and I know I ought not to think that. Grumpy incense, he thinks; whenever I see these two the phrase "grumpy incense" comes to mind. I find it comforting, even though I don't actually know what it means.

The altar server rings the hand bell. Her mother works in reception at the Hotel Wertzer on the lake. She has a little brother and lives in one of the blocks of flats in Furth-Nord. What's her name? He goes mad when he cannot remember things. Names, for example. The little girl is wearing ankle boots with a speckled fur trim. The altar smock is too short for her.

My son is called Jakob, he thinks, he is five years old. My wife is called Sophie and works as an assistant pharmacist. I've never forgotten their names. They will come and I'll collect them from the station. But not until it gets warmer.

For on the same night that he was betrayed he took bread and, after giving thanks, he gave it to the disciples.

As always when he raises the host, he cannot help thinking of Padre Pio, whose stigmata opened up during the consecration, it was claimed, and blood seeped into his bandages. He is sure the Weinbergers have a picture of him on the wall at home, above their dining table or bed. That bigoted, conceited, relentlessly self-obsessed Capuchin friar's face staring down at your soup bowl, he thinks, or at your conjugal duty.

Then he took the cup of wine and, after giving thanks, he gave it to the disciples.

He imagines a shadowy figure appearing on the organ platform, aiming a laser gun at the Padre, and burning holes in his hands and feet, where the paint marks had been before. Then the figure raises the barrel a little and blasts the priest's head off.

I must finish this quickly, he thinks. Afterwards I've got to take a pill and get some exercise. Then I'll lie down.

On bended knee. The mystery of faith. *We proclaim your death, Lord Jesus, we praise your resurrection, until you come in glory.* Wait. Deep breaths. Sometimes he reaches the point where he needs some instructions.

Christmas is an awkward time.

He sees himself running across the cemetery, under the railway line, along the sawmill. He can feel the gravel crunching under his feet. The flickering of television sets through the windows of people's homes. For a second he stares into a pair of headlights on full beam. The negative images remain in his eyes for a while afterwards. He is sure now that it was cloudy that night. No moon. No stars.

Before then, the Boxing Day visit to his mother and sister. Both staggeringly simple-minded. The fatty meal, the same old conversations. I can quite understand why my father disappeared; it had nothing to do with me, he thinks.

His iPod is in the sacristy. Once he even listened to music while celebrating mass. It must have been more than three years ago now. Afterwards, Clemens forced him to go to the clinic in Graz.

There are some funny things about my life, he thinks. My father disappeared from one day to the next and never got in touch again. I joined an order because I was on the verge of falling to pieces. But I still fall to pieces on a regular basis. I secretly believe that Bob Dylan is the reincarnation of Jesus Christ.

After the Lord's Prayer he offers the altar server his hand for the rite of peace. Her fingers are warm and podgy. Her name is Renate – he remembers it now.

The young lady at the back is standing alone. Nobody is going to shake her hand. He feels sorry for her. He would like to give her a hug. He would like to go up to her, give her a hug, and tell her about Sophie and Jakob.

Behold the Lamb of God. It takes away the sins of the world.

The Weinbergers, of course, come up to take communion. Old Kocic comes up, too, and finally Josephine Martin, a Filipino nurse who attends mass several times a week because her husband beats her and this makes her feel guilty. Frau Weinberger opens her mouth wide. She would never take the host in her hand. Her tongue has a yellow tinge, as if she were suffering from angina.

The host, a sip of wine. Wipe the rim of the cup. Cover the cup. Rituals keep us from falling apart. And the Rule. *Who has dashed his evil thoughts.*

He notices the change while uttering the blessing. There are now twelve people in the nave. At the back on the right, standing close to the young lady, is a small figure with a yellow headband over his blond hair. It is Björn.

SIX

The armchair she sat in was tiny. He had thought that ever since he first met her. An ancient, stained, reddish-brown bentwood chair, with a rip across the seat. Although Irene was slim, her hips protruded on either side.

As she played, she made slow circular movements with her torso. The neck of the instrument slid back and forth along her left collarbone. Her head was bowed, as if she were staring at a particular point on the floor. She had tied her medium-length hair into a ponytail that revealed just how much her ears stuck out.

Raffael Horn leaned against the door. He had an erection. It's Saturday morning, I'm watching my wife play music, and I've got an erection, he thought. Life could definitely be worse.

She was playing the Sarabande from Bach's *Suite in D Major*. When she played Bach she was at one with herself. That is the way it had always been. Her look turned inwards, the occasional hint of her tongue between her lips, the rims of her ears glowing red. In times gone by he would pounce on her in such moments. He did not do that any more.

He carefully closed the door to the stables. The building they had converted into a music room was at least fifty metres square; many years back it had housed cattle and sheep. That is why they had called it the stables from the start. Sometimes, visitors would sit inside on the long thin bench of unplaned fir; too seldom for Irene Horn's liking.

She seemed pleased with the bow; that made him happy. Through a viola player in her orchestra, he had bought it from an instrument maker in Hallein, near Salzburg. The bow had been crafted in Genoa 150 years ago, and had a very firm action; in the man's opinion it was flawless. He had not said anything else about it so Horn was willing to believe him. Irene had not said anything either when she took the bow out of its case on Christmas Eve. She tightened the adjuster with three or four turns and then played the *Xerxes* Largo without any warm-up. They had all sat there silently, and Tobias, that ultracool incarnation of puberty, had tears in his eyes.

Mimi crouched on the window sill, her teeth chattering. She wailed in indignation when he sat next to her. Two great tits sat on the platform of the bird box, cracking open sunflower seeds. "I'll let you have them," he said and stroked her neck. She just flicked her ear in his direction for a few seconds.

The outside thermometer was showing minus eleven. The pale yellow of the rising sun appeared through the tops of the spruces. The north-eastern part of town looked tangibly close. A veil of mist hung over the portion of the river visible from their house. A beautiful day, Horn thought, as if nothing could go wrong. He put some water on to boil. One of the sad facts of my life, he thought, is that during my ten years here each Saturday morning has come and gone without a newspaper, and in ten years I haven't got used to it. He fetched a tin of cat food from the larder, spooned a portion into Mimi's bowl, and mixed in a handful of cereal flakes. The cat leaped from the window sill and rubbed up against his ankles in excitement. Either I'm too lazy or it's not that important to me, he thought. He knew that he had only to get into the car, and that there was a newsagent's right by the road into town. Ten minutes there, ten minutes back. But he never did it.

He thought about their time in Vienna, about their flat in the second district and the old newsagent whose sight had become worse and worse each year. In the end he had to be told where the magazines and packets of cigarettes were on the shelves. But he always had Horn's newspapers ready, right to the very end. On Saturdays, the *Standard* and the *Presse*, that is how it had been.

He put rolls in the oven to warm up, and laid the table for two. Tobias would tumble down around midday, pour himself to a double helping of Coco Pops, and mumble something like, "Life is an imposition."

After he had put two eggs in the boiler he stood there for a moment and listened. He could hear very little: the bubbling of the water as it simmered in the kettle, and the cat munching at his feet.

"But you're the biggest townie in the world," his friends had said back then. "How can you move to the country?" His reply was that Furth am See was not the country, but a town with more than 35,000 inhabitants, a theatre, a symphony orchestra, a marina, a polytechnic, and a general hospital which not only planned to set up its own psychiatric department, but had also immediately agreed to his request to practise child psychiatry. "Admit it, it's because of Frege," some of them had said. He denied it, although of course it had been partly due to Frege. Frege was a psychopathic arsehole who had systematically ruined his chance of succeeding Böhler as head of department. "Horn is an extremely competent colleague, you know. This indecisiveness of his does not come into it." Or: "A mother took me aside yesterday and told me she didn't dare talk to Doctor Horn because she felt so stupid in his presence." Frege had gone a long time ago; two years after Horn left, he had moved to a clinic for addiction in Germany. But I still harbour the fantasy of smashing his teeth in, or driving a red-hot needle into his upper thigh, Horn thought. He spooned some coffee into the cafetière and poured over boiling water. "Bach and sex at the same time doesn't work."

He turned around. Irene was standing in the doorway, grinning.

"I didn't hear you coming," he said.

"I know. I like you making breakfast."

"I always make it. How long have you been up?"

"Two, three hours." She came over to him and kissed him gently on the mouth. "Bach with sex afterwards works fine," she said.

He took her right ear between his fingers. "You've got the sticky-outiest ears in the world," he said.

"I know," she said and kissed him again.

"Before or after breakfast?" he asked.

"Before," she said.

"The eggs are hard-boiled," Horn confirmed a while later. The egg boiler had buzzed just as they were getting to the fun part. He had yanked the plug out and the eggs had remained in the hot steam.

"In winter you should eat hard-boiled eggs," Irene said, placing a slice of salami between her teeth.

Horn nodded. "They're ballast for a snowstorm," he said. She laughed and blew a strand of hair from her forehead. She has red cheeks like a little girl, he thought. He knew that she had never considered moving back to Vienna, not for a second. "What do you want?" she said when the conversation turned to this topic. "Everything has got better." He had never tried to contest this. Michael had done, which had strained his relationship with his mother even more.

They talked about the bow and the quality of musical instruments in general. "Now and then it defies you," she said, "and that's good." For an instrument to be perfect for someone, it has to become an extension of their body. This was especially noticeable in the case of Yehudi Menuhin and his violin. "Or

John McLaughlin," he said.

"Who's John McLaughlin?"

"Philistine!" It was a sort of game between them. John McLaughlin's guitar was also like a part of his body. For the most part it was in complete unison with him; sometimes it did whatever it wanted.

"I want honey next," she said.

"Eat your egg first."

She held her empty shell in front of him. "Yuk!"

Horn stood up and shuffled off to the larder. "What are you doing?" she said.

"I'm getting Frau Cello Soloist her honey." She threw a scrunched-up napkin at him.

Horn rummaged through the jars of jam and bottles of home-made fruit juice. Right at the back of the shelf he found a small jar of thyme honey which they had brought back from a holiday in Turkey years before. "We're out of real honey," he said. She tried her best to twist open the lid, but in the end gave him back the jar to open.

"What was wrong with that little girl yesterday?" she asked.

"After breakfast I'll go to Joachim and Else's and fetch some."

"I mean the girl with the grandfather."

He took another roll from the basket, sliced it open, and started spreading it with butter. "Nothing wrong," he said.

"What do you mean nothing wrong?"

"Nothing. Absolutely nothing. Zilch."

"Didn't she come?"

"Yes, she came. Her mother brought her in, as arranged." He put a small slice of Stilton on the buttered half of the roll and took a bite. He always said that at breakfast on Saturdays you had the newspaper types and the conversation types, as well as the blue cheese types and the honey types. Newspaper and blue cheese usually went hand in hand, like conversation and honey. All that Irene would say to that was: "moron".

"What do you mean it was nothing? Wasn't she screaming her head off? Or were you called away to an emergency?"

Horn felt a slight irritation welling up inside him, as he always did when Irene's curiosity began to become intrusive. I've got to get out, he thought, otherwise we'll start rowing, despite our intimacy just now. "No," he said. "She just sat there silently."

"For a whole hour?"

"For a whole hour."

"So what did you do?"

"Waited. I waited, that's all."

She shook her head angrily. "What was the use of that?"

"None," he said. "It was no use at all."

She frowned and pointed a finger at him. "I don't believe a word you're saying, Herr Analyst," she objected. "You're forever telling me there's nothing more productive in therapy than silence, and suddenly the reverse is true?"

"With us psychos, there are no absolutes." He dipped a piece of roll into the honey and offered it to her. She took it carefully between her lips. Then she bit his finger. "Shall we do it again after breakfast?" he asked, surprised.

She laughed, shaking her head.

Irene Horn dropped her husband off just past the large roundabout and drove on into the town centre. They had agreed to meet in the Stiftscafé an hour and a half later.

Horn started southwards along the Severinstraße for a few hundred metres and then turned east. There were no clouds, the sun was at the mid-point in the sky, and in the distance he could see the peaks of the Limestone Alps shining above the town. Although the pavement outside the row of terraced houses had been cleared, it had not been gritted. Remnants of snow crunched under his shoes.

The girl had turned up to his surgery in fur-lined boots and a green quilted jacket with a squirrel on it. She had backed over to the wall and stood there motionless for ten minutes. Then she started to move slowly along the wall. She had not once taken her eyes off him.

Unusually for him, Horn had started after a while to talk. Remove the fear, he thought, you've got to take the fear away from her as quickly as possible. "Last time we met it was all pretty crazy," he said. "The paramedics and the ambulance, plus the police and those other people you didn't know." The girl continued to slide along the wall, past the toy shelf, over to the narrow wardrobe. There she had sat on the ground, her knees pulled up to her chest, and her arms wrapped around them. Her right hand was clenched. "You've still got a secret in your hand, haven't you?" he said, and the girl's expression did not change. He spoke, stopped talking, and then played with the puppets. The policeman told the crocodile off because he always gobbled the others up, and the witch let out a triumphant laugh. The girl looked straight through the puppets; she ran her eyes over his desk, over the pictures on the wall, over the bookcase. From time to time she would scrutinise him. He explained that death was largely an incomprehensible thing, and that some children had nice grandparents and others did not. The whole time he had felt powerless and superfluous. When he said, "Our time is up," the little girl stood up. She looked out of the window for a few seconds, at the river, the banks of reeds and the lake. "I wonder whether you can swim?" he asked, but thought it was a daft thing to say. It was winter, after all: in this weather, the lake would surely freeze over soon, and fathers would be hurrying to sand the rust off their children's skating boots. But the girl looked at him and, just for an instant, he noticed a quite different expression in her eyes from their previous session. Perhaps the two of them were the only people in the town who had been thinking of swimming at that moment.

Sitting on top of a conifer, a nutcracker was making a din. Horn stopped and tried to pack together a snowball, but it crumbled in his hand. These birds had all been around when he was a child, too: nutcrackers, fieldfares and hoopoes. He would sit for hours beneath the kitchen window and look over at the larches beyond the garden fence, at the bird house which had been fixed onto a wooden stake. Little by little his father had taught him the names: crested tit, bullfinch, waxwing. He thought of Heidemarie and how she sometimes felt as if all that was left of her was an empty sack. What people pompously referred to as identity was actually quite difficult to define; it was made up of everything that had been crammed into an individual over the course of their lifetime. In his case, for example, it even included a flock of waxwings which had landed in his parents' garden – a long way to the west of their customary route – and stayed there for a day and a half. He could recall how his father, a biology teacher, had been beside himself with excitement. The birds had crested feathers, bright stripes on their wings, and were almost tame. He was eight or nine at the time, and he remembered daydreaming about catching one of the waxwings, tying a thread to its leg, and flying it like a kite.

He wondered whether Heidemarie was sleeping better with the new pills, or whether she was still lying awake and being sucked into the emotional void of her parents as if into an enormous black funnel. He wondered why sons murdered their mothers and daughters did not, and why suicide fantasies were a huge relief to some people. People kill themselves on New Year's Eve, he thought. New Year's Eve was three days away.

The end of the terrace was also the end of the pavement. The street narrowed at this point, but continued in the same direction. He was approached by a thickset man with a pit bull on a leash. It was Konrad Seihs, the local secretary of the Business Party. They gave each other a polite greeting. "Fascist bastard," Horn muttered when Seihs was far enough away. The man was tipped to be the next council officer in charge of internal administration and security. He had been in the army before he started working for the party. Amongst other things, he was calling for an increase in police patrols on the town's council estates. Years before, he and Horn had clashed at a public meeting on the subject of care for the disabled. It was Irene who had prevented the matter from escalating. "Where's your professional distance?" she whispered to him, giving his lower arm a firm squeeze. "He's not my patient," he answered. "Pretend he is," she said, and so he ceased his verbal assault on Seihs. Later, when he had thought about it, he realised of course that calling the Chancellor a deranged narcissist, or the Finance Minister a compulsive neurotic stuck in the pregenital phase did not alter things one jot. But it had helped at the time. He thought of Schmidinger and pictured people like him and Seihs perched at the sports club bar, their conversation switching from shagging Thai girls to problems with asylum seekers to how impossible it was to tell which elements of the so-called youth scene on the Walzwerk estate were involved in drug dealing and street prostitution. He felt pangs of guilt whenever he thought of Schmidinger, both on account of the latter's wife and daughters, and due to his own strong desire to sedate the man and lock him away. "I'm a doctor," he said to himself. But he also knew that made no difference at all.

Joachim and Else Fux's house was right by the Mühlaubach, so close in fact that the lower of the two barns was flooded every time there was high water. For this reason the barn was empty save for a pile of old bricks and roof tiles. Fux had shown it to him years ago. When Horn asked him why he had not torn it down he said, "because it's always been there." Horn leaned on the wooden railings of the bridge. There was little gradient to the stream at this point. Tongues of ice lapped down at the water from the granite blocks which bolstered the stream's banks. My whole life is a play between town and country, he thought. I go back and forth, but I don't feel at home anywhere.

When he opened the front door he was assailed by the scent of cinnamon. Whenever a special occasion was impending, you could be sure that Else would be baking. She had no doubt just made tons of biscuits and cakes for Christmas, and was now preparing for New Year.

The two of them were sitting at the dining table, sorting through photographs. Horn sniffed, wrinkling his nose.

"Red wine cake with cinnamon," Else said, getting up. "Are you out visiting patients?"

Horn laughed. "Exactly, I'm going from house to house treating post-Christmas depression." She fetched him a stool. She's seventy-five and still a beautiful woman, he thought.

Fux gathered the photographs together.

"Leave them, I'm not staying long," Horn said. He reached for one of the pictures. A few soldiers: young men in badly fitting uniform. "It's astonishing that photographs do actually turn yellow with age," he said.

"Our skin turns yellow and so do photographs," Fux said tersely. The soldiers in the photograph all looked the same. "Who's that?" Horn asked.

"I was enlisted in 1945," Fux said. Two of the soldiers looked very alike, as if twins. They all have the same unhappy expression, Horn thought. Right at the front was one whose face was no longer recognisable. In its place was a white mark, as if it had been fingered often. It's him, Horn thought. He looks at the picture over and over again, and each time he taps his finger on his face, as if he has to make sure that he was there. Over the course of time he's rubbing himself out.

Horn pointed to the man. "And that's you there, is it?" he asked.

Fux promptly took the photographs and put them back in the box on the table. "It wasn't nice back then," he said. His hand was trembling. I've upset him and asked too much, Horn thought. He doesn't want to talk or show me the pictures.

"Does it go away with time?" he asked cautiously.

Fux looked at him. He had turned pale and his jaw muscles had tensed. He gave an almost imperceptible nod.

"I'm seventy-seven now. I was seventeen then."

Seventeen. A child. Sometimes there's nothing you can say, Horn thought. He could well believe that it had not been nice then; he could understand Fux's desire to erase himself from that era. He knew that post-traumatic symptoms could crop up decades later, quite severe ones too.

Else passed him a plate of Christmas biscuits. He ran his eyes over them.

"You don't have to take one," she said. "It's just something I do automatically when visitors come."

"How's your shoulder?" Horn asked. He wanted to get away from war stories. Fux slowly stretched out his right arm, clenched his fist, and then stretched again. "Better?"

"A little."

For several months now, Horn had been treating Fux for shoulder-arm syndrome, which was as persistent as shoulder-arm syndromes tend to be. "I only dabble in neurology," he said, and Fux said that he didn't mind – he wouldn't dream of letting another doctor look at him. Recently Horn had given him a corticoid depot injection in the upper part of the deltoid muscle, and had said that if that did not help then all that was left was dear old Frau Limnig from Waiern with her pebbles and pendulum. Horn felt the upper arm. He could see the medication was working. It was less painful when touched. There was still a small tender area on the back of the shoulder. "You're a tough nut," he said. Fux stood up, looked at him, and said nothing in reply. He was half a head shorter than Horn, wiry and tanned. When he stood his body was slightly bent and twisted to the right, an idiosyncrasy which vanished as soon as he moved. "That's from my work," he had said when Horn mentioned it once. Fux had been a postman in Furth for almost thirty years and had always carried his large black shoulder bag on the left, which explained the anomaly in his posture, at least in part. And yet, even at the end of his career he was still speedier than all his colleagues. When he retired he was presented with the black and yellow Puch moped which had assisted him on his round for fifteen years. He was the only postman who had regularly used one. Now he used it to go to his beehives, whenever the weather permitted. Apart from that he drove a dark-green Opel Astra Combi.

"Do you want some honey?" Fux asked.

"How did you guess?"

"Everybody who comes here wants honey."

"Am I everybody?"

Else laughed out loud. "No, you're not," she said.

As if it were a scene from a film Horn could still recall that clearing to the south of the town. Nobody knew him at the time, and they had only sent for him because he was the new psychiatrist. A forestry worker had driven him up a winding farm road in an ancient Lada Niva with zero suspension, and he remembered being delighted when finally he got out of it. In front of them was a timber barn, a brownish-black, weathered log building in the old Alpine style, only slightly taller. To its left were ten or twelve colourful beehives, some of which stood in isolation, while others were stacked on top of each other. In the middle of these was a group of people, only two of whom – both uniformed policemen – had bothered to greet him at first. Then a strong-looking, bald-headed man in civilian clothes had come up to him and offered his hand. "Ludwig Kovacs, Kriminalpolizei," he said. An elderly lady, a former nurse in fact, had rung the police: she had found a note at home from her husband saying he was going to hang himself. After she had searched the house and outbuildings without finding him, there was only one other place she could imagine he might do it. "When my colleagues arrived he was in the middle of cleaning out one of his hives, as if everything were normal," Kovacs said. Appearing very relaxed, the man had chatted with them. He had said that the whole thing was a big mistake; his wife had just been over concerned. They were about to leave when, by chance, one of them peered into the barn and noticed the stepladder on the cargo bed of the old truck and the steel sling at the top of the lifting arm. When Kovacs had returned to the barn with the wife, the man was distraught.

Horn had approached the group of people and saw that the policemen were still restraining the man by his arms. His wife was on her knees, trying to talk to him. Kovacs' brusque comment – "That's the neurologist" – was still as vivid in Horn's mind as the expression on Fux's face. It was the look of somebody who had wanted to die there and then.

Perhaps it was because he had spared Fux a spell in a psychiatric institution that Horn had struck up a kind of friendship with him and his wife. It was also perhaps because he had never asked about the reasons behind the planned suicide, and that he had accepted Fux's rejection of every type of psychotherapy. "Give me medication so that the urge to hang myself goes away,"

Fux had said. "And don't try to delve inside me – it's not going to happen, you understand?" He had given him medication, all sorts of stuff, especially in the early days, and in time Fux no longer had any objection to remaining alive. They talked about different things, about the problems relating to forced and voluntary psychiatric treatment, about the fact that cats and bees were not so different as pets, and about the population of Furth am See, these strange urban–Alpine people, about whom nobody could know quite as much as a former postman. At some point their wives had got to know each other, and before long they were all good friends – it had been a logical and natural development. Fux had added more bee colonies, one after another, and each time Horn had been able to reduce the dose of psychotropic drugs. Eventually Fux said that he had more clarity in his life, and Horn had thought that this was as good an outcome as he could have hoped for.

"Of course I'd like some honey," Horn said, taking a rum truffle from the plate of biscuits.

"Everybody wants honey," Fux said.

Horn crushed the truffle with his tongue against the roof of his mouth. Else Fux watched him in anticipation. "Well?" she asked.

Horn swallowed. "You know damn well. The best rum truffle in the world. Mostly walnuts and butter. Fat content: 59 per cent. As ever."

"You can afford it."

"Yes, because Irene doesn't make rum truffles."

Else laughed. "Poor man," she said. Horn drew back when she shoved the plate of biscuits under his nose. "It's honey I'm after, not biscuits."

Fux went to the door. "Are you coming, or will you tell me what you want?" he asked. Horn said goodbye to Else.

"Old people lose their patience," she said glancing at her

husband. She knew that Horn always accompanied him to the barn where he kept his equipment.

There was an intense smell of wax, which was both soft and strong. At the far end of the room was the centrifuge, partially covered by a white blanket. It drew your attention as soon as the door was opened. Frames in need of repair were leaning up against the wall immediately to the left. Above them hung a pair of ochre-coloured overalls and the beekeeping hat with its protective veil. On the shelf stretching along the entire right-hand wall were stacked jars, arranged according to the honey's origin. In front of this Fux had built a sort of bar out of larch wood. This is where he let his customers try the honeys. Horn sat down on one of the stools. He liked the wooden panelling on the walls and under the roof, as well as the smell, and the sunlight on the jars of honey. He especially liked the large heater, painted rust brown, which Fux had connected to the central heating system of the main house so that the room had at least some warmth in winter.

Fux talked about a new spot above Sankt Christoph, on the southern side of the lake. A young farmer had offered him this site in the middle of a larch forest, which had been used to store wood but was now abandoned. All he wanted in return was honey for himself and his family. He had settled a first lot of bees there one and three-quarter years ago, only five colonies to start with, as he always did before he could gauge how much a site would yield. The harvest from the first two seasons had been quite incredible – an especially clear and fruity forest honey, very granulated with medium viscosity. He placed a jar in front of Horn together with a small spoon and paper napkin.

Horn unscrewed the lid, dipped the spoon in and took it out again slowly. The thread of honey became thinner and thinner. The tiny spiral which he had made when he had scraped the surface disappeared within a second.

"Can you imagine anybody in this town driving over an old man's head?" he asked.

Fux looked at him in surprise. "How can you be so blunt?"

"You know the people here," Horn said. An uncomfortable feeling came over him. All I'm doing is treating this little girl, he thought. It's not good to want to know too much more.

"I could imagine a few people being capable of it, if they were drunk enough," Fux said after a while.

Perhaps it is as simple as that, Horn thought: someone's had a bit to drink, like most people round here they're pretty unobservant anyway, they put the car into reverse by mistake, knock the old man down, and run over his face. "You're right," he said. "I can imagine it, too."

Horn put the spoon into his mouth. The honey tasted spicy and new. "White bread honey," he said. Fux nodded in satisfaction. Horn looked at him. He's wearing glasses, he thought. He didn't before. He's getting old.

"How are you?" he asked.

"Is this a medical visit after all then?"

Horn licked the spoon clean. "You'd never tell the truth in front of Else."

"You're right," Fux said. "I'm fine – that's the truth. I'm starting to discover that certain things are untrue, but otherwise I'm fine."

"What do you mean certain things are untrue?"

"It's untrue, for example, that you forget everything as you get older. The opposite is the case: suddenly you see some things with such clarity that it hurts."

"Perhaps that's got something to do with your new glasses."

Fux smiled, grinned and took them off. "I know they're ugly," he said. "But I can't do without them in artificial light." In the last few days he had been recalling that time – in his very early days of keeping bees – when several colonies succumbed to the varroa mite. He had stood in front of the hives, looking at all the dead and deformed bees; it had almost broken his heart. Or the business with Wertzer's youngest son, who had climbed onto Fux's work moped in front of the hotel and then just driven off. He had come back with a huge burn on his calf, howling that he would report Fux and the entire postal service because there was no way that moped's exhaust was in proper working order – Fux would have to pay him compensation and a disability pension. This boy, only just sixteen, had stood on the hotel forecourt and yelled at him in the most disrespectful manner; Fux was too baffled to say anything in reply. Suddenly, the main door to the hotel had swung open and old Wertzer – quite a small, stocky man – stormed out, stepped between them and, without a single word, gave his grandson a powerful slap in the face, the classic combination: left to right; the flat of the hand first, then the back. Still silent, he pointed to the door, and the youngster marched off without hesitation, his head bowed, and his grandfather's handprints on his face.

"Until a few weeks ago these things were buried," Fux said. "Then they turn up again – you've no idea where they come from."

Horn placed the spoon on his napkin and screwed the lid back on the jar. "Did you ever have anything to do with old Wilfert?" he asked.

"Wilfert?" For a second Fux gave him a horrified look. Then he stared into space as if he were having to think about it. "His house was not on my postal round," he said at last. "From time to time his daughter used to buy honey from me, like lots of other people."

"Any stories?"

"About him, you mean?"

Horn nodded. Fux took off his glasses and pressed his fingertips against his eyelids. He now looked very tired. Horn thought back to the episode in front of the barn. Death is still very much on his mind – I should have thought of that. "We can change the subject if you like," he said. Fux dismissed this suggestion with a wave of his hand.

"His wife died not so long ago," Fux said in a soft voice. "It was quite sudden, thrombosis, or something like that. His daughter looked after him, his son-in-law works at the sawmill, there are a few grandchildren. Just a normal old man, people say."

"Nothing particular?"

"He was a hunter, but so are lots of people round here."

Cejpek is a hunter, Horn thought; and Martin Schwarz, his neighbour, went hunting too sometimes. Tobias said that all hunters ought to be strapped to a tree and left to the mercy of the animals. When he was older and stronger he would definitely be a vegetarian. At the moment, thought Horn, my love towards my son mainly manifests itself in a clip round the ear, but I suppose this is always the case with the real love of fathers for their sons at a certain point in the relationship.

Horn took two jars of the new forest honey and a jar of an almost white, creamy rape honey that Irene liked. Fux wrapped the jars carefully in tissue paper and, as usual, refused to allow Horn to pay. Horn had learned that it was useless to protest, so he put his wallet away.

"What is the varroa mite?" he asked as he was leaving.

"Something which sits in your neck, sucks out your blood, and turns you into a cripple," Joachim Fux said. He still seemed exhausted.

"Me?"

"If you're a bee, yes." They looked at each other. Horn laughed.

As Raffael Horn headed back towards the centre of town, breathing out the occasional small cloud of mist, he thought that the last thing he wanted to do was to bump into Konrad Seihs and his pit bull again. I'll smash his face in with this bag of honey jars, he thought, and in his daydream neither Seihs nor the dog were expecting it; both of them looked extremely stupid.

A while later, as he was crossing the river over the Severin bridge and gazing at the hospital to the west, he realised that he had forgotten to ask Fux how bees overwinter.

SEVEN

"Lefti, do I look funny?" Kovacs asked. Lefti, the owner, placed a glass of unfiltered Pils in front of Kovacs and took a good look at him.

"Of course you look funny, Kommissar," he said. "I mean, not you personally, but the fact that you're sitting here on my terrace with your beer in the depths of winter, wearing your black woolly hat, at this table that's been put out especially for you, with all this snow around, and the lake down there that's already half frozen. Now, if you also take into account that this is a Moroccan restaurant, and that in Morocco people in thick, blue, padded jackets who don't know whether or not to take off their gloves to drink are quite a rarity; if you take all this into consideration then, yes, you do look funny."

"Well, that makes me feel much better," Kovacs said. He slipped off his right glove.

"*Prost!*"

"Although I suppose that there are some parts of Morocco where they do wear black woolly hats, up in the Atlas mountains, in Ifrane for example, or around the Jbel Toubkal."

"Well, it also makes me feel better that I'm not so different in every respect."

"You don't understand me, Kommissar."

"As usual."

"Yes, as usual."

Kovacs and Lefti got on well. The fact that skinhead gangs had stopped attacking the "Tin" since Kovacs started turning up there on a regular basis with his team was only part of the reason. There was something more personal too. Lefti had an instinct for whether a customer wanted a full meal with a long story, or just a glass of beer. Kovacs valued that highly. Lefti was a curious type, but never intrusive. He loved football and was at war with every kind of bureaucracy, which meant that people trusted him and that he was always well informed. Kovacs valued that too, at least sometimes. And there was also Szarah, Lefti's wife. She worked in the kitchen day in, day out, and was a total blessing for the business. She had been a particular godsend to Kovacs since his wife had divorced him four years ago. "I would have starved without Szarah," he sometimes said. Lefti would reply, "No way would you have starved. Look at yourself: you might have got the odd stomach ulcer, but you'd never have starved." Kovacs would then say, "But Szarah's carrot puree with mint saved my life." Lefti would keep arguing for a while but he let Kovacs win in the end. He kept an eye on his wife, but everybody could see that this was totally unnecessary: her cypress-like figure and the large curve in the bridge of her nose combined to make her seem so inaccessible that nobody would have tried anything on with her.

The lake will certainly freeze, Kovacs thought. Until recently nobody believed it possible, but the skies have cleared and temperatures are well below freezing. He scanned the municipal outdoor swimming pool, now under a blanket of snow, the indoor pool with its low sunken roof, the narrow jetties of the boat hire place, the two blocks of the old lakeside hotels, and the marina which was currently empty of masts. Kovacs thought of his own dinghy which he had left with Fred Ley under cover in Waiern, on the northern side of the lake. It was a nice old boat made of false acacia, with a clear varnish; the covered bow and the seating were teak. Over the past few years he had more often rented the boat out than used it himself, even though he had imagined that after his divorce he would be out in it all the time, to fish or just to sail. Yvonne, his wife, had hated the lake, the tourists who came every year, the fish, and the cool westerly wind which she blamed for her joint troubles. It had been no different with Charlotte, their daughter. From this point of view it was only logical that Charlotte now lived with her mother and Yvonne's new husband in Traun near Linz, an area devoid of any large bodies of water.

He put his hand in his jacket and felt for the retractable pencil he always carried. In the past, whenever he had been working on a case, he had written notes in a thick D.I.N. A6 book with an orange cover. He caught Bitterle and Demski in a huddle once, laughing about his notebook, and after that he had left it at home. Occasionally he still wrote on napkins or tabletops, drew diagrams or sketched ideas. But just having the pencil in his hand was usually enough to give some structure to his thoughts.

The spate of car break-ins since the end of November was relatively clear-cut. Always at night, always close to an arterial road – in one of the side streets or in the nearest parallel street. They came in the evenings, checked to see which cars had things in them – clothes, bags, electronic gadgets – and, a few hours later, picked the locks. They probably drove around in a car with a stolen number plate, most likely they came from Romania or Moldova, and worked from an unknown headquarters. These crooks preferred the medium-sized towns in the south and east of the country: Wiener Neustadt, Krems, Steyr, Bruck an der Mur, Villach, Furth. They worked exceptionally quickly and left no significant clues. People speculated as to what they might do if somebody caught them in the act. As this was yet to happen, no-one could tell. None of that interests me, thought Kovacs. Let the police patrols do their work – I'm sick to death of outraged people who've been daft enough to leave their laptop in the car.

He noticed his beer getting colder, so put his pencil away and his glove back on. I couldn't give a monkey's if people see me, he thought. You can't always worry about what other people think of you.

There were several small groups of people on the promenade, including a pair of joggers. The sun was a hand's width above the peak of the Kammwand; it bathed most of the town in a whitish-yellow, shimmering light. It would be dusk in about an hour's time.

Kovacs got a shock when the door to the terrace opened behind him. It was Lefti. He placed the chair he was carrying beside the table and sat down. He had put on a thick, grey-brown jumper and fingerless, woollen gloves.

"Brilliant," Kovacs said. "I see you're used to eating outside when it's freezing." Lefti laughed. Behind him came Szarah with two large china bowls, spoons and a white flatbread. She greeted Kovacs with a discreet nod of the head. She's a goddess, he thought, not immediately beautiful, but there's an intelligence in her face and an independence in her figure that just knock you down. "What is it?" he asked.

"Red lentil soup," she said. She put the bowls down in a rapid but careful movement. Then she disappeared.

"*Bismillah*," Lefti said.

"Same to you, *Mahlzeit*," Kovacs answered. The soup tasted of chilli, cumin and cinnamon. Lefti dunked bread into it, hardly using his spoon.

"How come you always know what I need?" Kovacs asked.

"It wasn't so hard this time. What does a Kommissar who sits on my terrace in winter need? Anyway, the soup was Szarah's idea, not mine."

He's making a huge effort, Kovacs thought. He trusts me.

"You're a lucky man to have a wife like that," he said.

"Yes, I'm lucky to have her, my daughters, and you, Kommissar."

"Your Oriental politeness sometimes gets on my nerves."

"You were less fortunate with your wife and daughter; why shouldn't I be polite?"

For a while Kovacs remained silent. He thought of Yvonne's coldness, and of Charlotte, who over time had become ever more like a sack of potatoes, formless and passive. I was never able to connect with her, he thought; at least Yvonne and I had something for a while. He bit into a large piece of chilli and could feel the tears welling in his eyes.

"Sorry, Kommissar," Lefti said.

"You lot just have fewer nerves in your mouths," Kovacs said. "Far fewer."

Lefti paused for a moment. "I meant that about your wife and daughter."

Kovacs sipped his beer. It was now so cold that it hurt his teeth. "It's been a long time since I've cried over it. Anyway, do you really believe that it's all down to luck whether a relationship works or not?"

"Allah gives you eyes, ears and the humility to wait."

"And Maghrebin landlords who talk in riddles whenever you ask them a concrete question."

Lefti bowed his head. "Whatever you say, Kommissar."

He may well be right about the eyes and ears, Kovacs thought; my lack of attentiveness may have been a problem from the very start. It's my job to be far more perceptive than other people, and yet when I met this woman I relied on a vague hunch that she was the right one.

Twenty years earlier Yvonne had done an internship at the Fernkorn as part of her hotel management training, and on summer evenings she used to turn up at Manolo's Strandcafé.

Kovacs had been a regular at the café, because of the Italian coffee, because of the grappa selection, and because of the rattan chairs which were exceptionally comfortable. Best of all, however, the place was free of the young wannabes or the semi-crooked business set who filled the terraces of the Wertzer or the Fernkorn. Instead it attracted people who swam in the municipal lido and a few individuals whose modest boats were moored in the marina. He recalled that Yvonne had worn a tight-fitting, egg-yolk yellow top, and there were plasters on her heels, under the straps of her sandals. I stared at her tits, Kovacs thought, and the tits stared back, then I noticed the plasters and then I looked at her face. You put one and one together and know that the best-case scenario would be some satisfactory sex, but no more than that. Perhaps the contempt she had expressed fifteen years later for the lake and the people sitting around the tables was already present then, but he had not noticed anything. In hindsight everybody had been much wiser than him; they claimed it had been obvious right from the start that nothing could come of it. He had just sat there, drinking beer, then schnapps. In the end he had turned to his telescope. How infantile, he had thought, but in some way it had calmed him down.

The beer foam which stuck to the sides of the glass had now frozen. Kovacs scraped at it a little, then broke off a piece of the flatbread and mopped up the rest of his soup. "In the old days I would have said I was a Kriminalkommissar first, a husband and father second, and a beer-garden man third," he said. "Now I'd say I'm mainly a beer-garden man and a Kriminalkommissar on the side. It's irrelevant whether you get along with your wife or not; if she leaves you, a part of your identity is lost."

Lefti turned round and looked towards the restaurant. "I've been living in this country for twelve years now. I wear woollen jumpers and gloves, I drink your wine, I think in your terms,

I say 'shit' and 'arsehole', but I'll never understand this identity business of yours."

"You don't need to, because your wife will never leave you," said Kovacs.

"True. She won't."

I'm a beer-garden man, a sometime Kriminalkommissar, and third, someone who screws the owner of a second-hand clothes shop twice a week, Kovacs thought. The last of these activities operates on the basis of mutual satisfaction, he thought, nothing more. Not the remotest trace of anything like love. Kovacs knew that Lefti knew, and that was reason enough not to waste any breath on the subject.

He slipped off his glove to shake hands and say goodbye. "What are you doing for New Year?" he asked.

"Nothing at all," Lefti said. "We're still in 1426 and the end of our year is in a month's time. We're closing the place. Experience tells us it's a good move."

Kovacs nodded. He had a distinct memory of the time he went into the "Tin" on the morning of 1 January, seven years earlier. Lefti was standing, deathly pale, in the middle of the restaurant, wearing a makeshift bandage on his head. Everything around him was a total mess. The ringleader of the gang which had smashed the place up at about two in the morning had been the son of a Freedom Party deputy in the provincial assembly; there had been plenty of witnesses to this. The skinheads had necked champagne from the bottle, then they had hurled all the chairs to the floor. Finally, they'd smeared "Foreigners Out!" on the walls with red candle stubs, and given a rendition of the old S.A. anthem, "The rotten bones are trembling". When one old man objected that he'd had quite enough of this song during his lifetime, they broke his nose with a peppermill.

The chief culprit's father had sought out the judge, which meant that the sentence was a joke: six months suspended. The deputy's son spent the whole trial grinning, and after the sentence was passed he said that Lefti should just be happy that they hadn't fucked his wife as well. At the time Kovacs thought what a good thing it was that he did not have a weapon on him some days.

"I'm just going to thank Szarah again," he said, zipping up his jacket.

"I'm sure it was a great pleasure for her."

"If only you could be a little less polite ..."

"Then you'd know you'd have to be on your guard," Lefti said. He raised his hand and bent over to clear away the soup bowls.

Kovacs made for the promenade. He walked quickly, as was his habit, not because he was cold. I'm a fast walker, he thought, that's also part of my identity. Charlotte had endlessly moaned about it, and he reckoned that Yvonne had only kept her mouth shut because she was so keen to show how sporty she was.

He reached the lake in front of the boat hire place. Where Manolo's beach café had once stood was now Franz Holdegger's water sports shop. Holdegger had started with a surfing centre on Cyprus, then for many years he had run a diving school in the Maldives. After accumulating enough money he returned to the town of his birth when the first opening presented itself. The opportunity was somewhat tarnished by the fact that it was the result of Manolo's accident; but someone else would have moved into the premises if Holdegger had not seized the chance. In any case, there was no way Manolo was coming back from the dead. In his Corvette one sunny October morning, he had taken a bend on the Kanaltal motorway too quickly, careered effortlessly over the crash barrier, and landed in a river bed 150 metres below – a tributary of the Tagliamento. Some people considered this death in Italy to be highly romantic. They were probably the same individuals who used to bitch about Manolo's homosexuality: it's a good thing that faggot went back home to die. They were not bothered by the fact that that Manolo was actually from Naples, about a thousand kilometres from the Kanaltal. Anyway, Holdegger did not seem to be queer, and the town was happy about that. In the few years since his return home, moreover, he had become one of the leading experts on the fish and bird populations of the lake, as well as on its climatic peculiarities. Fishermen and surfers would approach him for advice, and he had an excellent relationship with the wildlife observation centre. For those tourists who toyed with the idea of doing a dive, meanwhile, he devised a compendium of wild stories. He particularly enjoyed rubbishing the rumour about Nazi gold in the Toplitzsee, insisting that the treasures of the Third Reich had, in fact, disappeared almost in eyeshot of his shop: the transport ship, he claimed, had been scuttled at the foot of the Kammwand, then it disappeared under an avalanche triggered by a controlled explosion. On the back of his story people would sign up in droves; he would lead them to a fishing cutter which had sunk a good thirty years before, and announce that this was the pilot boat that the treasure ship had once followed. The boulders nearby were the result of the avalanche, he maintained. Nobody ever complained about these dives; on the contrary, there were so many enthusiastic testimonies from happy customers on Holdegger's web site that even the town council decided not to put the story straight.

In my line of work I'm seeking out the so-called facts, Kovacs thought, whereas people just want to be deceived. People always opt for what isn't true.

The salt that had been scattered on the promenade had eaten up the rest of the snow and ice. Suitable for everybody to walk on, whatever their mobility, he thought. Maybe there'll come a time when I'll be pleased about that. He headed south, past the boat hire place, past the driveway up to the Wertzer, and past the landing stage for the ferries to Sankt Christoph and Mooshaim. At the marina he entered the shade thrown by the mountain. All of a sudden the wind picked up. He pulled his cap down over his ears. At the furthest point of the jetty five or six seagulls were sitting motionless. Each year a few birds stayed here over winter. He felt some sort of connection to them.

He walked the entire arc of the eastern shore, beyond the end of the asphalt path to where the Fürstenaubach emptied into the lake as a waterfall. There he stood on the bridge and looked back at the town.

The business with the old man had not yet been cleared up, although he felt that they would soon find an explanation. For example: the son-in-law had been loading wood for the stove on to the back of the old, green Steyr tractor. As it was only a short distance, he had not bothered to tie the logs securely, and so had to keep on looking round to make sure they were not sliding off. This meant he had not seen the old man. Case closed. It would be something simple like that. It was hardly surprising that the man's face had looked so horrific; any face which had been run over by a tractor was bound to look gruesome. He thought of Mauritz cursing because it was almost impossible to do anything with the splashes of blood in the snow, and because the tyre marks had distorted everything even more. And he thought of Wieck, how she had walked beside him, her face pale and yet determined, how her uniform had been a size too large. He would get her onto his team; she had exactly the same energy and urge to uncover the truth that he had had when he turned thirty. And he liked her. I'd love to have a daughter like her, he thought, she's nothing like a sack of potatoes, not a bit. I'll call Mauritz, he thought, perhaps he's already got some results. I know he hates being disturbed at the weekend, but I hate having nothing to go on. I also hate it when it starts getting dark at three in the afternoon and there's nothing else to do but go home.

He could hear the bangs from far away. It was the same every year. A few days before New Year's Eve the local youngsters herded together – even those who had nothing to do with each other for the rest of the year – and started unleashing their arsenal of firecrackers, bangers and rockets. Although their offerings were no competition for the big fireworks at midnight, by letting off the entire collection ahead of time they could be sure of provoking a reaction from certain residents. There would be the same complaints this year, too; his fellow officers would be called out, reprimand the usual suspects, and carry out at least one confiscation for infringement of the Fireworks and Pyrotechnics Law. This satisfied people like Alexander Koesten, who lived in one of the apartments below Kovacs.

Seven or eight young people were squatting on the railings of the long, rectangular fountain. When they saw Kovacs coming most of them disappeared. Only Matthias Fries, a pale-faced, red-haired seventeen-year-old who bragged that he only wore stolen gear, and Sharif Erdoyan, an unbelievably fat Turkish boy who everybody called "Sheriff", remained sitting there. It was quite obvious they were smoking hash. "Hi, Kommissar. How's it going?" Erdoyan said, trying to look serious.

"Hello, Sheriff," Kovacs replied. "Very kind of you to ask."

"People should have some responsibility for the wellbeing of their neighbours."

"You're right there. By the way, just tell me quickly – what is the legal limit for personal consumption of marijuana?"

"Oh, you've put me on the spot there, Kommissar. I think it depends on your body weight."

Sheriff was twenty-one, he came from Konya, and for the last two years or so he had got his hands on every sort of cannabinoid to be found in the south of the town. As they were convinced he was not into anything else they had left him in peace until now, even though council demands for police intervention had become ever louder. Konrad Seihs, that ghastly secretary of the Business Party, had been particularly vocal on the matter. Mike Dassler, who headed the department for "addiction and habits", had till now remained calm. Interference from all quarters was part of his daily routine.

"You can generally rely on fat people," Kovacs said.

Erdoyan nodded. "One hundred per cent, Kommissar."

"Do you know what might make me set these pit bull types at your throats?"

"Opiates and children, Kommissar. How could I forget that?"

"Excellent." Kovacs raised his hand. "Happy New Year, gentle-men."

Matthias Fries spat provocatively at the fountain pipes which rose vertically from the middle of the basin. Fries liked pretending to be dangerous, but in fact he was quite harmless. All the same, Kovacs could not stand the boy; there was something of the ferret about him. Erdoyan bellowed something behind him. Not catching what it was he turned round and cupped his hand to his ear. "I might be a father myself soon!" That's all this town needs, thought Kovacs. He saw a troop of small, chubby Turkish boys, all carrying their hash pipes, and then he pictured Charlotte, who would have no idea what a hash pipe was, and who had never been satisfied in her life.

Kovacs was approaching block B. He had lived in this former industrial building for three years, and for the first time in ages he had felt at home from day one. He had taken an instant liking to the black and red brick walls, the arched windows with their small mosaic patterns, and the enormous grey steel door at the entrance. What is more, he had never minded the few trendies who rented in his area. The divorce had left him with no choice but to sell the family apartment in Furth-Nord. The Walzwerk estate project had turned out to be a highly convenient solution, overcoming all the scepticism he had harboured beforehand. As was to be expected, the social housing in the former workers' quarters had been allocated quickly. This had further reduced the already questionable appeal of those units left for general occupation in the three former factory buildings, and had kept the prices down. It suited Kovacs fine; he had found a nice seventy square metres with four-metre high ceilings, direct access to the communal roof terrace garden, and a window by his bed that faced south-east. If she wanted to, Charlotte could sleep on the small mezzanine which had been intended as a work area, but which he never used as such. Charlotte never wanted to. He was pleased about that.

He looked at the Christmas tree which stood on a low side table in front of the bookcase. A present from Marlene. Although the agreement they had for satisfying their mutual needs worked fine, her interpretation of it clearly included the urge to give unattached men Christmas trees with glass baubles and golden angels. There was also the business with New Year's Eve. She told him she had read something in a magazine about a tiny hotel in the Lungau. Actually it was a renovated forester's lodge, and as it only had nine rooms she had booked one, just in case. This in spite of the fact that she knew damn well he would prefer to stay at home drinking bock beer and – at most – go up to the roof terrace at midnight. He felt really uncomfortable. It began with nothing more than sex; now there were Christmas trees and romantic arrangements for New Year's Eve. I'll tell her now, he thought. Right now. He remembered that he wanted to call Mauritz, too. He picked up the handset. Marlene first. He punched in the number.

Her mobile was set to voicemail. "Call me," he said, nothing more.

He went into the kitchen, put some water on to boil, and dropped some dried mint leaves and a few lumps of sugar into the teapot. This was another thing he had learned from Lefti: peppermint tea instead of an afternoon schnapps. I'm turning Oriental, he thought. But his headaches had become less frequent since he had adopted this routine.

The sky had remained clear. From the kitchen window he could see the pale-red tint of the evening in the south-west. The first stars would soon be visible. The telescope was beside his bed; the last few times he had not bothered to put it away. Tonight he would go up to the roof, take his time, and align it properly. He would start by looking at the zenith, where at this time of year Andromeda was in view. As always he would look for M31 and, as always, he would get annoyed that he could not make out the spiral structure of the galaxy, even at the highest magnification. Then he would turn eastwards and start by searching for some of his favourite objects, for example Capella in Auriga, or Aldebaran in Taurus. Of course he was upset when Eleonore Bitterle had joked, "My boss has become a stargazer," and of course it had bothered him when his other colleagues kept on taking the piss. But when Strack had asked him what the point was of spending hours staring through a tube, he had said, "I'm looking for God, that's the point," and all of them had shut up, for good.

The triumphal march from *Aida*, slightly muffled. He had to get his bearings. The mobile was in his inside jacket pocket, in the wardrobe. He had decided that he needed a martial ring-tone, and Demski had helped him to download it. He flipped the phone open.

"I hope you're not going to get too upset about this, but New Year's Eve is not going to be as you planned," he said.

"I'm very sad about that," said the voice at the other end.

85

It definitely was not Marlene's.

"I'm sorry you're sad," he said. "Who is this?" On the display there was a landline number that he recognised.

"But Kommissar?"

The smug tone, the slight Swiss twang – it was Patrizia Fleurin, the forensic pathologist. She had been in charge of the district for years, and whenever possible she carried out her post-mortems at the pathology unit of the town's hospital; she sent corpses to the Vienna University institute in Sensengasse only in special circumstances. Much to the chagrin of the pathology assistants she loved unconventional working hours. "As I can't believe you'd call me on a private matter, Frau Doktor, I assume that you're standing by the post-mortem table," he said.

"Precisely," she said. "Do you know what? I wouldn't dare call you on a private matter." A body was lying in front of her: an old man who had once had a head. At the bottom of this former head there was something significant. She thought he ought to take a look at it.

EIGHT

I'm sleeping just in my black cloak. The mask is on the floor next to the bed. They were presents from Daniel. He said they cost a load of money, but he has inexhaustible reserves. Our mother reckons he must be stealing, but she can't prove anything; and our father says that if he catches him nicking anything, he'll chop his hand off. Our father's the biggest car dealer in the area. He sells Jaguars, Rolls Royces and Range Rovers, and once he shot somebody in the leg while out hunting, but it was an accident. Not long ago he sold young Stuchlik a Dodge Viper. He made the worst profit of his life on this deal, although he did give him a 12 per cent discount. He sat in the sitting room and roared with laughter the whole time. Daniel says that if our father dies he's going to take over the business, but only for a short time, because then he's going to sell it for shedloads of money.

It's silent in the house. It's always like this on Sunday mornings. If I look out of my window I can see the roof of the assembly hangar, above it the hill that looks like the pointy end of a lemon, and further above that the sky.

I go into the larder and cut myself a slice of the marble cake that our mother got from the shop yesterday. She can't cook or bake herself. She says that her own mother was a failure and never taught her how to do it. I really want to make myself a hot chocolate, but something's bound to go wrong and I'd wake everybody in the house, so I leave it.

The fridge in the kitchen is buzzing. If no-one else is around I just stay there until it stops again. I watch the red second hand of the clock on the wall. Three minutes and twenty-one seconds. Not even as long as school break. And then everything is at the right temperature again: the mineral water and the milk and the Christmas salami with the mini Christmas tree or bell pattern inside. Daniel says they were fed this salami inside, on his last few days, and he thinks it's horrid because it's the same bog-standard, low-quality Extrawurst; it's just that the mini trees or bells are darker than the bits around them. Daniel says that there's no difference in taste between the light bits and dark bits.

My clothes are ready. The gloves, the headband. And my boots in the hall, too. I'm wearing the cloak under my coat. I've got a mission.

Daniel gave me another present. It's heavy. I try to put it in my waistband, but it won't go. So I take my rucksack.

Daniel said I can choose the first target. It's a practice. Vader also needed a bit of time to get where he is. Daniel says that you don't know you can do something until you've tried. He says that it's only when you can do things that you can defend yourself, and he says that's the only important thing in life: to be able to fight.

It's not yet fully light and it's cold. The first thing that happens is that I bump into Frau Reithbauer with her really fat half-breed collie. That fuck-awful face and then the inevitable question: "Where on earth are you going at this ungodly hour?" I smile like C-3PO and say, "To church," and she says, "Well, it is Sunday, but you're rather early," and I say, "There's a requiem mass beforehand," and she asks, "For whom?" and I say, "I don't know."

I go along Ettrichgasse as far as the newspaper kiosk. The dark-green shutters are pulled down. I turn into Lorenzgasse. You can easily spot Roland's house by the red postbox which looks like the postboxes in American films. Roland says his dad once drove through America on a motorbike, that's where they got the postbox. I don't believe him but it doesn't matter now. Roland's a useless bastard, I've known that since the cinema story. Daniel says that when someone lies to you, you either smash his face in or you pronounce him dead in your mind – that helps too. Right now Roland is skiing in the Zillertal with his parents and his unnecessary sister, and that's just as good. His granny, who's looking after the house, lives in Mühlau and, as I can't see her car anywhere, she won't be there.

A footpath that runs between the second and third house takes me to the back of the estate. I go the other way along the fence and climb over with the help of an old cherry tree. Daniel says that if you don't fight this bunch of lesbians, gays, and wogs then you've had it. It's intuition – that's how he knows it, he says, and he also says that if you want to fight then the very first thing you've got to do is to send the right signals.

The nature reserve is covered in snow; the reeds next to it are almost all broken. One of the ornamental balls is missing a piece as big as my hand. Roland knocked it out with his catapult, but no-one else knows that except me. A pretty brilliant shot to just graze it like that, anybody else would have destroyed the ball outright.

The key to the garden shed is under an old brick slab on the woodpile. Any old idiot could find it.

When I go in, the rabbits and guinea pigs hop around nervously in their cages. I shut the door behind me and sit on an old garden chair. I tell them the story of Anakin Skywalker who becomes Darth Vader, and how after the battle with Obi-Wan he's lying there on the lava bank, nothing left of him – no arms, no legs, no breath – just burnt skin, and how the Emperor comes and gives him a new face. The animals calm down while I'm talking. They all listen to me.

Twelve rabbits: five black and white, two white with red eyes, one white with blue eyes, one black with white on its chest, three grey. Seven guinea pigs: five with smooth coats, two curly ones. The white rabbit with the blue eyes is called Kylie Minogue. Roland's sister christened it.

I open the rucksack. I put the thing that Daniel gave me on the ground. It's a warhammer. It's got an oval wooden handle.

I put on the Darth Vader mask. I start breathing like him. Then I open the guinea pig cage and take out one of the animals. It's grey and dark-brown at the back. It doesn't squeal. It doesn't even look at me.

NINE

The dark-green Golf has been on new winter tyres for a week and a half. They still stand out – they look as if they have been painted black. A young policewoman, who obviously has no idea about our special agreement, stopped Robert and measured the tread. Robert, who always knows everything better, stands there and pays the forty-five Euro fine; what a picture it makes! Clemens then sorted it all out over the phone. That is why you have an abbot – to sort out these things.

It crunches when he changes gear from first to second. The Golf has already racked up 160,000 kilometres; that may be the reason. Out of the car park, right into Stiftsallee, along the Rathausplatz, Severinstraße, over the bridge up to the large roundabout. He drives round it three times. He sometimes does this if nobody is coming. Off towards the west, petrol station, the junction off to the wildlife observation centre. Two kilometres later the fast road begins.

The rosemary chicken he had for lunch is sitting in his stomach. But it tasted good, and Irma had made a real effort. The chickens that his mother cooks are always repulsive: unseasoned and raw inside. She usually accompanies it with rice that has been boiled to a mush. Then his sister laughs and says that he used to like chicken with rice when he was a child.

There are sections where the hard shoulder has not been properly cleared. If one were to come off the outside lane it would be dangerous. A silver-grey BMW overtakes him. In the rear-view mirror the car's headlights are yellow circles. The Golf chugs like a tractor. It does not go faster than 140 kph.

At lunch they talked about the programme for New Year. The Service of Thanks on New Year's Eve. The High Mass on New Year's Day. They will all be there, the Bürgermeister and councillors will sit in the first few rows; in his sermon Clemens will try to make diplomatic references to the issue of the socially disadvantaged, as he does every year; and, as every year, he will lose all contact with reality as soon as he looks into one of those piggy faces. Otherwise there is nothing special over the coming days: no weddings, no baptisms, no funerals. Sebastian Wilfert's body has not been released yet. A squashed face – the notion of it is quite cheery, in a funny way.

To the left, the flat sheds of the poultry farm emerge above an oak-covered hill, followed by the church spire in Waiern. In the bend of the exit lane he takes his foot off the accelerator only when he feels the back of the car starting to move sideways. By his standards he has not had an accident for a long time; the last was more than two years ago when he crashed the Volvo estate into a milk tanker.

In the car park of the old people's home there are thirty-one vehicles; in the front row on the very left there is a VW Toureg which he has not seen here before. Most of the lines marking the parking bays are covered by the remains of old snow. That is not good. The whole of life runs along demarcation lines. He parks next to the blue-grey Renault Megane. It belongs to a landlord from Sankt Christoph who put his mother in this home and visits her more or less every other Sunday.

The air is dry and packed with frost. Sometimes he gets these images: the air in the depths of winter, consisting of nothing but densely packed, bright blue blocks. Or very narrow passageways that run under the surface of the snow, kilometres long, tiny creatures scurrying along them from A to B with unimaginable speed.

The building has that intrinsic ugliness common to all Austrian old people's homes. To be fair, old people's homes in Switzerland, Germany or Norway might be just as ugly, but he has no experience of them. No, in Norway it is very unlikely; but in Germany, definitely. Anyway, this one has endless balconies which it is strictly forbidden to use, for fear that the old people will climb over those green railings by mistake and fall to their deaths. An entrance hall in which yucca palms and huge fig-type specimens planted in hydroculture clay pebbles strain towards the light of high-output plant lamps, cloth parrots perch on top of wooden poles, and a reception booth staffed by someone to whom everybody entering the building is an imposition.

Here he comes to see people who receive no other visitors: Franziska Zillinger from Mooshaim, and Leopold Rödl from Furth. But right now Leopold Rödl is in hospital with circulation problems in his legs. He sometimes gives a service in the chapel at the home; scarcely anybody attends.

Franziska Zillinger is ninety-eight and almost blind. Her daughter died some years ago from heart failure – actually from excessive obesity – and her granddaughter, who is a successful bank clerk, has no time to visit. Frau Zillinger loves hymns; it makes the whole thing fairly easy. He hums "A House of Glory Watches" when he enters her unit, and she says, "Yes – a house of glory watches," and starts to sing. She knows approximately eight to ten verses; he knows three, but that does not matter. She becomes quite passionate during the chorus, and she rapturously belts out the "O let us all be safe in thy house" as if at that moment she were singing for the benefit of heaven itself.

"How are you, Frau Zillinger?" he asks. She turns her face towards him and her right hand creeps in his direction. Her hand is a little like an old branch. "If that's you, Herr Kaplan, I'm well." Although he is not actually a chaplain he likes being addressed as such. She knew a chaplain once, he thinks. He imagines how they fell in love; it was like something from a Heimatfilm. At this point the memory of Sophie does not intrude, which sort of amazes him, but sometimes there is a certain distance. He looks into those eyes with their whitish, sad lenses and wonders whether old people's irises tend to turn blue again like small children's, or whether that is a just figment of the imagination.

He talks to her about the approaching year's end, and she says that she has never liked New Year's Eve – all that noise really gets on her nerves, particularly since she lost her sight. Mind you, it is not as bad here in Waiern as it was in Mooshaim where they used to live by the lake, right next to the jetty where the big fireworks were let off at midnight. For days afterwards the cats would not come out from under the cupboards; it was the same every year. She had stopped asking whether it would be her last New Year; since the loss of her daughter it was irrelevant. Her happiness had vanished with the death of her husband shortly after the war, and with the death of her daughter her life had lost its meaning – that was the truth. "The 'safe in thy house' is like a lovely fairy tale," she says. "I picture a house in which everybody's together and happy, and you don't feel so alone. Just like a fairy tale. But I shouldn't be saying these things to a priest."

Something begins to dash around in circles inside his head. He realises that he can still resist it quite well. Two questions enter his mind. First: What has happened recently? Second: What is meaningful in my life? The Rule, the Redeemer, the mother and the child.

"By the way, did you ever know anybody by the name of Sebastian Wilfert?" he asks.

At first something flashes over the lady's face like a breeze, fleeting and indefinite. Then it is as if somebody had held her under her elbows and slowly straightened her. She is sitting there in her armchair, her eyes open wide and her fingers digging into the arms. She looks like she's just met the Devil, he thinks. After a while, her face relaxes again and she sinks back into the chair. She shakes her head. "No, I never knew anybody by that name," she says softly. "But my husband. All those years ago."

"Somebody drove over his head, probably with a tractor," he says. She closes her eyes and says nothing.

The bag with his trousers, jumper and shoes is on the back seat. His iPod is in the glove compartment. He must get away from here. He must run, it does not matter where.

TEN

This year is not ending well, thought Raffael Horn. Lying on his stomach, he shifted his body to the right and tried to reach the receiver. He dreamed he had arrived at a station, totally out of breath, only to watch the train pull away from him. His heart was pounding. The digital alarm clock on his bedside table showed 4.47.

It was Brunner. Her voice was strained. "I'm sorry, Raffael, but I think you ought to come in." Apparently, Caroline Weber had become more tense and paranoid since the previous evening. Amongst other things, she was convinced that her little daughter was standing outside the door downstairs, just waiting for the opportunity to slip in. The invisible girl was going to come up to the ward and tear her mother's soul from her body. They had tried everything to calm the woman down – close personal attention, all sorts of medication – but without any success.

"Where is she now?" Horn said.

"In the kitchen."

"How did she get in there?"

"She elbowed Lydia in the face and took her key to get in."

Lydia was a Chilean nurse, one metre sixty at most, but a fighter nonetheless. Anybody getting past her must have a mountain of energy.

"Have you called the locksmith?"

"She said that if anybody tries to fiddle with the door she'll slit her wrists."

"Call him anyway. Tell him to wait until I get there," said Horn, and hung up.

Irene sat up beside him and looked at him, still half asleep. "Who?" she asked.

"Caroline Weber," he said.

"Is it serious?"

"If Lili Brunner can't disguise her concern on the phone then it's serious."

"Be nice to her," she said.

"To who?"

"Frau Weber. She thinks her child's the Devil."

She kissed him on the cheek before he climbed out of bed, groaning. She notices everything, he thought, and I tell her far too much.

The thermometer in the Volvo said it was minus thirteen outside. The sky was cloudless. Steady high pressure. According to the weather forecast it would not change much over the coming days. Caroline Weber's crisis could not be explained from a purely psycho-meteorological perspective. Horn was careful to take the bends to the highway slowly. It's five o'clock in the morning and I'm taking into consideration the possibility that deer may cross the road, he thought. I'm getting old. A shooting star flashed across the sky in a shallow arc and disappeared behind the ridge of the Kammwand. He knew he ought to make a wish, but apart from bed nothing entered his head.

The petrol station by the western slip road was bathed in a green night light. It looked to him as if a figure was moving between the petrol pumps. I'm seeing ghosts, he thought, I keep on dreaming of railways, and I'm incapable of wishing for something useful.

On his arrival the porter momentarily turned his gaze from the television set to wave hello. "The locksmith will be here soon," he said. Why do porters always have to know everything? Horn asked himself. I should have taken the side entrance, as usual. Two ambulance men came out of the lift with an empty stretcher on wheels. He entered the compartment and pressed the button. He was too tired to climb the stairs and, anyway, at this time of the day he could shelve all his compulsive rituals, thank goodness.

Hrachovec, a tall, thin trainee doctor, was sitting outside the door to the kitchen, keeping watch. He stood up when he saw Horn enter the ward. "She's not doing anything in there," he said. Sometimes it was when there was nothing to be heard outside that the critical things were happening on the inside. But Horn did not tell Hrachovec that because, on the whole, he was alright.

The others were sitting in the staffroom. Brunner was smoking, Lydia was holding an ice pack to her right eye, and Christina, who also looked like she had been called in out of hours, was sorting the day medication into pill dispensers. Lydia attempted a smile when Horn examined her face. "The elbow, I gather," he said. She nodded. It had hit her right in the cheekbone. The swelling extended to her lower eyelid and the purple bruising was already showing. At the morning meeting Leithner would say, "That's why people on I23 get their hardship allowance." Horn could already hear his voice and picture his stupid grin. "Go home," he said.

Lydia shook her head. "I want to see what happens."

Once again Horn started imagining Lydia's past life: she was the oldest of five or six siblings, her mother had to go out to work, and from an early age she had to look after the little ones. All this had taken place in a suburb of Santiago. The heroism of this story is so beguiling, he thought, that it prevents me from asking her what it was really like.

Brunner handed him Frau Weber's medical notes and said the whole thing must have started when her husband came to visit in the afternoon, accompanied by their daughter. Throughout the visit Frau Weber refused to hold the child. Her husband cradled the little girl in his arms, said a few things to his wife, and at the end he just blubbered helplessly. Frau Weber gave the impression of feeling more and more threatened by the minute. At the start she spent short periods sitting opposite her husband, in between which she would jump up again and run to the door. By the end she was making large circles around the two of them, her eyes wide open, and saying nothing. When her husband finally left with their daughter, it was clearly too late to start calming her down.

The door to the ward was pushed open. Lydia winced in pain.

"Are you sure you don't want to go home?" Horn asked.

"I'm going," she said. She was trembling.

The locksmith was stocky, red-faced and short of breath. He put down his tool bag with a gesture that suggested that he was not at all pleased to have been called out at this time of day. Christina stood up. "One of the reasons we all earn our money is that unexpected things happen from time to time. This includes you, I believe," she said. Sometimes her words were as spiky as her physiognomy. Horn was full of admiration.

"We'll have to break it open," the locksmith said when they explained the situation to him. If the key really was inside the room then there was no other solution. He could not do it now, however, as he needed some heavy-duty tools – a crowbar at least – and he had none of these on him. "You're best off calling the fire brigade," he said.

Once, more than six years earlier, they had been forced to break open a door. Willy Röder, a long-term junkie with a personality disorder, had stolen the master key off Martha, the duty casualty sister, and had locked himself in the orthopaedic examination room. There he had screamed "I'm going to kill myself!" a number of times, and gave himself a jab which could have easily done the job. Horn had always hated breaking things; he could not even stand the term "break open". After this episode he swore never again to use a crowbar, especially as Röder died of hepatitis soon afterwards.

"Who was the last person to try talking to her?" he said.

Hrachovec put up his hand. "Me," he said.

"And?"

"I said, 'What's the point in doing this, Frau Weber?' and things like that, but she didn't answer me."

"When was that, roughly?"

Hrachovec looked at the clock. "Half an hour ago, perhaps," he said.

Horn leaned against the wall and gazed along the corridor. The far end of the ward was in total darkness. He tried to gather his thoughts together. A little girl who was barely two months old was certainly not the Devil. The most likely explanation was that the mother was trying to get rid of the negative elements inside her by detaching them and projecting them onto her daughter. The Catholic technique – so popular in this country – of uprooting what is bad in oneself and planting it on another person. The problem with detaching things from yourself, thought Horn, is that they always come in through the back door.

"What comes in through the back door?" Christina asked. Horn was startled.

"Did I say something?"

She laughed and grabbed his arm. "You're always doing it," she said.

I'm thinking aloud without realising it, Horn thought. I'm doing things I'm not even aware of. That's not good.

"The Devil comes in the back door," he said. "I meant it." But you couldn't phrase it like that, as nobody knew what the Devil was or looked like. For a while nobody said anything. Then Lydia said, "Basically I believe that the Devil's bad. He looks nice, but he's bad. It can't be any other way."

Brunner shook her head. "The Devil isn't nice," she said.

Horn looked right through her. Perhaps Lydia was right, perhaps it was a case of displacement; and the Devil that Caroline Weber had planted into her daughter had its origins in a different person altogether: someone who seemed nice, but was bad.

Horn raised his hand. "Wait a moment," he said. He went over to the kitchen door and knocked twice. "Frau Weber," he said in a loud voice. "It's Doctor Horn here. I know you're in a bad way, and I know that because you feel all alone you want to be on your own at the moment. But I'm worried that your desire to be alone is now getting quite extreme, so I can't let it to go any further. In any case, I don't like it when the fire brigade comes and smashes down the door, and everybody on the ward wakes up and then the next day they're talking about it all around the hospital. Please open the door. I also know that the root of your problem is not your daughter but your husband, at least that's what I think."

Brunner looked at him in surprise. Horn raised his shoulders and put his finger to his lips.

After about twenty seconds the key turned in the lock. Caroline Weber stood in the doorway, her arms hanging by her side. Horn tried to work out what had happened. Out of the corner of his eye he could see that the locksmith next to him had turned as white as a sheet. The first person to say something was Christina, and it was a single word: "Casualty".

An hour and a half later the drama was over. The cuts on both Caroline Weber's lower arms and on the left-hand side of her neck, which she had made with a shard from a broken side plate, had been seen to, and the patient was in a sleep which they reckoned would last at least twenty-four hours. Leuweritz, the duty casualty surgeon, had not grumbled because he was awake anyway. In fact he had stitched and stuck with patience and commitment. He said that the whole thing was a sort of relaxation; he had just operated on a five-year-old girl whose lower legs had both been shattered by a car. According to the girl's father, the driver had just put his foot down and disappeared. Obviously, in his state of agitation he had not noted the registration number, but he knew it was a dark-blue estate car.

Horn lay on the sofa in his office. There was still an hour to go until the morning meeting. The year is really not ending well, he thought. People are driving into children's legs and then vanishing; other people are running over old men's heads; young mothers are cutting themselves; and my wife is having the most destructive arguments with my son. His gaze fell on the Kasperl puppets on the shelf opposite him. Those were the days – the time in his life when nobody questioned anything: Seppel was good, because he was Kasperl's best friend; the Robber was bad, because robbers are bad; and the Constable with the spiked helmet was good, because constables are the arm of the law. And that was that. Deep down he knew he had become a child psychiatrist in order to salvage some of this simplicity for himself. That people by and large did not conform to it was another thing entirely.

For the most part the morning passed peacefully. Leithner had spent the weekend at his house in Kitzbühel, and had got sunburned on his forehead and nose while skiing. During the staff meeting he said nothing about hardship allowance on I23, but spoke only about Melitta Steinböck, the Bürgermeister's wife, who would be admitted at some point that morning with unidentified respiratory problems. Prinz, the consultant on the private ward, made a few smutty comments, a symptom of the persistent battle between him and Leithner over the allocation of special fees. It was a quarrel that everybody else had lost interest in a long time ago. Brunner produced several loud yawns, and Broschek was somewhat bad tempered, as she was most Mondays.

Although it was the start of the week there was not much happening in the outpatient department. Most of those waiting had come to see Cejpek for a check-up on their blood clots. Among them Horn could see Marianne Schwarz, the wife of his neighbour, Martin. She had recently had a deep-vein thrombosis in her leg, as a result of which she suffered several pulmonary infarctions, and so had been put on blood-thinning medication. It was the usual combination: pills plus cigarettes plus being overweight. Even afterwards, neither of them had understood just how serious it could have been.

Horn had called in two patients for check-ups: an elderly man with Alzheimer's-related dementia who had started seeing strange people in his garden; and Elena Weitbrecht, a supermarket manager who had been a long-term sufferer from complex motor tics. Just before Christmas she had decided against psychotherapy in favour of treatment by medication. Both were feeling well: the man said that, apart from a young lady with glasses, the people in his garden had disappeared; and the only side-effect Elena Weitbrecht had had from the pills was a reduction in her appetite, and that was fine by her. She also had the impression that the eye-twitching and shoulder spasms had already got a bit better. Horn did not share that impression.

Linda was on holiday; Ingeborg, her stand-in, was a skeletal, humourless individual with a grey crew cut. It was said that she used to work as a housekeeper in a rectory. Everybody could picture her in the role, and nobody dared ask whether it was the truth. As Horn was leaving to begin his round of the wards she handed him a bright blue envelope. "This was left for you," she said. Inside there was a card with a Mondrian picture on the front and a few lines on the back: "I tried to leave early. It didn't work out. I imagine I'm going to sleep as badly in Vienna as I do here, but it won't bother me as much. I hope you enjoy the music. H." Heidemarie. He remembered the package: dark blue with small, bright stars. He must have taken it out of his jacket pocket at home and put it down somewhere. Dvořák, he thought, or Tchaikovsky – something Slavonic at any rate. Music that does not end well. Like life. Life never ends well. In truth, all I do as a psychiatrist is to kid people that it isn't like that. I'm a fraud, he thought. The fact that life never ends well is reason enough to go mad, slash your wrists, or pump heroin into your veins; but you can't say that aloud. "Do you know what's sometimes quite difficult?" he asked Ingeborg. She looked at him, at a loss. "Trying to hide just how big a cynic you are."

She shrugged. "Whatever," she said.

The young mother in obstetrics who had recently showed signs of becoming depressive was sitting beside the bed, breastfeeding her child, and complaining in great detail that the baby's father had not looked in since the day before. Horn said that young fathers sometimes felt very threatened by their newborn children; he got the feeling that this was not what the lady wanted to hear just now. She talked of her boyfriend's continual unreliability, and of his tendency to jump into the car and drive away at the first sign of stress. With each sentence Horn was more assured that the danger of depression had passed. As he left he wondered what name the woman would give to her son. An answer eluded him.

I22 had admitted a man from the old people's home in Waiern who, as a result of huge circulation problems in his legs, was no longer capable of taking even a single step without serious pain. The man used to work as roofer, and after he retired his favourite activity was to walk in the local woods. He had never smoked; on the contrary, he had always tried to lead a healthy life, and the vascular damage was due to diabetes which had been diagnosed too late. Anyhow, the man's desperation was totally understandable, as was the fact that he refused outright to take anti-depressants. Horn talked to him about the demise of medium-sized businesses in the region, and about how politicians over the years had turned from people with an idea of how the population lived into soulless robots. At the end he asked him whether he had known Sebastian Wilfert, and the man said no, he had not known him personally. Then the man looked him in the eyes for a second and said, "His head was crushed to nothing and my lower leg's going to be amputated, maybe even both of them." Horn said that justice was problematic, and the man nodded.

Horn resisted the strong impulse to perform an unscheduled check-up on the official from the highways agency in the room next door. Sometimes it was hard not to be a sadist.

Nobody objected when Horn declared that he was going to keep the visits short. Only five of Horn's twelve beds were occupied, and he also believed that the team had every right to work in low gear around New Year. What is more, Herbert, a former chef, had brought in a large pot of chicken curry which everybody was looking forward to.

Caroline Weber lay there, quite relaxed in a pharmacogenic sleep. Horn had ordered two litres of electrolyte solution to be infused into her, and Verena, the most circumspect nurse on the team, had insisted that her vital functions be observed by monitor. As expected, everything was working optimally: 76 per minute, 115 over 70, 97 per cent oxygen saturation.

"By the way, what did you mean when you said that her husband was the root of the problem?" Brunner asked.

"It was more intuition than anything else," Horn said. "The husband plants the child inside the woman; at the same time he is planting something evil in her. Perhaps she didn't want a baby;

perhaps she didn't want one by this man."

"And you think it's more difficult for her to direct her anger at her husband than her child?"

"Or more dangerous."

"But he seems such a harmless type."

"So do I," Horn said.

Benedikt Ley was much better. He lay on his bed, playing with his mobile. "Can I get out for New Year?" he asked.

Horn nodded. "If you promise me you won't take any narcotic substances."

The thin, dark-haired boy winked. "You always speak so pompously, Dottore."

"I prize the fact that I do not belong to your crowd, not even linguistically." I can't bear people who try to get me on their side, he thought. I can't bear Marilyn Manson T-shirts, and I really can't bear it when he calls me "Dottore".

"O.K. I won't take anything."

Horn looked at him doubtfully.

"One or two beers at most. I don't like sekt anyway."

Horn shrugged. As Ley had now come of age, there was no legal way of keeping him here against his will. If he insisted on it, he could go right away. He just had to sign a declaration that it was against medical advice. The young man looked a little confused. "What does that mean?"

"From a medical point of view it means that the probability of having flashbacks in two days' time is lower than for tomorrow. For this reason it would be more prudent to stay for a while longer. But you're no longer in such serious danger."

"And who's responsible then, Dottore?"

"You are, you alone."

Ley shut his eyes. Like a little child who thinks that if they can't see anybody then there's nobody there, Horn thought.

"Is he staying or going?" Herbert asked from outside the room. "He's staying," said Verena. "He doesn't know what he took, and he's worried he'll end up in the same mess as last time." Herbert was not so sure, but was inclined to think that Ley would leave. "He doesn't have any notion of responsibility so thinks it's outrageous he should be expected to take any." All Horn said was, "There's some truth in that." He did not add that he was pretty sure Ley would ring his mother straight away, and pester her to pick him up as soon as possible. The woman would arrive at the ward soon afterwards in her purple dress, stare at the ground and say, "But if he really wants to go." Horn would ask whether his father would beat him up, and the woman would go on staring at the ground, shaking her head.

There was nothing particularly wrong with the other three, either. After a reduction in his neuroleptic drugs, Stefan Reisinger, the early retired electrician with schizoaffective psychosis, was exhibiting less inhibition in his movement than before; Friedrich Helm, the court usher with bi-polar disorder, seemed to be on a nice, gradual path towards a level tolerable for both him and those around him; and Liane Bäuerle, the chronically pre-suicidal Latin and Greek schoolteacher, had received sufficient distraction from the back-to-back visits her relatives made. There had been no new admissions or transfers. Horn knew he could clear up the Caroline Weber incident without the need for the public health officer or a compulsory transferral to the clinic in Vienna. So he could conclude his visits with a good conscience and turn his attentions to the chicken curry.

When Horn arrived on the paediatric ward at ten to two, the girl was sitting next to her mother in the visitors' corner. As before, she was wearing the green quilted jacket, fur boots, and her right hand was still clenched. Her mother stood up to greet Horn.

"We can't get her to take the things off," she said, giving a helpless shrug of her shoulders.

"Don't worry," he said. "We'll straighten that out soon enough." The woman directed a long, doubting glance at her daughter. Horn said, "Shall we go?" and gestured to her to go in. The girl put her left hand around her right fist, stood, and followed him. Something interests her, Horn thought, that's a start at least. He remembered the paralysis of their previous session and how his professional reasoning had only been of partial assistance: inhibition is a phenomenon that results from unconquered ambivalence or fear. Take the inhibition right inside you; only then can you feel its cause. In children fear manifests itself in many different ways, but rarely in eyes opened wide with horror. Etc. etc. He had been least troubled by the idea of himself standing in front of an old man whose head had been run over by a tractor, and feeling temporarily speechless. I'm forty-eight, and the truth is that I'm still too impatient, he thought. I've got two sons, one of whom has already left home, and when a child says nothing the first words that spring to mind are "petulant" and "stubborn".

After Horn had closed the door behind them, the girl remained in the doorframe as if in a picture. She let her gaze wander slowly around the room.

"Last time, Katharina, I asked you whether you could swim," he said. "And then I thought to myself, look, it's winter. At this time of year people are interested in skiing and ice-skating, and we might be the only ones talking about swimming." Something flickered in the girl's face, the hint of a change in expression, but nothing more, just like the last time.

"If you'd like to talk about swimming, it might be smart to take off your thick jacket and fur boots first."

The girl did not react.

"Shall I help you take them off?"

Katharina Maywald made it quite plain that Horn should not attempt this; she threw her arms around her own body as if to protect herself, and froze. She did not relax until Horn moved away and sat behind his desk. Her arms slipped down and she started to move along the wall again, past the toy shelf, as far as the wardrobe. With her back pressed up against the wardrobe door, she slowly slid to the floor, not letting Horn out of her sight for a second. She can't gauge me, he thought, she doesn't know who I really am. She knows that I work here in the hospital, and she knows that people die in hospital. Perhaps I'm the one who let her grandfather die, and it's her turn next.

Horn looked at the rack with the Kasperl puppets and wondered who it would be best to let die. The policeman? The robber? Kasperl or Seppel? The magician? There were no other male figures in his collection. It's a disgrace, he thought, that there's always a Grandmother in the Kasperl theatre, whereas you never find a Grandfather. There were no mothers, nor fathers, and certainly no grandfathers. The robber was closest in terms of age, but he was a very unsympathetic figure. The same was true of the magician. There was no way that Kasperl or Sepperl could be allowed to die and, in view of the events of the last few days, the police had to be ruled out. I'm already feeling quite inhibited, Horn thought. I'm completely incapable of making a decision. He took the five figures from the rack and laid them side by side on the floor. I'll leave it up to her, he thought. I'll ask her, "Which of the five should we let die?" and she'll point to one of them.

As it happened, Horn did not have to do anything else at that point; he was spared the dilemma when Katharina began to slide across the room on her backside, straight over to the bookshelf. Books, he thought, and picked up the hand puppets off the floor. First year at primary school – she'll be able to read a bit; and he remembered what a struggle the whole notion of school and learning to read had been for him since Michael's disastrous experiences.

Michael suffered from a serious perception disorder, which in the early days meant he had never been able to put the letters of the alphabet in the correct order. Fate decreed that his disorder would converge with a teacher whose saccharine manner was the product of pedagogic cluelessness and hidden aggression. Irene had staggered from one crisis to the next; when the teacher refused to stop marking Michael's exercise book with a thick red pen, she offloaded her anger first in the headmaster's office, and then – when the latter proved to be a nervous, coughing wimp – in that of the district school inspector. The upshot of this was that the teacher used to call Irene before each assessment and ask her to suggest the grade she should assign to Michael's work. They arranged for Michael to change schools for the third year, which had led to bucketfuls of tears, as he was leaving behind a number of friends. By the end of the fourth year, on the other hand, he was halfway to being able to read. Writing was, of course, still a disaster, and the irreparable rift in his relationship with Irene must have already begun to develop. Horn had not been aware of the problem until Michael himself articulated it to his mother a few years later: "Who I am has never been good enough for you!" There and then Horn had understood that he could have done nothing – indeed, nothing could have been done at all – to prevent this rupture. Michael had slogged his way through secondary school; over time he became a shy, ill-adjusted boy. It was only when he left school – if they were honest they would have to admit that it was only after he realised it was possible to escape some of the pressures of family life – that things had taken a turn for the better. Michael's employer, the owner of a small carpentry firm in Mooshaim, had liked his new apprentice from day one, and could not care less if "rafter" was written with two Fs. Michael had since become a foreman, he was content, well paid, and had met Gabriele. She was the other piece of fortune in Michael's life besides his work, although Irene had a different opinion on this. She blames Gabriele for Michael's having moved out of home, Horn thought. It's the same old story: Irene has a highly ambivalent relationship with her difficult son, and holds it against her rival that it is not any better. Moreover, a Viennese-born symphony orchestra player manqué had little in common with a farmer's daughter from a tiny village in the upper Styrian Ennsthal. The fact that the farmer's daughter taught at the town's agricultural college and had all the academic qualifications, seemed to exacerbate matters. Cows' udders – even from a scientific perspective – and Genoese cello bows are quite incompatible, he thought. Gabriele was also seven years older than Michael, and Irene was not happy about that either.

Katharina sat on the ground in front of the bookshelves and looked back and forth between her clenched right fist and the book spines. If she were to take what she wants, and do this in the way she'd like to, she would reveal something valuable to her, Horn thought. In other words: she's right-handed and there's no way she's going to swap what she's clutching from one hand to the other. The mother had said it was two Ludo pieces: one yellow and one blue. He stood up, crouched down next to the girl, took a handful of books from the shelf, and placed them in a row on the floor. They included Maurice Sendak's *In the Night Kitchen*, Astrid Lindgren's *Rasmus and the Vagabond*, a Winnie the Pooh collection, and two volumes of Christine Nöstlinger's Franz stories. After a little hesitation, Katharina took hold of the books with her left hand, placed one on top of the other, very neatly, with *My First Animal Dictionary* on top, and pushed the pile to one side. Then she flicked Mira Lobe's *The Geggis* off the shelf, glanced at the cover, and placed it on the pile. She did the same with Otfried Preußler's *The Little Ghost*, Donald Duck books

29, 30 and 41, a volume of *Tales from Iceland* with a horrible troll on the cover, and Lindgren's *The Children of Noisy Village*. Then there was a Donauland book club edition of *German Heroic Legends*, a good forty years old, which Horn's mother had given him for Christmas one year because she believed that nine-year-olds ought to be interested in knights. Horn had always been more of the Red Indian persuasion, and had preferred tomahawks and bowie knives to lances and swords. That is why he had never liked the book much; the only reason he had not thrown it away was because it was a present from his mother. In his early days as a child psychiatrist he was happy to be able to put the book to good use, and also get it out of his house. It was not just in psychoanalytical theory but in real life, too, that there were boys who got excited about knights and their weapons. A knight in silver armour swished his mighty sword from the book's cover towards the reader through a transparent protective sheet. He crouched behind a shield decorated with a midnight-blue dragon, his head protected by a tufted helmet with closed visor. Katharina stroked the figure with the index and middle fingers of her left hand, as if she were checking how real it was, and then pushed the book next to her. One by one, she carefully put the other books back onto the shelf with her left hand. She's going to open the book, thought Horn, and see that there's a lot of text, and I'll ask her if she can read such small type. She would shake her head and he would offer to read to her. She would not know what to think, freeze, and he would just start reading to her. There was something lovely about the idea of reading to this girl, and Horn did not mind in the slightest that he would be doing it from a book that he did not like.

The telephone was not supposed to ring during a therapy session, so Horn got a big fright. Katharina looked up, but only for a second. Dressler, the blind telephonist, who usually knew

Horn's timetable by heart, made profuse apologies and said that this time there was no way he could have fobbed the caller off. Horn thought first of Irene and Michael, then of Heidemarie, and felt his throat tightening. Something had happened.

When he heard the voice of Ludwig Kovacs, the head of the serious crime unit in Furth's Kriminalpolizei, he did not relax. He grabbed at his neck. After some throat-clearing, Kovacs said, "How's it going with the little girl?" Perhaps nothing had happened after all. Horn started to breathe more easily again.

"I'm in the middle of a session."

"I only need a second of your time, and I shouldn't be telling you this, really, but I think it might be important: Wilfert's murder was premeditated."

They're wrong, Horn thought at first. Nobody kills someone on purpose by driving over their head. People shoot other people, batter each other to death, or hold each other underwater until the weaker one dies, but like that? No.

Katharina had started to look through the book and had got to the first illustration. Sigmund with the grey horse. It did not appear to interest her much.

"Are you sure?" Horn said.

"Absolutely."

"I can't ask any questions now, I hope you understand."

"Of course. Just call me if there's anything you want to know, and call me if the girl says anything."

"Does that mean you don't know anything? I mean, who did it."

"No, we know nothing yet," Kovacs said. Then he hung up.

Katharina was looking the picture in which Siegfried is face to face with Kriemhild. Out of good manners he has removed his helmet and carries it on his arm. He bows to Kriemhild. Katharina placed the index finger of her left hand first on the lady's head, then on that of the hero. She looked very concentrated. It's all about the heads, Horn thought. By touching them she's making sure that they're still O.K. – like a small child. She's worried that the same might happen to their heads as to her grandfather's; this fear makes her silent. Perhaps there would be no reason to ring Kovacs, and that was fine. Psychotherapy worked best without police involvement.

Horn watched the girl turn the page illustrating Siegfried's battle with the dragon. The next one was the picture in which Hagen sinks his spear between Siegfried's shoulders. This one did not arouse much interest either. Horn knew how consistent traumatised people could be in their denial, and so was not that surprised. Hagen is a murderer, he thought, and Wilfert was murdered. There is a logical connection there, but nothing more. Looking at the girl, a thought sparked in his mind, and he wrote the word "accident" on the yellow notepad on his desk. He suddenly felt very hungry.

The knight Katharina was now looking at was similar to the one on the cover: huge sword, shield with coat of arms, closed visor, a plume on the helmet. He was from the story "The Tournament in King Laurin's Rose Garden". Horn was not certain who this knight was. Perhaps Dietrich of Bern, or Ilsan, the militant monk. The only thing that he could remember was that the prize for the victor was a kiss from the princess.

"Our time is up," Horn said at last. Katharina shut the book and put it back on the shelf. She's going to leave the heads with me, Horn thought. That's good.

The mother wore exactly the same sceptical expression as fifty minutes previously. Again, she stood up. "Is she talking yet?" she asked.

"Of course she's talking," Horn said. "She's talking through her actions."

As they left he saw that the girl must have at some point

unzipped her squirrel jacket. He had not noticed her doing it.

There's a murderer in town, Horn thought after a while. He scrunched up the yellow note and grabbed the phone.

Accident and Emergency. Mike, the ward orderly, answered in U14.

"Leuweritz told me he operated on a five-year-old girl last night, comminuted fractures of both lower legs. A road accident, I think," Horn said. "Can you find out her name for me?"

"I know it already."

"And?"

"Birgit Schmidinger."

Horn felt unable to breathe. Then his chest swelled with anger.

"Are you still there?" Mike asked.

"Yes, I'm here. I think I'll come over your way."

"There's huge amounts of herring salad," Mike said. "A sort of early New Year's celebration."

I'd like to stay here by the window and watch the lake freeze over, Horn thought. I'd like not to have to contemplate who might kill an old man. And I'd like the Schmidinger case to be over, I don't care how. He'd ring Kovacs, that was the first thing he decided to do. And he'd do it straight way.

ELEVEN

Aldebaran, the reddish star in the eye of Taurus, was low down in that V-shaped gap which defined the contour of the mountains over the western end of the lake. A little further south, Sirius was just touching the horizon, and Betelgeuse, Orion's shoulder, was approaching it.

Freezing, Kovacs paced up and down on the flat roof of his apartment block. His telescope was focused on Gamma Leonis, a double star which made up the neck of Leo. He had only looked through the lens once, and then he gazed, lost in his thoughts, at a thin, wispy sheet of fog which crept over the lake towards Furth. It was just before half-past five, and time passed even more slowly in the cold of an early morning. Over the course of the night Kovacs had spent perhaps two hours in his bed. He felt as if he had not slept a wink. I can't see anything, he thought, no pattern, no motive, no clue. I can't extract any meaning from this case.

After Patrizia Fleurin's phone call on Saturday evening, he had got into the car and driven to the hospital. When an ambulance had flashed him several times as he turned into the car park, he realised that he only had his sidelights on. Herr Kommissar is driving through the town without his lights on – none of his colleagues were around, but he still felt bad.

Viktor Groh, the colossal pathology assistant, had opened the door for him. With his piggy eyes he looked down at Kovacs rather disparagingly and said, "Today me good friend, Commissario."

Once, several years previously, Kovacs had arrested Groh after he had rammed a broken tequila bottle into the shoulder of a Dutch tourist during a scuffle in a pub. In the end Groh had got away with a suspended sentence because there were ample witnesses to the fact that he had been provoked by his victim. "Yes, today good friend," Kovacs said, and he followed Groh, who looked like a run-down sumo wrestler in his stained, sandy work outfit, through the corridors.

Fleurin was wearing a white doctor's coat under a transparent plastic apron that reached down to her calves, and disposable gloves. She was in the middle of labelling different-sized specimen containers. She must already have finished the rougher work. Her red hair was tied into a bun, and she looked devastating with her freckles and the little bunches of laughter lines at the corners of her eyes. I have a satisfying sexual relationship on a contractual basis, thought Kovacs, and yet I can't help imagining what it would be like to get my hands on this woman.

"Don't beam at me like that, Kommissar," she said. "First, there's no way I'm going to spend New Year with you, and second, you've got work to do, I believe." She pointed to the autopsy table. There lay the body of Sebastian Wilfert under some washed-out green cloths.

Kovacs bowed his head, put on the apron that Fleurin handed to him, and slipped some artificial blue footlets over his boots. He declined the gloves. "Don't touch anything if you're a stranger! That's what my mum always used to say."

"You say that every time you come here."

He said nothing. She is so damn precise in her observations and has a memory like an elephant, he thought.

"Let's get to the important stuff straight away." Kovacs looked at her left collarbone and nodded.

Fleurin took away one of the cloths. Using a piece of cling film, she had shifted upwards the mass that was once Wilfert's chin and lower jaw, thus exposing the neck section. Underneath, as far as the voice box, everything had been completely wrecked; the lingual bone had been broken several times and pushed back. However, a centimetre below the thyroid cartilage – itself undamaged apart from some torn tissue right at the top – there was a wide, crossways slit. Because it been covered by the crushed chin, she explained, it had not been visible at first.

"And?" Kovacs said.

"A very sharp tool and a very definite cut."

Kovacs shut his eyes for a moment. He had been worried that he would be sick but the moment passed.

Fleurin took two long pairs of tweezers from her instrument tray and pulled apart the two sides of the wound. The cut was almost horizontal, she explained, perhaps angled just a touch from top left to bottom right and, apart from the strand of blood vessels on the right, it had severed all the organs of the throat, including the oesophagus and the left-hand sternocleidomastoid muscle. If one assumed that the cut was made from behind, then this pointed to a right-handed suspect. She showed him the cut marks in the depths of the wound, which ran across the front of the fourth cervical vertebra like a notch. All one could infer from this was that the perpetrator had used a very well-sharpened blade-like tool.

"What you're saying is that the neck was cut through, so to speak," Kovacs said. He did not know where to put his hands.

"So to speak, yes."

"And then the guy's head was run over."

"No," the forensic pathologist said. "Certainly not."

For a few seconds Kovacs stared straight at her. She looked absolutely sure of herself. She's wrong, he thought, she's utterly wrong. The one thing I've taken for granted up till now was the tractor tyres grinding over the old man's head. Fleurin said she had not found traces of earth or gravel anywhere around the shattered skull; on the contrary, the wound area was astonishingly clean – an impossibility if the head had been run over. What was more, Mauritz had come to the same conclusion; she had talked to him on the phone about an hour ago. I wanted to ring Mauritz; she did it, Kovacs thought – I'm too slow.

"How then?" he said, putting his arms to his sides beneath the apron.

"I don't know," she said. "There is a large dent at the front of the skullcap, and it burst at the lambdoid and sagittal sutures because of the internal pressure. Perhaps a huge sledgehammer. From the few spatterings of blood and brain he was able to analyse, Mauritz says it looks in all seriousness as if the poor old chap was hit bang in the face by a meteorite."

Kovacs closed his eyes again. Mauritz had never joked about his astrophilia. I've got to keep a clear head, he thought, and I mustn't allow myself to become paranoid.

"A meteorite?" he said. "And Mauritz took it home with him I suppose!"

Fleurin shrugged. "Mauritz says that meteorites vaporise on impact with the earth." Sometimes they make a crater, Kovacs thought, and sometimes they leave behind tiny clumps of ice.

"Who is capable of doing such a thing?" he said. "What monster could do something like that?" And he recalled how Wieck had vomited over the yellow police tape that early morning. He would ask for her. Demski was still on holiday and it would not work with Eleonore Bitterle alone. He would also ask for young Lipp. Lipp was fearless and he listened.

"Why ask me?"

"They say pathologists always know everything."

". . . but always too late. Very original!"

Kovacs was close to apologising, even though that old chestnut had not crossed his mind. He felt comfortable in this woman's presence, and that unnerved him. It might have been her freckles and the red hair, but more likely it was the way her presence radiated. You could put her behind an electronic microscope or the wheel of a mechanical digger, hand her a garden rake or a Glock 17 pistol – she would always look right.

"I know that ultimately it's up to me to find the answer to that question," he said. "But sometimes there are just certain situations . . ."

Fleurin made a placatory gesture with her hand and then pulled away the cloth that covered the rest of Wilfert's head. "That's alright," she said. "I think that people who do things like that must either harbour a huge amount of hatred . . ."

"Or?"

She hesitated. "Or nothing at all. Actually there's no 'or'. I know that's not much help at the moment, but I can't think of anything else."

The old man's skull had changed quite a lot, as if the whole thing had shrunk, not just the freely dangling eyeball that had lost all its lustre and now looked like a light-grey shrivelled fruit. You could hardly distinguish Wilfert's hair from its surroundings, and the dried blood had coloured it blackish-brown. The artificial denture, the only solid thing in the mush of tissue, had been removed.

"How strong does someone have to be to cause that much damage?" Kovacs asked. Fleurin stared at him.

"You've wielded a sledgehammer before, haven't you?"

Kovacs nodded. "It was meant to be a rhetorical question," he said. She covered the head and neck again.

"You'd need less power after having slit his throat."

What makes an attractive woman become a forensic pathologist? he wondered. He then remembered how he had driven the
wooden stakes into the frozen ground by the ramp up to the barn,
one after the other, but with the head of an axe, not a sledge-
hammer. He looked at Groh, who was sitting on a yellow plastic
chair by the wall of the room, leafing through a motorbike magazine. Groh noticed that Kovacs was looking at him. He grinned
from ear to ear. "One metre ninety-eight and 119 kilos," he said.
"I'd be a fantastic murderer."

On the drive back he had started to make his calls. Mauritz
answered straight away, as if he had been expecting it. "Aren't
you amazed?" he asked, and Kovacs said that was the most stupid
remark he had heard recently. Mauritz apologised and sum-
marised what he knew at present: tons of blood-stained slush,
more in evidence to the left of the skull and shoulder than the
right because of the severed vessel in the neck, no hint of a struggle. Also, the pattern of the splattered tissue on the ground looked
as if Wilfert had suffered a single, powerful blow. So much for
the meteorite, Kovacs said, and Mauritz ignored the comment,
as if it had not been made. Overall the case was anything but
clear-cut, and there was even something peculiar about the tyre
marks which were all over the place. After the initial examination
Mauritz had insisted that the large tracks must have been made
by the back wheel of a tractor, but these were the only ones that
had been found near the body. From this one had to conclude
that it must have been a vehicle with four equally large wheels,
and not a tractor normally found around these parts. "What else?"
Kovacs asked. Mauritz said that it was most likely to have been a
type of lorry. Also, it was pretty certain that where the body had
been found was also the scene of the crime, and that the frozen
ground had provided an ideal level of resistance for the mass

that had come smashing down onto Wilfert's skull, be it a sledge-hammer or anything else. "You know what that means, don't you?" Kovacs said, and Mauritz sighed deeply. "Sunday duty, the little shovel and sieve, on my knees the whole time, just like an archae-ologist." Kovacs promised to ensure that nobody disturbed him, and Mauritz said, "Great!"

Philipp Eyltz, the local police chief, had been in the tearoom of the Hotel Bauriedl with a former school friend to celebrate the birth of the latter's granddaughter. Kovacs had uttered the words "Code Red" on his voicemail, and so the call was returned in an instant. The system worked, even though Kovacs thought Eyltz a fraud, while Eyltz, in turn, never missed an opportunity to describe Kovacs as a "highly misanthropic investigative machine".

They had settled the matter in a seating area of the Bauriedl lobby, Eyltz with an armagnac, Kovacs with nothing. Mauritz would get the assistance of a uniformed officer, and another would be sent to guard the crime scene at night, just in case. They would leave it until Monday before passing any information to the media – the run-up to New Year was expected to be a pretty quiet time, anyway. Kovacs could of course carry on investigating however he liked, while the secondment of Lipp and Wieck was fine for the duration of the investigation. Eyltz wore a white and yellow striped shirt under a dark-blue blazer with golden buttons, as well as handmade, black, lace-up ankle boots. He had his usual supportive smile, an expression which Kovacs always felt the urge to wipe off with a high-pressure water blaster. I'm getting more and more sensitive, he thought. I'm not as tolerant as I once was. Eyltz is trying to be constructive and yet he's driving me round the bend.

The duty clerk at the public prosecutor's office had asked, "Are you sure?", and Kovacs came close to saying for a second time that evening that it was the most stupid comment he'd heard for some time. But he bit his lip and just barked back that yes, he was sure, and that everything would be faxed over: forensic pathologist's findings, investigative report, etc.

Late that evening he had called Eleonore Bitterle again. She had sounded sleepy, and when he apologised she explained that she had dozed off in her steam room. "I'd like you just to think about it," he said. "You've got the whole of Sunday." It was only afterwards that he realised he was ordering her back from holiday. She was always there, holiday or no holiday.

Bitterle was a gaunt, grey-haired woman of forty-two – if you believed her file – and she had been single since the death of her husband. At work they called her "Mrs Brain", and it did sometimes seem as if she knew everything. It was said she had embarked on several degrees – history, philosophy, and whatever else – and abandoned them all just before completion. Psychologically this could be linked to her father, who was a professor of administrative law at Salzburg University, and known to be a dictatorial arsehole. She had landed up at the Bundeskriminalamt, probably thanks to her father's intervention, and had started working in Vienna, first in the criminal statistical office, later in victim support. She had then met her husband, a civil engineer from Upper Austria, and moved with him to Furth. It was plain to everybody that he had been the love of her life. The two of them had bought into an ecological housing project in the north-east of the city, and they had been in the middle of planting a hornbeam hedge along the garden fence when a lump appeared on the front of his right lower leg. First they thought it was an injury, a bruise between the muscles, then an infection of the bone marrow, and when he was finally diagnosed with osteosarcoma, the cancer had already spread throughout his body. Thanks to the widow's pension that she received in addition to her salary, she had been able to finish planting the hedge and keep the house. But overnight she had become a different person. Her hesitant intellectual approach to things had become even more accentuated, and sometimes it seemed as if she were all fear and uncertainty, even in the most harmless of situations. Kovacs tried to treat her gently, as he knew that a single flash of inspirational thinking was sometimes worth more than twenty-four hours of steel nerves. If he could say to her, as in this instance, "I'd like you just to think about it," it was the best approach.

Kovacs had spent most of Sunday at Marlene's. For lunch she had cooked lemon chicken with rosemary potatoes, and a hazelnut soufflé with orange brittle for pudding. In spite of a double Pernod afterwards, they were both so full that the coitus could not take place until much later, after the siesta and short stroll. It had been leisurely and somewhat routine, and in the middle of it he had thought: those are the most wonderful breasts in the world. The scene was clear in his mind. In that same instant he had looked into Marlene's face, but her eyes were shut.

A little earlier they had walked downstream along the river, past the rafting camp, to where the strip of woodland by the bank became very narrow and where the drop started. Marlene talked about how the shop's turnover had been on the increase again for some months – not a dramatic rise, but consistent – and how the chamber of commerce, which had promised her assistance for the rental of additional storage space, was now behaving as if it knew nothing about the matter. He said, "It's quite simple: people are feeling the pinch again, so they're buying second-hand things," and she nodded. He could not think of anything to say about the chamber of commerce. When they turned back, he looked at the mountains in the south-east. The sky above the peaks had been glowing yellow; this picture was also vivid in his mind.

The tension had first stung him when he was back alone in his flat. He had sat in front of a piece of paper and scribbled meaning-less rings on it, the image of Wilfert's gaping neck ever present in his mind. In the end he wrote a single sentence: a right-handed person slices through the throat of an old man. He read it out loud several times, until it sounded to him like a practice sentence from a German lesson. He then stood up, chucked the pen in the air, and put on his jacket.

As Lefti was closed on Sunday he had gone to the Piccola Cucina, a tiny trattoria on the Rathausplatz. He ordered a small carafe of house red wine, a coarse Apulian Primitivo which he knew would not fog his head up. He also ordered a plate of marinated anchovies, even though he was not in the least bit hungry yet. A young woman was sitting at one of the brown tables by the wall, wearing a dark-red jumper with gold stars. She looked a broken woman, and was knocking back one limoncello after the other. She seemed to get on well with Daniela, the round waitress with black curly hair, and from time to time they exchanged a few quiet words. Kovacs thought hard, but he could not recall where he knew the woman from.

He broke off a piece of white bread and dipped it in the oil. Whenever he was unhappy with something he would often think of thousands of other unrelated things: Yvonne, who had pushed his life in a strange direction; Charlotte, who would always look like a vegetable, even in a red angora jumper; the town, which held him in its claws; the damp winter in the Furth basin; Marlene with her housewifey ideas for New Year; the Romanians, who only came over here to break into cars; the gold buttons on Philipp Fyltz's blazer; the Business Party, which was preying mercilessly on the country; the millions of people who refused to grasp this; his own lethargy, which hung over him every winter like a huge, languid bank of fog. He asked Daniela for a waiter's pad, took his pen out of his pocket, and wrote things on the narrow paper, such as: "Mauritz is lazy", "Let Eleonore think!", or "People usually kill a member of their own family." In the end he tried to sketch Wilfert's body from memory, lying there upside down on the ramp up to the barn with arms stretched out wide. Daniela glanced over his shoulder and said, "Looks like someone crucified," but he could not escape the feeling that he had not progressed one jot.

Kovacs paced up and down, clapping his hands together. He had felt a similar unease over six years before when a taxman from Wels who had taken early retirement had left a trail of sexual crimes throughout the Salzkammergut and Upper Styria. In the end, ten-year-old Michaela Moor from Waiern had been raped and then strangled, and although they had a sample of the man's sperm, and hence his D.N.A., there was nothing else to go on. In a very rare moment of lucidity, Strack had then come up with the camper van idea. Soon afterwards they had caught the perpetrator in a dark-blue camper, just as he was tucking an envelope with photographs of his last victim into the first aid compartment. In spite of this the man had the audacity to deny everything, causing Kurt Niemayer to explode on the spot. The man's nose was pulp before the others could even blink, and it was only then that that Demski had been able to restrain Niemayer from behind with both arms. His overreaction was understandable: at the time both of Niemayer's daughters had been of primary-school age, as well as the fact that he left the Kriminaldienst when he finished his law studies soon afterwards. Niemayer was now a judge in a juvenile court in Innsbruck. He would phone Kovacs from time to time, and once or twice a year he used to make an appearance at his former workplace.

Kovacs walked over to the railings on the roof terrace and looked out eastwards over the roofs of the Walzwerk estate. In two hours' time the sun would rise over the jagged peaks of the Ennsthal mountains. A white column of smoke rose vertically from one of the chimneys of the woodworking factory. The first lorries could be heard chugging on the roads into town. I'm not going to leave Furth, Kovacs thought. I'm going to continue sleeping with Marlene, probably with greater regularity, I'm going to continue gazing into the sky, and I'll be the only person who retires here.

He did not adjust the telescope's focus. The eyepiece was icy cold. He imagined his eyeball freezing solid to it, and remaining attached to the black metal cylinder when he pulled his head away. Regulus in Leo. The pale speck of the spiral nebulus M35. Castor and Pollux. I've got a brother, Kovacs thought. He coaches second-rate football sides and gets pissed; every time I see him he has a go at me; I don't want anything to do with him. Kovacs loved Castor, one of the two principal stars in the Gemini constellation. What looked to the naked eye like an average, medium-sized, white, fixed star, was revealed, even at low magnification, to be a cluster of six individual stars. Things are generally more complex than they seem, he thought. He put his hand into his pocket and felt the waiter's pad he had written on. In front of him he could see the dark-red jumper with golden stars worn by the young woman with the sad expression and succession of limoncellos. Stars, he thought, stars everywhere – a distraction which is not getting me anywhere.

He knocked the snow off his boots before going down the steps to his flat. He stood for a second in front of the hall mirror. Below his left eye he saw an age spot which was slowly getting bigger. He would not take off his jacket, but go straight into the office; he would put the lights on in most of the rooms and turn on the espresso machine; then he would stand by the board and start drawing.

As usual, it was Bitterle who was the first to make an appearance, but not by much on this occasion – hardly had she removed her fake-fur coat than young Lipp was at the door. He was wearing a thickly padded lumberjack's coat over a light-grey woollen jumper. "This is a bit odd," he said. "I almost feel like I'm on holiday." Eyltz had emailed him, he said, in that peremptory tone he always used: with immediate effect and for the duration of the investigation, Lipp was assigned to the serious crime squad of the Kriminalpolizei for the Wilfert case. He was to show up at eight o'clock on Monday, 30 December at the office of the chief Kommissar in charge of the case, to whom he would be provisionally reporting. "At least you know where you stand," Kovacs said. Lipp pulled a sour grin.

Wieck arrived in uniform, including regulation winter coat, and immediately turned red when she saw Lipp in civvies. She had not known what was expected, she stammered, and she had thought it silly to phone somebody just to ask what she should wear. "It doesn't matter," Bitterle said. She was wearing olive-green woollen trousers and a black roll neck-jumper. She looks like a secondary-school teacher, Kovacs thought. Latin and Greek, perhaps. He was also relieved that she was not going to be troubled by the presence of a second woman. It must have something to do with me, he thought: this conviction that two women in the same place must herald the start of a disaster. "We're missing Mauritz," he said, because he could not think of anything else. "The fat guy from forensics?" Lipp asked.

"Exactly, the fat guy."

"He's usually very punctual." Bitterle looked at the clock.

"Perhaps he's got a cold," Kovacs said. "He was working yesterday, I hope."

"Great," Lipp said, beaming. Lipp's first name was Florian, he had moved out of his parents' house nine months ago, and lived alone. He had attended a technical school for metalworking, but did not go on to study engineering at college as his father, a director at a large lift manufacturer, would have wished. Instead he had joined the police force. During his job interview he had said that he did not want to be one of those millions who abandon their childhood dreams. He had wanted to be a policeman from the age of five, and he had stuck with the idea. At the bottom of the employment form there was a note written by Rahberger, head of the personnel department: "Infantile?" They had taken him on anyway. The only thing there was no information on was Lipp's sexual orientation. It was alleged that in his first year of police training he'd had a relationship with a schoolgirl, but that was more a rumour than anything else. It bothered Kovacs that he knew nothing, and also that he was bothered by this. In the past I could sniff out a queer ten kilometres away, he thought. It's not like that any more. Either they've changed or I have.

Kovacs dragged the rectangular whiteboard from the other end of the room to the meeting table. He took a sponge and wiped off the Christmas tree which he had drawn an hour or so before. Then, using a thick, dark-blue marker, he made a vertical and horizontal line to divide the board into four boxes.

"What's that supposed to be?" Lipp said.

"A home-made structuring system," Kovacs answered. "As simple as my provincial criminologist's brain." At the top of the four boxes he wrote: "What have we got?", "What do we need?", "Who's doing what?" and "Notes". Lipp copied the whole thing into his notebook. Bitterle had her head bowed and was looking at the palms of her hands. Kovacs was annoyed that he had run himself down yet again. "Basically, violence is simple," he said.

Mauritz was at the door when Kovacs was noting "right-handed" in the "What have we got?" box. He held up a white paper bag and said, "Breakfast!" The others looked at Kovacs. He sighed out loud and put the pen down.

"Go and make us all a cup of coffee," he said.

Kovacs had already forgotten that Lipp and Bitterle both wanted tea rather than coffee, when Christine Strobl, the departmental secretary, rushed in and passed him the telephone. "The fourth attempt," she said. "No name and very annoying." He went out into the corridor.

The woman had a shrill voice, and the first thing she said was, "The next time it'll be the head!" Kovacs shut his eyes. Things leak out, he thought, especially at weekends. He said nothing. After a while the woman seemed to realise that he was listening to her, and she began to give some order to her flow of words. She wanted to remain anonymous and was calling from a phone box, as she suspected that the police would do nothing this time, either. She'd heard of people who'd tried in the past to do something and had only got themselves into the most awful difficulties. It had happened three days ago, on Friday afternoon, maybe at four o'clock, but while it was still light, anyway. She'd been out walking her dog, just wandering around you might say, and by chance she'd come along Bergheimstraße, a couple of minutes on the Graz highway, then east – but she didn't need to explain that to a member of the police force. From there the road sloped down towards the town, and in the garden of number four there was a mound, two or at most three metres high – maybe it was earth excavated from the cellar that they hadn't cleared away. A little girl had trudged up this hillock, pulling a blue sledge behind her, a short, flat, one-man type. At the top the girl sat on the sledge and slid down right to the end of the garden, which you could do because the whole thing was on a slope. Then she turned round, plodded back up the garden and up the mound, and tried to slide down again. But this time she only got as far as the bottom of the hillock, because all of a sudden a man was standing in her way. With a face like thunder he stopped the girl in mid-slide, yelling, "I told you to stay in your room!" He yanked the sledge from under her, so that she fell on her back in the snow. He took the blue sledge in both hands and swung it sideways, smashing it against one of two T-shaped iron washing stands which were fixed into the ground. He let the pieces fall to the ground, hurried back over to the crying girl, lifted her up, and did the same with her. He grabbed the child under her armpits, twirled her through the air and crashed her legs – well, the bits below her knees – against the iron pole, just like that. For a moment the girl stopped crying. She was wearing a grey anorak with white polar bears on it; the woman had noticed that quite clearly. She had watched the episode from the street, ducking behind a barberry bush, and holding her dog's mouth shut, a small dachshund cross. She'd rarely been as frightened in her life and didn't move until the man had disappeared into the house with the child in his arms. She'd imagined he might appear again with a gun, looking for witnesses, so she'd run away. Then, about an hour later, she'd come back, this time without her dog, as she'd been wracked with guilt. The ambulance and police cars were outside the house, so she'd turned back, convinced that somebody else had seen the incident, too. Yesterday she'd heard from a friend who helped out in the kitchens at the hospital that the girl was in casualty, but had been admitted as the victim of a "car accident". That was the reason why she wanted to report this man to the police. His name was Norbert Schmidinger.

Kovacs moved his legs wider apart. He felt he had not had enough sleep. From the kitchenette came the clattering of cutlery. He lied to the woman on the end of the phone that he had jotted down some notes, but for them to be able to use her statement she would either have to tell the story again to one of his colleagues, exactly as she had told it to him, one thing at a time, or bring in a written version herself. If she was worried about remaining anonymous she could just send somebody else. The woman breathed deeply. She had already written something, she said, it was as good as sent.

Life is like a piece of knotted string – nothing for long periods of time, then it all happens at once. For a short while Kovacs felt the urge to smash the phone against the wall. "It's the neighbour, simple as that," he said out loud.

Mauritz, who was just coming past with a full pot of coffee, asked, "Which neighbour?"

"Tell you later," Kovacs said.

A man who breaks his own daughter's legs, he thought – everybody knows him yet nobody dares do a thing about him. They'd had endless dealings with him for years, and in all that time nobody had attempted to make a useable statement against him. Psychopaths scare people, he thought, irrespective of whether they're fathers, teachers or politicians. Psychopaths intimidate, humiliate and beat people up. People are afraid of these things, of being intimidated, humiliated and beaten up. Deep down, fear is always rational.

While he was demolishing a plaited brioche in three mouthfuls, Mauritz told him how the day before he had taken imprints of the tyre marks, and then dug in the snow around where the body had been found, square metre by square metre. In total he had found four nails – two eighty-millimetre ones, one hundred-millimetre one with a countersunk head, and a zinc-coated roofing nail – the remains of a sack of chemical fertiliser, a rusted door fitting, a green Lego brick – a four piece as he recalled from his childhood – and finally, perhaps the most interesting find in his opinion, a brown leather button you might find on a loden coat or a sports jacket. He could not of course say how long it had been lying there. In any case, no button had been missing from Wilfert's jacket;

he had checked that again. Georg, the Maywalds' son, had turned up at regular intervals, circling the tape around the sealed-off area and asking questions like, "Can you find anything at all in the snow?", or "What if you don't find out what happened?" He, Mauritz, had remained silent even though curious children like that could trick you into chattering away. As agreed, he had refrained from mentioning that Wilfert had been murdered; not a hint of it, not even to Georg's mother, who invited him in for lunch. There had been a perfectly decent chilli con carne with home-made bread and cider. Ernst Maywald was not there; they said he had gone to his brother's to help cut up some larch branches. The smaller of the two daughters spent the whole time staring at the wall and not saying a word.

Their discussion then turned to how even body-temperature blood freezes rapidly when the temperature is minus ten degrees; the totally uncharacteristic fragments of footprints – Vibram soles, size forty-two – which had been found here and there; and the fact that this vehicle, whatever it was, looked to have stopped at the ramp up to the barn and not driven up it. It was still unclear what had actually pulverised Wilfert's skull. Kovacs did not mention the meteorite and Mauritz also remained silent on this point. Bitterle's research had shown that the severing of a head or the mutilation of a face was a characteristic behaviour of mentally ill people or people with serious personality disorders, and that the literature on the subject showed that an astonishingly high proportion of these offenders were sons who felt compelled to annihilate their mothers, something which did not apply in this case, of course. But one could still infer that a considerable amount of energy had gone into the violence, which was expressed not least by its absurd aesthetic. "Aesthetic?" asked Wieck, and Bitterle said, "Yes, aesthetic. Like a bloody painting." Kovacs wrote aesthetic on the board, Wieck shook her head and all of a sudden

Lipp put up his hand like a schoolboy. "I've thought of something," he said. "There was an episode of *Father Brown* on telly in which someone was murdered by a hammer that had been dropped on his head from a steeple." None of the others could recall the episode. "Well, I was at the crime scene all of yesterday and I didn't see any steeple," Mauritz said, "even though it was Sunday." Lipp looked a little offended. "I was only saying," he said.

In the end Lipp was given the job of asking around in the hunting club and O.A.P. association, the two places where Wilfert often socialised with people outside the family. Bitterle was to check Wilfert's financial affairs and savings, and draft a press release for issue later on in the afternoon. Mauritz announced he was going to look through all available data on tyre treads. Then he planned to jump into the car and drive to Salzburg, where one of his aunts had a shop that sold tailoring accessories. She was the right person to answer any questions about buttons.

TWELVE

It's snowing. If I look up I can see a hundred thousand million of them. Sometimes a flake lands on my eye. Then I have to blink.

Beyond the snowdrifts and the thick, grey clouds and the thin, blue clouds and the stratosphere, there is the universe. Geonosis and Coruscant and Naboo and the four suns which shine for ever and for ever again.

This is the mission: sit on one of the tree trunks lying next to the wildlife observation centre, where they cut down the reeds from a boat in late autumn. Read the newspaper article again and look out at the lake. Feel it penetrating you. You are a tool. That's what he said – penetrating you – and he kneed me in the ribcage to expel any foreign air from my lungs. I fainted.

You can't go out onto the lake from here. The ice is thin and part of it, towards town, beyond the dark observation centre building, has disappeared completely. The ducks and greylag geese are gathering at the point where the river flows out of the lake. Two swans pass by from time to time.

A kilometre to the west they say the ice is twenty centimetres thick. They drilled down and measured it before they let the fireworks off there on New Year's Eve. We were all there. Dad was in a really good mood but Mum made a mistake. His clients are his clients, says Daniel, and he can drink as much punch with them as he wants, and she shouldn't get involved. She did get involved and said that yes, young Grosser was right: a silver Z3 is a nicer car for a woman than a dark-green M.G. Cabrio. Basically she flirted with young Grosser, which meant that the next day her face looked like a blueberry flan. That's what my dad said at breakfast the next day, "Your face looks like a blueberry flan." And later Daniel told me, "B.H. instead of S.I." Then he punched me because I didn't know that S.I. means sexual intercourse. So I thought I deserved it.

I put the page from the newspaper into a transparent sleeve so it wouldn't get wet. The sleeve is from my dad's office, but it's best he doesn't know. He goes through phases where he couldn't care less if you took sleeves from his office, and then at other times he's not like that at all. You never know which phase he's going through at any one time. I think that that's what he means when he talks about his personality. He says that the personality of a successful car dealer is to pretend you're predictable, whereas actually the opposite is true.

The headline is not nice: "Town Gripped by Fear." It hits you hard. Underneath is a large picture of a slope covered in snow, a barn behind – where the body was found, apparently. The article says that it's not just a simple murder, but a monstrous crime which should make everybody afraid. "The victim's windpipe and artery were slashed with a razor-sharp instrument." Underlined with a thick red marker. It says the daughter is completely devastated; she can't understand how someone could have done that to her father who'd been a kind and gentle man all his life. The whole family is in counselling. "The world is unfair," Daniel says. "The world couldn't care less whether you're a kind and gentle person or not. Inside, for instance, they make you eat shit or they fuck you up the arse, and nobody asks you what you were like before." Then he pinches my chest hard and twists it until I start screaming. At the end of the article there is a lot of stuff about the lack of a motive, the fact that the man had no money – neither in his wallet nor in his bank account – that his will had

136

been sorted out a long time ago, and that in the hunting club and wherever else he used to go he'd always been a respected and well-loved individual, from which, the paper said, one had to conclude that the murderer must be sick and full of hatred.

I sit there looking out over the lake. It starts to snow more heavily and I picture a thick, fluffy layer soon forming on the ice, and the snow crystals right at the bottom sinking into the ice and fusing with it.

To my left, where the dark water begins, the ducks are making a hell of a noise. Some of them disappear into the boathouse and then come out again soon after. There's a small gap in the bars below the planks inside the boathouse. I've no idea if the people at the wildlife observation station are aware of it. The coots, for example, pass through the opening with ease, although the geese can't do it any more and the swans are much too big anyway.

It was Daniel who gave me the Stanley knife. It's the middle one of a set of three, it's got a retractable blade you can fix and a red plastic handle. Special offer, he said, four Euro ninety. But it's as sharp as an expensive one. Inside it's just teeming with weapons, he said. You imagine that it's a safe place, but that's completely wrong. "If someone presses a blade into your back, you drop your trousers there and then, or open your mouth wide or whatever," he says. Then he shows me what it's like and he's right.

It doesn't matter whether it's holiday time or not. In term time I sit in class and there are certain things I don't understand. In the holidays my dad walks round the flat five times every morning and Daniel teaches me stuff.

The ferry only operates from March to October. I imagine them deciding to use an ice-breaker so that people can go to Mooshaim and Sankt Christoph in winter as well, and I picture everybody standing on the lake on New Year's Eve, glasses of sekt in their hands, waiting for the fireworks, when suddenly this huge boat comes up to them with its steel shell and many thousands of horsepower.

I'm going to put on the cloak and mask, then I'll be so dark that I don't stand out against the background. I'll go over to the boathouse under the cover of the trees. Around the back of it I'll get the Phillips screwdriver from my rucksack and unscrew the padlock fitting from the door. As the boathouse has four windows – two facing south, one east and one west – it'll be light enough inside, Daniel said. There'll be two or three plastic dinghies inside. At first the ducks will get a fright and try to escape through the gap in the bars, but as soon as I offer them some white bread they'll turn back and come over to me. I'll lay the Stanley knife and warhammer on the main plank, next to the water's edge. Ducks like white bread, Daniel said. He also said a bit more over to the left-hand side of the neck. If something happens it doesn't matter; you won't see any spots on the black cloak.

THIRTEEN

It is as if he were running inside a room. The snowflakes are thick and falling straight downwards, and the sky begins a few arm-lengths above his head. The wind is quite still. The noise of the waterfall coming from below to the left is muted. The cliff face, which towers up vertically on the other side, fades to grey in the void. Here and there a branch deposits its load.

Number nine. The longest one of all.

They're sellin', postcards of the hanging, they're painting the passports brown.

Every morning one of the council workers drives here with the snowcat and turns half of the path into a track for cross-country skiers. The rest is flattened for those who walk here. There is now five centimetres of new snow on the compacted base. This makes the run a bit awkward. Nonetheless, he manages the long climb without reducing his speed. The elders and willows become denser. In clear weather one would be able to see the gleaming chimneys of the woodworking factory between the trees and, a little further to the west, the steeples of the abbey church. Now he notices a flock of blue tits flying past him from the hazelnut bushes.

He can just about make out his footprints from the way there, but nothing else. Since he left the road he has not met a soul. Other people would be afraid to be alone in this winter wood, on the edge of a town where people have their throats slit. His fear always comes from within, from the fissure where he is ripped

139

apart. Whenever he tries to explain it, nobody understands. People are too accustomed to identifying only with their own feelings.

The boy will sit on the toboggan and demand to be pulled up the hill. At first the woman will say no, and then she will do it after all. Her frizzy black hair will flow out from under her headband. There will be a soft layer of snow on her hair and shoulders. She will throw snowballs at the boy. He will laugh out loud and topple over backwards from the toboggan.

Sometimes he has the feeling that his entire body is artificial: joints, bones, teeth, skin, eyeballs. His windpipe becomes a flexible hose and his lungs two semi-transparent sacks divided into tiny cube-shaped chambers. He cannot picture his brain. At any rate, it is the place where the thoughts are generated.

A fresh set of tracks crosses his path. Some hoofed game, most likely a young hind. She has probably not yet had any young and she is on her own. That happens.

Down to the left now, on the other side of the bank, the rafting centre. Both its jetties are covered in a thick layer of snow. The river waltzes languidly in front of it. Not a single rafting or canyoning accident in their eight years; they make quite a show of broadcasting this fact. One of the safest outdoor activity firms in Europe. Robert went with them once last year; he did the four kilometres below the rapids, the standard option for beginners. He was so excited about it afterwards and spouted all sorts of pathetic nonsense – "An experience which expands your horizons" etc.

Left over the footbridge. The planks under the new snow are frozen over. He slips and curses. Along Imhofstraße. The tanning studio. A man with a precision-trimmed moustache walks on to the street. The studio manager is a platinum-blonde Slovak woman, who is said to have once been a well-known model. One day a persistent fan attacked her with an ice pick and that was her career over.

Up on the cemetery wall two crows are fighting over something that looks like a piece of skin. They move towards each other in a weird symmetry, then away from each other, then towards each other again, not making a sound all the while. The occasional spray of snow.

His favourite bit: *Across the street they've nailed the curtains, they're getting ready for the feast, The Phantom of the Opera, A perfect image of a priest.* Casanova is poisoned with words, T. S. Eliot and Ezra Pound fight in the captain's tower of the *Titanic*, and then the end. More than eleven minutes. He feels for his waistband and turns off his iPod.

Wilfert's body has been released. Given that the affair has caused such a stir, a lot of people will to come to the funeral; the television cameras might be there, too. Clemens will insist on leading the ceremony. He will find some comforting words and, as always, will quote St Augustine. Everything will appear in the newspaper the following day.

West into Weyrer Straße. The headlights of the cars grope their way along the ground through the snowfall. Kurt Neulinger, the head of I.T. at the district authority, is clearing his drive with a mechanical tiller. Since it got out that his wife would sometimes bring a student back to their apartment, he comes home from work earlier, and everything is kept even tidier than usual. Although he looks as if he would freeze to death, he does not wear gloves while pushing the tiller. The machine makes a hell of a din. It occurs to him that on the night Wilfert died there was also some sort of noise.

He turns left into Orangerie-Straße, runs along the wall of the abbey park for about a couple of hundred metres, and then takes the east gate. The round conifers on either side of the path, the stone giant with the cudgel, the nymphs in the middle of the mussel-shaped fountain. The glass panels of the greenhouse are covered all over with ice flowers. Not even right at the top, where the gable is flat, does the snow seem to be settling. It must be due to the warm air rising inside. The image of Clemens strutting through the greenhouse with Sterck, the gardener, peering into hidden corners, and being taught about palms and orchids. You take a stone, and another one, throw them as hard as you can, and you hit them both in the temple, right by the ear. They collapse, and the holes in the panes are so small that nobody notices them. He speeds up until the end of the greenhouse. The cold burns his lungs. People take holy orders for different reasons, he thinks. Some because they need security; some because the idea of lots of men in one place makes them excited; and some because they would otherwise kill their mothers and sisters sooner or later.

Wilhelm, who is sitting by the gate reading a motorcycle magazine, tells him that the team of cleaners are doing the floors in the school, which is why the key is not hanging up on the board. He takes the corridor to the left, walks to the main stairwell, goes up to the first floor and through the frosted glass door, which is open. His classroom is the first after the bend in the corridor. The strong stench of floor polish hangs in the air.

He closes the door behind him. On the wall to the left are twenty-three photographic portraits of children; at the back of the room a board with the basic laws of mathematics on it, and another showing a school project in Ethiopia. He goes over to the window. In the beam of the floodlights which illuminate the abbey courtyard the snow looks completely artificial.

He sits down on the teacher's table, his legs dangling over the edge. From here he has a view of all of them. Directly in front of him is Lisa, who is afraid of many things such as squirrels and P. E. Next to her is Veronika, the only real swot in the class. Some of them like her nevertheless. Michael Streiter, and next to him, Konstantin, who by the time he reaches the fifth year will probably be three metres tall. Hans-Peter; Leo; Markus, who never says anything. Ewald, the cellist; Rudolf, who always asks if he can bring his rat into class; Katharina Jordak, who has the breasts of an eighteen-year-old; little, thin Jaqueline; Jennifer, who is always scratching her arms; Günseli and Leyla, the two Turkish girls; Nora; red-haired Johanna with her translucent skin; Benedikt; Michael Wontok, who everybody calls "piggy" because of his rosy, moonlike face; Katharina Scheffberger; the hyperactive Annabelle; Björn; tiny Anatolij from Georgia, who can work out complicated multiplication sums in his head; and Dominik, who only has one arm because he reached into a straw cutter when he was a small child.

Two children were missing before the holidays: Jennifer, because of an inflammation of the appendix; and Leo, who overestimated his snowboard jumping skills, and bruised his ribs. They did not do any maths in the last lesson; instead they sang Christmas carols. Ewald played his cello and Jaqueline an alto recorder. Björn sat there the whole time staring at the floor. He spotted the change in him at once. Afterwards he took Björn aside and asked him what Christmas would be like at home. All he said was, "Daniel's back."

He thinks of the couple of years that he taught Björn's brother divinity, of the small, hard fists, of the thin scar on his left upper lip, and of those empty eyes which sparkled only when somebody else in the class was crying. He thinks of the ripped-up books belonging to Daniel's classmates, of the cupboard door that was kicked in, and how relieved his colleagues were when the headmaster managed to persuade the boy's parents to remove him from their school and put him in the less academic Hauptschule. Finally, he thinks of that morning when the twelve-year-old boy came right up to him, looked up into his eyes, and said very softly, "Priests ought to be nailed to a cross – that's what my dad says and I think so too." He has no ideas for the rest of the lesson; he

143

can hear a squeaking in his right ear that gets louder and softer, and the children go haywire.

Loud laughter from outside the classroom. The cleaners. He slides off the desk, takes off his shoes and goes to the door in his socks. He does not open it. He stands flat against the wall right next to the door. He stays like that for some time.

FOURTEEN

Madeleine Peyroux. He had never heard the name before. The cover photo shows a young woman in a baggy dress. She is lounging about and looking defiantly into the camera. An unaffected, somewhat smoky soul voice, reminiscent of Billie Holiday. Track four was his favourite by far: "You're Gonna Make Me Lonesome When You Go". This was the second time he had listened to the C.D.

Irene sometimes claimed that there was a slight echo in the stables, particularly with middle notes. Horn did not notice it at all, but there were lots of things Irene heard that he could not. He sat in the old, wine-coloured velvet armchair, stared at the ceiling, and wondered what sort of people Heidemarie mixed with. He imagined her inviting some fellow students to her small Viennese flat and cooking them pasta, everyone very jolly and having a good old laugh.

The cat came miaowing over to him and rubbed the side of her head against his calf. He patted his thigh to invite her up. She jumped into his lap, made herself comfortable, and began to purr like a small engine. He had never had a pet as a child, and felt his mother was probably to blame for this. She had grown up on a large farm in the Innviertel where everything had revolved around livestock. Roland, his childhood friend, had a dachshund which they used to make sit up and beg and play at hunting rabbits with. Once they had tied the dog's ears together with a string of cooked spaghetti. They were caught by Margit, Roland's big sister, who had belted her brother one without saying anything. Horn escaped with a ferocious stare.

"Just heavenly!" Irene was standing by the door, her arms crossed. Once again he had not heard her coming. "What *is* that music?" she asked.

"Madeleine Peyroux."

"Since when have you liked that sort of stuff?"

He raised his hands to silence her.

"Got it as a present," he said.

"I see. So what's her name?"

"I told you, Madeleine Peyroux."

"No, I mean the woman who gave it to you."

He sat up straight. The cat purred again, very loudly. "Don't be silly," he said. Irene took the case. "*Careless Love*," she read out, "I see . . ."

"A patient!"

"Very nice dress."

"A rather depressive patient."

"Extremely pretty!"

"For God's sake!" He placed the cat on the floor and stood up.

"Poor Mimi," Irene said. He went over and tried to put his arms around her, but she started to back away. "Is that the reason people become psychiatrists?" she asked.

"What reason?"

"So they can accept love tokens from depressive patients."

"Daft cow," he said, grabbing her bum. She laughed and pulled herself away from him.

"Why are you here, anyway?" she said.

"I'd just had enough," he said. "Come on, let's go and cook." She came into the room and picked up the cat.

"We'll take Mimi with us," she said. She never usually did that.

146

They agreed on an omelette. Two days before, Marianne Schwarz had brought round forty fresh eggs, so it was an obvious choice. Irene cleaned some spring onions, Horn cut crosses in the skins of some tomatoes and waited for the water in the pan to come to the boil. He began talking about his morning. It had started with Leithner having a fit, because Melitta Steinböck, the Bürgermeister's wife, had complained about the timing and quality of the evening meal, as well as about how long she had to wait for the computer tomography. It had been one of Leithner's rather unpleasant fits, which were not actually fits but endless, superfluous tirades, delivered in a nerve-shatteringly baleful tone. As expected, Prinz retaliated: they could not stop the world spinning round, not even for the Bürgermeister's wife; in any case the whole team was already attending to her every whim. His protest did not improve the situation. On the contrary, Leithner hit them all with a general ban on leave.

"He always does that," Irene said.

"Yes," Horn said. "He always does that because he doesn't know what else to do; and nobody takes him seriously any more when he talks like this. The fact that he realises it himself doesn't make him any less tense."

Horn dropped the tomatoes into the boiling water, waited twenty seconds, and scooped them out again with a soup spoon.

"Not long enough," Irene said.

"No, it's definitely long enough," he said. It was one of those rituals whose only function was to prove that cooking together was an impossibility. Irene never peeled the tomatoes, so how did she know the amount of time they needed in boiling water? But in these situations she liked to play the pig-headed dilettante. Horn speared the tomatoes onto a skewer and removed the skin with a small, sharp knife. "You see?" he said.

"It's still wrong," she said, chopping up the spring onion stalks. He laughed, and put the peeled tomatoes next to each other on a board.

"Five naked Indians," he said.

Irene had not yet calmed down. "You psychoanalysts with your smug metaphors."

"That's why we do what we do," he said, and began chopping the tomatoes into large chunks. The only positive thing about the morning had been Caroline Weber's condition, he went on. Either the neuroleptic drug had worked, or her paranoia had diminished by itself. In any case, according to the duty sister's report she had held her daughter for a quarter of an hour the evening before, without any negative reaction. Since the last incident they had kept a closer watch on the husband, and they had indeed observed an increased level of nasty, subtle aggression.

"I also think my child's the Devil sometimes, and you're always full of subtle aggression," Irene said. He did not react; he just tilted the pan and watched as the olive oil slowly coated the surface. On the instruction of the voices he had started to hear again, Reisinger, the early retired electrician, had tried to drink a bottle of concentrated cleaner, badly scorching his oesophagus and gullet. Liu Pjong, the Korean partner of Jurowetz the haulier, was writing about twenty daily letters of complaint in her manic state. As these letters were also being posted the situation had got quite unpleasant. The patient support office had been making endless calls to the ward over the past few days. During her four-day stay, moreover, she had managed to turn even the most amicable members of the nursing staff against her. "She goes over to Herbert, pulls up her jumper and says, 'I saw your wife recently in the café, Herbert – pure coincidence – and now I understand why you don't want to fuck her any more. Have me instead.'" Herbert had stood there staring at the first pair of Korean breasts he had seen in his life. There were worse things in life than staring at those breasts, but he was already so paralysed with pent-up aggression that they had to lead him out of the room by his arm.

"Outside he grabbed me and screamed that if I didn't give her an injection right away he would resign and then wring her neck."

"So what did you do?"

Horn took the chopping board from her and pushed the sliced onions into the pan with the back of his knife.

"What would you have done if you were me?" he said.

"I'd have given Herbert an injection," Irene said, closing a half-open drawer with a shove of her hip.

"The female solution."

"And yours? The male one?"

"The pragmatic solution," Horn said, shrugging his shoulders. "What else could I do?"

Breasts plus aggression versus helplessness and responsibility – it's somehow a classic dilemma, Irene said, and now she also understood why he had chosen to go home through the ice and snow. She violently whisked some eggs in a medium-sized plastic bowl. Then she tipped the tomato chunks onto the fried onions which were now translucent, and gave a good stir. Horn sat at the table watching her. He noticed that her movements were more hurried than usual. Of course she was right about the classic dilemma. Sex drive and cultural achievement – the old cliché. A psychiatrist is nothing more than a policeman who pretends that he isn't one, he thought.

"Exactly," Irene said.

"What do you mean 'exactly'?"

"You're a policeman who pretends that he's not one."

Horn felt himself turning red. "Did I say that out loud?"

Irene laughed. "You're always doing it," she said.

Things happen to me that I can't control, he thought, and other people laugh at me.

He looked over towards the window. The snow was falling even more heavily. The day before, Tobias had gone to Obertauern on a school ski course. "Who needs ski courses?" he said when he left, kicking his suitcase into the luggage compartment of the coach. Tobias hated his gym teacher, he hated some of his fellow pupils, and he struggled in deep snow.

Crap self-control, he thought, and he recalled those months of his analysis training when he would regularly get an erection on the couch. He would lie down, then bang, there it was – a stiffy. In the beginning he had almost died of embarrassment, then it made him aggressive, finally he tried to ignore it. His analyst had been pretty relaxed about it. When one day he asked her, "Does it make you happy then?" she said, "Well, what do you think? Of course it makes a woman of my age happy." At the time she was somewhere between seventy and seventy-five, tall, slim and quite frail looking. She always wore her hair pinned up stylishly. He remembered that later he had had all sorts of thoughts about closeness, touching and masturbation, and his automatic erections had disappeared by themselves.

Irene put down her knife and fork and looked at him. "I've been feeling scared recently," she said. Horn dipped a bit of baguette into the fluffy mass of tomato and egg.

"Because of Michael?" he asked, putting it into his mouth and chewing with pleasure. She shook her head.

"Because of Gabriele?"

"No, not worried, I mean scared."

"But you're never scared," Horn said. "You pick up sea urchins with your bare hands. You sit alone on stage and play Bach or Saint-Saëns. You leave Vienna for the provinces. Being scared doesn't suit you. In our relationship I'm the one who's scared." She shook her head again and swallowed. Horn put down the pepper mill he had just reached for. "Are you being serious?"

She nodded. "It's the animal thing," she said.

"What animal thing?"

"The thing that's in the paper."

His instinctive reaction was to turn around. The cat was lying asleep in front of the heater. "It's about Mimi, too, of course," Irene said. "But not just her." Every night she had bad dreams, and the first thing she thought about in the morning were those dead animals: chickens, ducks, hamsters, guinea pigs, cats. She had read in the paper that four cats had now been killed. "Who could do a thing like that?" Horn shrugged. The strange thing was that the deaths of those animals scared her more than the Wilfert case.

"A psychopath could," Horn said finally. "A real psychopath." Irene said that she did not know any psychopaths, but Horn said that he knew plenty.

Horn stood up, fetched a side plate from the cupboard, shovelled on some omelette, and gave it to the cat. She opened one eye and sniffed. Psychopaths are all about terror and destruction, Horn said, about scaring other people, then destroying them. By contrast, most were incapable of feeling fear themselves. "Put a knife to their chests and they'll laugh in your face," he said. "If you take the knife away, they'll kill you." The cat arched its back, took a few exploratory licks at the mass of egg, and started eating. We'll keep her locked in, Horn thought, we won't let her outside any more. The person responsible had not gone into anybody's house. Into open stables and boathouses, yes; into closed buildings, no. He thought of the description of the half-severed and crushed duck heads in the last *Kurier* article, and he thought of somebody he could imagine doing such things, but that person was unlikely to be responsible in this instance as he was sitting in prison.

"Do psychopaths like music?" Irene said.

Horn looked surprised. "What a ridiculous question!" he said.

"It's not a ridiculous question at all."

"Yes it is, it reminds me of those painted wooden signs you could buy when I was a boy: 'Make your home where you hear song . . .'"

"'. . . for bad men never sing along.' Precisely. My aunt had it hanging in her hallway, together with a pair of mice."

"There you go then. How ridiculous is that?"

"It might just be true," she said. Next school year, the psychopathic minister of education of this psychopathic province wanted to cut one third of music lessons for the younger school pupils, which must mean the loss of at least one full-time post at her school; as she was the only one of the three music teachers without a teaching qualification, it was obvious who would get the chop. "You're absolutely right," she said. "First they scare me, then they do away with me." Horn put down his fork and offered her his hand.

"Don't talk nonsense," he said. "You'll take on more private pupils, you'll have more spare time, and I'll do more work." Irene raised an eyebrow and said nothing. She's depressed, he thought, a number of things frighten her and I don't know what to do.

He had wrapped a scarf around his face, pulled the hood of his coat down over his ears, and braced himself against the snow which was drifting horizontally towards him. Irene had asked him again whether he would like a lift into town, but he declined. There was nothing more sublime than a snowstorm, and very few things to which he felt so physically close. Even as a child he had loved bad weather, and even then nobody had understood him. Time after time he would run in the rain until his entire body was drenched, and one winter while he was still at primary school he had gone outside into several snowfalls and played "I'm freezing". He had been able to feel the gradual fading of the warmth from his fingers and toes, and he had always ignored his parents' nagging.

Now he pulled the peak of his hood right down over his forehead. In spite of this, snowflakes hung on his eyelids the moment he lifted his head even slightly. The wind sang as it hit the edge of the transformer station roof, and clouds of new snow sprayed from the young spruces by the roadside. Nothing further in the distance was visible: not the town, not the lake, not even the small pine wood to the south-west of the house.

In the end he had been able to soothe Irene's fears somewhat. They had agreed to wait and see what happened before worrying about her possible redundancy, and they had devised a surveillance and provisioning plan for Mimi which was watertight until Tobias got back. Irene had, of course, refused to accept his argument that it was only pets in the town itself which had been killed up to now. Her geography was not that bad, she said; although the wildlife observation centre was close to the town's outer limits, it was still quite clearly outside the boundary. And when he said that snow and freezing temperatures were bound to prevent cats from going outside, she retaliated with, "You obviously don't know your own pet." But he found himself mentally scanning the building from top to bottom, hunting for holes through which the cat could sneak out. He was relieved when he could not find any.

While he fought his way along the highway he could not help thinking of Daniel Gasselik, in spite of all efforts to the contrary. He remembered his sparing movements, his uncannily stilted speech, and the way in which he used to crack his right middle finger. Horn had come into contact with him twice. The first time was three years before, when the then thirteen-year-old kept on bragging at school that he was going to get the green Grand Cherokee with the chrome bull bars from his father's firm, and mow down the parents and siblings of some of his classmates. The youth welfare service had said that he ought to undergo immediate and intensive psychotherapy, and had issued written instructions to that effect. When the boy appeared before him he told Horn to go fuck a pumpkin – a yellow butternut squash would be best because it was suitable for floppy dicks. He could shove his psychotherapy up his arse, as far as his appendix; he had just learned in biology that the appendix was at the beginning of the colon.

The second encounter had taken place about eight months ago, during criminal proceedings that resulted in Gasselik's going to prison. The youth had driven through town on a Vespa which he had taken from one of the mechanics at his father's firm. Along the lake, then up Fürstenaustraße to the Walzwerk estate. There, he was forced to brake in front of a ten-year-old Turkish boy crossing the road. He came to an abrupt halt, turned off the Vespa, ran over to the boy, and floored him beside a large fountain with a kick to the chest. When the boy grasped the edge of the fountain to pull himself up, Gasselik said that if he did not put his hand back down on the ground as if he were dead, he would break his arm. In tears, the boy ignored the threat and continued trying to stand, so Gasselik leaped on his lower arm with both feet. The boy had let out a scream which witnesses claimed sounded like an Asiatic war cry.

The proceedings had come to a very speedy conclusion. At the trial, Gasselik's father said that he couldn't stand it when a wog got in his way either, while Gasselik himself remained silent for the most part, smirking his way through the trial. It was Gasselik's lawyer who came up with the idea of a neurological examination. He said that they might find a fault in the workings of his client's brain, or a minor trauma, and this might provide some mitigating circumstances. It was no surprise that Horn had landed the job. Apart from the fact that he already knew of Gasselik, he was the only trained child psychiatrist in the surrounding area, giving him no chance to duck out of it. In the end he had written a pointedly neutral report: although it underlined the complete lack of any emotional attachment to his parents as a fundamental psychodynamic element of Daniel Gasselik's personality disorder, it emphasised that this could not be equated with a reduced capacity for reasoning and judgement. Not least because he had two previous convictions for theft and attempted robbery, Gasselik was sentenced to three years' imprisonment – nine months of which was suspended – for grievous bodily harm with intent, as it was called. Everybody considered that a fair outcome. Even Seihs, the secretary of the Business Party, had said in a newspaper interview, "Nobody breaks people's arms in our town, not even Turkish people's arms."

Right next to the signpost pointing to the hospital, a grey estate car which must have taken the bend too quickly was stuck in snow. To the eye the car seemed to blend in perfectly with its surroundings and, as the wind kept on blowing over the warning triangle, the driver stood there alerting other cars to the hazard by waving. Horn passed by without asking whether he could be of assistance. The man would have contacted the breakdown service long ago, and the only thing which interested Horn was whether or not the car was on summer tyres. I'm just as much of a psychopath as all the rest, he thought.

At the entrance to the children's ward, Magdalena, the red-haired sister with the pierced upper lip, was trying to explain to a girl, perhaps six years of age and bawling her eyes out, that visiting time had not yet begun and that her parents would come soon.

The little girl did not appear to believe her, and she was not placated when Horn bent down as he passed and said, "My cat sends its love." Magdalena shrugged, gave a somewhat resigned smile, and pointed to the other end of the ward.

"Both your ladies are here already," she said.

Luise Maywald had called the previous day and requested an extra session for Katharina. Unlike the other occasions, she had sounded rather confused and hysterical, and it had taken Horn some time to grasp that that the reason for this was her father's impending funeral. It would be fine with the two older children, she had said, they understood what had happened. They had been told that it was an evil person; there were such people around who could just appear from somewhere and kill somebody. And she had explained in great detail about the brass band and the coffin being lowered into the ground and flowers being thrown on top. But she was very unsure about Katharina, as the child was still saying nothing at all. She might start howling at the graveside, behave in a peculiar fashion, or even run away. She was afraid of all these things, because after all it was her father, and even though she had already said goodbye to him inside and was ready for the moment the gravedigger started turning the crank handle, she knew she would be deeply affected by the occasion and would not have the nerves to cope with a daughter going crackers. "Teach her," she had said again and again. "Please, teach her!" and he had asked himself: what?

For the first time since he had met her the woman was wearing black – a long woollen skirt and a very loosely knitted roll-neck jumper. The day before the funeral, he thought, getting in the mood. Then he thought of *Careless Love* and track four, and how Heidemarie was depressed because of unconscious death wishes directed towards her parents, and that there was nobody who was even dreaming of slitting *her* father's throat. There was no justice in the world, particularly in who got killed and who did not, but doctors should not think like that.

Katharina had put the yellow toy box beside her. Its contents were supposed to make the wait more bearable for children. On the small, low table in front of her a princess doll in a pink tulle dress lay on its back. Using everything that was to hand – toy bricks, Playmobil trees, dolls' crockery – she had started to build an arch-shaped construction by the doll's head. It's still about heads, Horn thought. At the same time something flashed through his mind, at the very edge of his consciousness. Then it disappeared again. He could not work out what it was; that annoyed him.

"Thank you for taking the time," Luise Maywald said.

"It sounded like it was urgent," said Horn. He was pleased that she was no longer asking him to teach the girl something.

She nodded. "It's all a bit too much for us."

Maybe that's part of it, too, he thought: she's no less inhibited than her daughter. Her father is the victim of a grisly murder, and she says, "It's all a bit too much for us." She looks like a strong woman, but in fact she's just got a tough protective exterior.

Katharina grabbed the princess doll by the legs and took it into Horn's room. As soon as she got through the door she took her boots off. Things are changing, Horn noted with satisfaction. She's taking off her boots and leaving the green squirrel jacket with her mum. She kneeled by the bookshelves, at the spot where she had spent most of the previous therapy sessions, crouched on her heels, and put the doll on the ground in front of her. She looked at it, and slowly turned its body around, carefully feeling the tiara and tulle dress. It was then that Horn realised what had escaped his mind before: the girl was no longer clenching her fist. She was using both hands. She had put the two pieces down somewhere. It's not going to be long now before she starts talking, he thought. Perhaps it had something to do with the funeral.

Horn fetched two boxes of Lego from the cupboard, and also a large Lego base which had a pond, a river and a street printed on it. "Out there you started building something around the puppet. I thought you might want to continue with these," he said. She bent the puppet at the waist, put it on the shelf, and rearranged the skirt. He recalled that there were children – in such a bad state that they could not even play any more – who would at some point in their therapy start to play "playing".

"Would you like a comb for your doll?" he said. She ignored him.

When he was a child, there had only been the normal Lego bricks in the usual sizes, as well as windows, doors, roofs, wheels and fences. The bases were only small, thirty by thirty centimetres at most. This meant you built houses or cars, maybe trains if you had a lot of wheel bits, but definitely no spaceships, submarines or complete football stadiums, as was now possible. "I played with Lego when I was a child, too," he said. She looked at him. "Shall we play?" he asked. She shook her head.

It's for these sorts of moments that you practise psychotherapy, he thought – there's a little girl not saying a single word, spending the whole day as if under a bell jar, and at some point you ask her, "Shall we play?" and just like that she shakes her head. He sat down on the ground facing Katharina, picked up one of the two Lego boxes, and emptied it. "Shall we make something?" he said. She pulled her legs up to her chest. "I'll make something," he said. Take the inhibition into yourself, he thought. Do what the girl can't do yet.

Michael had hated Lego from day one. It had taken some time before Horn had grasped this, and for somebody who had always loved Lego such antipathy was incomprehensible. He had connected it to Michael's dyslexia, thinking that he did not understand the instructions, or that he had poor spatial awareness. Both of these turned out to be untrue. The simple fact of the matter was that Michael loathed Lego; it seemed as if he would not dream of liking the same things as his father.

Horn began building a wall, straight up without any fancy bits. He only used the yellow and green bricks, alternately – one yellow one, one green one. He also started talking about funerals. He told her about cremations and burials. Around here, he said, people preferred burials, because it seemed they were alarmed by the idea of their body being burnt, whereas lying in a grave must be like lying in bed. This was also why you had to be silent in graveyards. Of course people knew that the bodies in the graves were dead, but everybody appeared to want to keep up the idea of the big sleep. "The gravedigger digs the hole with a small excavator," he said. Katharina was looking straight past him. The princess doll was lying to her right. She had closed her hand around its body. Is she listening to me, he wondered? He imagined her looking at her grandfather's shattered face, and then standing beside the grave, her doll in her hand, and being afraid that she might fall in. He added the last bricks; there were only green ones left at the end. The wall was seven rows high. He had only managed to start the eighth one. "Finished," he said, then asked, without expecting any reaction, "Where did you leave your two Ludo pieces?"

Katharina looked around for a while, as if the pieces were hidden somewhere in the room, then she shuffled over to the bookshelf and took out the volume of heroic tales. Not again! he thought. He knew what would follow: endless leafing through the pages from one picture to the other, and whenever she came across a knight with an open visor she would place her finger on his head for thirty seconds or so. I've lost her, he thought. For a split second she was connected, and now she's gone away again. He explained that everybody would be sad at the funeral, and some people would cry – her mum, her dad, sister and brother. The coffin would look pretty large, almost like a house, with a wreath of flowers on the top, and there would be many other wreaths lying around. People would give speeches, they would sing songs, and then somebody would give the sign, and somebody else would go to the crank and start turning the handle, and the coffin would slowly be lowered into the hole that the small excavator had dug.

While Horn spoke, Katharina got about as far as the twentieth illustration. Contrary to his expectations, she had sped up as she leafed through the book. She turned to the pages with the pictures, tapped on the knights' heads, each time casting a brief glance at the doll as if she wanted to make sure of something, and then kept on turning the pages. At the end, Horn said, everybody would drop a flower into the grave, right on to the coffin lid, like a final farewell. And then they all go to the pub, Horn thought, wondering after whether he had said this out loud. But there was no reaction from Katharina. She had rushed through the last few pages and she shut the book with a loud crack. Then she put the doll on the cover and gazed at it for a while. Horn said that graveyards were particularly cold in winter; an icy wind would whistle between the tombstones, so she should not forget her scarf, hat and muffler. And then the gravedigger will be standing there, he thought, and he'll be offering out his cap, and people will scrabble around inside their purses, and half of them won't have the right coin.

Suddenly, Katharina looked at him. For a second he thought: this is it, now. Now she's going to speak. But she grabbed the doll, put both arms down to the side of the body, and pulled up the outer of the two layers of the tulle dress so that it covered the arms, torso and also the princess's head. Of course it's still all about heads, Horn thought. Heads must be covered, the memory of the crushed head has to disappear. Katharina put the covered doll back onto the book which she then lifted up with both hands, and carefully pushed into a gap on the bookshelf. While doing this she gave a contented smile. A sort of funeral, Horn thought. She's laying out the doll and putting it into a slot.

"It'll be alright," Horn said outside to Katharina's mother. "You've no need to worry." Luise Maywald thanked him.

"Do you know what I'm pleased about?" she said as they were leaving. "I'm pleased that we don't have to see him again." Horn nodded, but said nothing. He had just noticed Katharina opening the zip of her right jacket pocket, putting in her hand, and pulling out a clenched fist. The pieces, he thought. Everything's alright.

Horn stood by the window. It was still snowing. It seemed to be settling even on the dried-out reeds around the river outlet. He could not make out the rock falls on the south side of the lake. He thought of Irene and Tobias. He reckoned she would be sitting in the stables, practising Tchaikovsky's Rococo Variations, which she was due to perform at the Furth Symphony Orchestra's Carnival concert; and maybe Tobias was falling in love. He remembered that falling in love was what you did on ski courses. During the day you larked around in the snow, and in the evenings you noticed that the girls came to dinner with freshly washed hair. Irene hated Tchaikovsky, but Rauter, the musical leader of the orchestra, insisted that it got bums on seats, and she could not refuse. Horn knew she would turn out a brilliant performance, playing the piece with an aggressive passion. She sits down, plays, and in between she's afraid, he thought. He thought of Gasselik, whom he could well imagine slitting the throats of animals and then crushing their skulls. The Wilfert thing is a bit out of his league, he thought afterwards. He's too young for it. He gave a cursory glance around the room and was happy that nobody else was there. I bet I've been thinking aloud again the whole time, he thought.

The couple that came for family therapy shortly afterwards bored him senseless. They had done from the very start. The husband was a biochemist at Veropharm, a pharmaceutical company based in the town. His main job was the production of phytotherapeutic medicines. His wife was the manager of a small business which manufactured orthopaedic aids. The couple had two children: a fourteen-year-old daughter and an eleven-year-old son, both of whom had made unsuccessful attempts over the years to combat their parents' obsessive behaviour and academic ambitions by developing a range of different symptoms. At present the boy was suffering from a nervous cough, while the girl was attending school every other day at most. These people are so painfully conventional, Horn thought. When he asked them what strategies they used for their children, the wife said they had advised their son to suppress his cough whenever he felt it coming. They were clueless vis-à-vis their daughter; they had no ideas at all. She did what she wanted anyway – punk hairstyle, piercings, pentagram pendants and all that sort of stuff. I hope she does what she wants, thought Horn, and then he imagined this boy lying in his bed at night, confronted by the fantasy of his naked sister, trying as hard as he could to cough away the impulse to masturbate. If he gave in to his urge, he would be forced to do one hundred squats, or say seven prayers seven times. He would end up as obsessive as his father.

"Did you masturbate when you were a boy?" Horn asked. The woman's face turned ashen, and she looked as if she wanted to ground to swallow her up. The man went beetroot colour and cleared his throat several times. It's all so obvious, Horn thought, and it's all so damn conventional that I'd welcome a migraine attack on the spot.

"What do you mean?" the man said.

"Masturbation, wanking, self-gratification," he said. The two of them sat there in silence, both in a state of excruciating embarrassment. I'm an arsehole and I enjoy it, Horn thought. Finally, the woman lifted her head.

"I don't think we're at that stage yet," she said. She would not look at her husband.

"What do you talk about at home?" Horn said.

"Work, the children, what's in the newspaper."

What's in the newspaper, Horn repeated to himself. The man's tie was greyish-brown with pink diagonal stripes. He had not seen anything that ugly for a long time.

"Do you have any pets?" Horn wanted to know at the end. Yes, a pair of budgies, the two of them answered; the male one is blue, the female one yellow, and both birds are fine. A yellow budgie and a blue budgie, he thought. A yellow Ludo piece and a blue Ludo piece. These things are unconnected. Coincidence creates meaning.

Afterwards he opened the window. He leaned out into the snowfall, stuck out his tongue and was pleased when the first flakes settled on it. If someone sees me they'll think I'm mad, he thought.

FIFTEEN

He had woken with Marlene in his arms, a strand of her hair between his lips and her thumbs in his navel. He had lain there quite still, feeling the cool air in the room. For a minute he was almost happy. They ate boiled eggs and grilled bacon for breakfast, and wasted no more time discussing the subject of New Year's Eve. Afterwards they went up on to the roof and slowly spun around, arm in arm. It had stopped snowing overnight, and the town and lake were lit up by the rays of the morning sun, like a view straight from a postcard. I'm in a good mood, he thought, that's incredible.

Most of all it was the prospect of having to go to the office a few hours later that made Kovacs decide to see to the matter himself. What is more, he loved driving the Puch G., this powerful vehicle with its rough charm. Third, Demski had been back from holiday for two days, and anything which might come in would be in safe hands.

They drove south down Grazer Straße, out of town, and turned west after about four kilometres, just past the old customs house. The road had been well cleared, so there was no scope for four-wheel one-upmanship on the ascent to the Kammwand tunnel, as Kovacs had secretly hoped. The only things he overtook were a milk tanker and a B.M.W. seven series which crept up very tentatively.

The old man in the passenger seat had a sallow complexion and seemed to sink further into his grey coat with every bend.

"Why didn't you ring yesterday?" Wieck asked from the back. The man lifted his head slowly. "It was dark," he said after some time. "It would have been impossible to see anything." Outside, the yellow beams of the tunnel lighting rushed past. Every few hundred metres a huge ventilator spun on the ceiling. "Anyway, you can't be prepared for something like that," the man said. "You don't know what to do." It was his wife who had said that anybody who could demolish the heads of large animals was also capable of doing something like that; she insisted he notify the police.

"Was your wife there when you discovered it?" Wieck asked.

The man shook his head. "No. I usually go out driving on my own. Anyway, somebody else found it."

Kovacs looked sideways at the man. He's sinking, he thought. It's just like it was before. He asked him how he had coped during the night, and the man said it had been alright; his wife had been a great support, and he had an array of sedatives in the medicine cabinet for an emergency.

After the 2.6 kilometre mark in the tunnel, the road began to descend, and shortly afterwards they saw a white dot which was the exit. "Sometimes in life there are things that just happen to you and you're not prepared for them," the man said. And sometimes in life, Kovacs thought, nothing happens to you at all and you're not prepared for that either. He sped around the hairpin bends on the way down to Sankt Christoph, and enjoyed the sensation at the very edges of the curves that he was on the brink of flying out over the roofs of the restaurants and hotels. When they were at the bottom he muttered an apology but neither of the other two said anything.

They took a shortcut to the south around the centre of Sankt Christoph, thus avoiding the commuter traffic which usually clogged up the narrow streets at this time of day. They were nevertheless held up by a carriage of tourists wrapped up tight in thick clothes. Kovacs let out a quiet curse. After he had over-taken, Kovacs turned round. "Horses?" he asked. Wieck thought for a while. "No, not horses," she said. She's not 100 per cent sure, he thought.

They followed the lakeside road towards Mooshaim until they came to a shallow ravine which sloped down from the left. At the "Holiday Apartments" sign they turned into a road which went through the woods. In a long, rising loop, it led back to a hill directly above Sankt Christoph. About five hundred metres before a farmhouse, Fux instructed him to park the car next to a rectangular pile of beech logs.

"This is where the path begins," he said.

When they got out of the car, Kovacs could see the man trembling. "Are you sure you'll manage this?" he asked. Fux nodded.

Wieck walked up to him from behind and took his arm. She smiled. "I'll catch you if you faint," she said.

It was freezing. Kovacs put on his gloves and pulled up the quilted collar of his coat. Wieck stuffed her corduroy trousers into her boots. Fux was wearing a new black woolly hat with ear flaps. His overcoat, on the other hand, looked old – the buttons were worn and there was a rip in the left sleeve. Kovacs noted this after he had fetched the shoulder bag with camera, tape and Dictaphone from the car. Stakes, he thought. We haven't got any stakes or a tool to drive them in. It's always the same. He said nothing.

On the stretch where the path ran along open fields there were fierce gusts of wind. Fux said he always walked this bit; he did not dare drive his Astra further than the woodpile, not even with chains on, and he would never be able to afford a four-wheel drive. They walked in line, Fux at the front, until they came to a dense hedge of blackthorn and hazelnut at the edge of the forest. They stopped under cover of the hedge. Christoph Moser, who owned the woods all around, had discovered what had happened while taking away some larch logs and notified him. "He was in his large S.A.M.E. tractor and four-wheel trailer," Fux said, pointing to the deep tyre tracks by his feet. They cut wood in winter, Kovacs thought; people still stick to the old customs.

"When did Moser ring?" Wieck asked.

"At ten past two," Fux said. "From his tractor cabin. He always takes a mobile phone when he goes into the woods."

"And when did you get there?"

"Half-past three." Fux stood still for a second and raised his shoulders. "At first I really didn't want to go."

They walked the gentle incline up through the open larch woods, crossed a rocky ditch, and turned east after a spot where animals came to feed. When they stepped into the clearing the morning sun rather dazzled them. Fux stopped and stroked his cheeks with both hands.

"Is it over there?" Sabine Wieck asked. Fux nodded. "Will you be O.K.?" He stared silently at the snow. In the end, Kovacs pushed past him. "I'll take a look."

Fux grabbed him by the arm and shook his head.

"It'll be alright," he said.

The door to the shed was off its hinges, and the small, square window had been smashed in. On one of the side walls, all the wooden planks save for two small boards had been torn away. Fux pointed to the back of the shed. "It's behind there," he said.

The moment they turned the corner Kovacs looked over at Wieck. Sometimes people behave as if they're in a film, he thought. She stood there, her eyes like saucers, a hand slapped in front of her mouth. The snow in front of them was black from dead bees. In the middle was about a metre's length of splintered wood; bits of its bright paintwork could still be made out here and there. "They freeze to death instantly in these temperatures,"

Fux said. Kovacs took off his gloves, bent over, picked up one of the bees and put it in the palm of his hand. He held it in front of his face – it came into focus a good half metre away – and he examined the compound eyes, the sting and the fine veining of the wings. "How many of them were there?" he asked.

Fux stared at him. "Hundreds of thousands," he said.

Kovacs put the bee back in the snow, carefully, as if it were still alive. Sabine Wieck bent over to him.

"Sixteen," she whispered. "Sixteen hives, if I counted correctly."

Whoever did it must have gone about the job with incredible thoroughness. The beehives had been lined up in a row, and then demolished, one after the other. Levelled to the ground, Kovacs thought, that's what they say, and he thought of a huge sledge-hammer crashing down onto the wooden cubes.

"Who could do a thing like that?" Wieck said. "Who kills bees?" I don't imagine anyone who slits the throats of cats and mallards would have a problem doing it, Kovacs thought. He had no idea why she always asked, "Who could do a thing like that?" and why it sounded so jolly when she said it.

"Someone who has a problem with the sweetness of life," he said, astonishing himself with his own words, because it was unlike him to tolerate such fanciful turns of phrase. Fux cast a glance at him, and he looked as if he had tears in his eyes, but perhaps it was just the cold.

Kovacs took the camera out of his shoulder bag and started taking photographs: the smashed-up hives, the shed, the surroundings. When he aimed the lens at the ground, Fux said, "He must have come with a tractor or a lorry." Kovacs put the camera back. "Why?" he asked. A second later he knew; he saw the ramp up to the barn with the old man whose neck was right on the cusp, and Lipp saying, "Like he's been crucified." Wieck got down on one knee and, with great care, fingered the large tyre prints before her in the snow. "We've got to get Mauritz," she said. Fux said, "These tracks are nothing to do with Moser's tractor," and Kovacs felt as if the ground were crumbling under his feet. The phrase "people and animals" came to mind, a phrase that people use without thinking. Another thought he had at that moment was that it was impossible to crush the heads of millions of bees.

Wieck called Mauritz. She explained the situation to him, described how to get there, and at Kovacs' bidding requested him to bring stakes and a tool to bash them in. At the end of the call she lifted her head to check and said, "Yes, it's very cold."

"Is he doing some prophylactic freezing again?" Kovacs asked. She laughed.

In places, the tyre tracks were covered all over with bees. Where they were exposed, the edges looked broken and the surface a little roughened. It was no longer possible to ascertain whether there had been a dusting of snow overnight or if the changes had occurred as a result of frost. The main thing was that they would be able to make a perfect copy of the tread. "It's the same," Kovacs said in a quiet voice so the others could not hear him.

They walked around the perimeter, to avoid stepping on the main area of devastation. Wieck kept on blowing into her gloves, and did kneebends to keep herself warm. She chatted to Fux about beekeeping, different types of honey, and the boom in royal jelly. She listened as he explained about swarming, how nervous the bees were beforehand, the division of the colony, and the fact that it was the old queens who defected, not the young ones. "So how do you get the swarm down from the branches?" she asked, and Fux said, "With a water sprinkler and a goose feather. You carefully wet the cluster of bees and then brush them off with the feather, into a bin or straight into the hives." She's talking as if she's going to take up beekeeping tomorrow, Kovacs thought. But in fact she's talking to him like that because she's afraid he might faint. Again he saw the old man with his arms stretched out on his back in the snow, a single eyeball staring at him from the amorphous surface of his face. Madeye, he thought, but could not fathom where this name came from.

"Did Sebastian Wilfert have anything at all to do with bees?" he asked.

Fux looked at him with wide eyes and then shook his head. "With bees?" he said. "No way. Not at all."

Mauritz was puffing huge white clouds when he got to them. A hefty man in a hefty quilted jacket on a bright winter's day, Kovacs thought, what an uplifting vision, but he hasn't got the stakes.

"Where are the stakes?" he said.

"There weren't any left in the depot," Mauritz replied. "I'd have had to rip out, separate and sharpen the snow poles by the side of the road. Number one, that's illegal; and number two, it would've meant that you lot would've had to wait an hour longer. What's more, the thing seems to be pretty clear anyway." He pointed to the tyre tracks.

"What do you mean, 'pretty clear anyway'?" Kovacs asked.

"An ancient Vredestein tyre, production ceased thirty-five years ago. Used to be fitted on to small military troop transporters, Bedford breakdown trucks, vehicles like that."

"How do you know all that?"

"From my contacts in the Danish Kriminalpolizei," Mauritz said. "Funnily enough, they're the experts in anything to do with tyres." Maybe there's a tyre specialist in Copenhagen or Växjö with blonde plaits and big hips, Kovacs thought, who's got something to offer her Austrian colleague Mauritz. He meets her once a year at an international forensics conference, and afterwards they discuss rubber compounds and the minutiae of tyre wear on whispering asphalt. He thought about Marlene's hips, which were also fairly broad, and about the slender figure of Elisabeth,

Mauritz's wife. "He treats her as if she's got brittle-bone disease," Frau Strobl, the secretary, had once whispered to him – a keen observation.

Mauritz dismissed Kovacs' suggestion that he should ask for Lipp if he needed help – he'd be fine on his own. Demski had already collared Lipp in any case, and it would be inadvisable to try competing with him.

On the walk back, Wieck and Fux discussed desensitisation to bee venom, which happened to some beekeepers and not to others. They also talked about the versatility of honey, and Fux told her about the classes of primary schoolchildren who visited him, the respect that they all had for the bees, and the reverence with which they put on the beekeeping hat. Kovacs walked behind them. They're behaving like they were father and daughter, he thought: a pretty, radiant daughter and a father in a ripped, threadbare coat. For a fraction of a second his eyes focused on a minute detail, and at the same time the recollection of an unresolved question flickered in his mind. The two were connected: a fleeting, shadowy double outline that he could not quite grasp.

When they emerged from the woods, they were blinded by the white expanse in front of them. A magnificent day, he thought. A day for sitting on Lefti's terrace and eating a decent portion of lamb tagine followed by one of Szarah's desserts that cemented your teeth together. Not at all a day for thinking about sending a representative to Wilfert's funeral, about who should deal with the New Year's Eve break-ins, or with a child's broken bones, and about how to bring some sort of order into the chaos of the world.

"It's still there," Kovacs said when the roof of the Puch G. emerged above a hilltop. Wieck gave him a confused look, and he felt that she was very close to asking, "What did you expect?" but had kept quiet given all that had happened. Anybody capable of flattening beehives would presumably not have a problem with stealing a police car. "The woodpile might have collapsed on it, too," Kovacs said, and she laughed. As he opened the passenger door for Fux, he reflected on the official name for the colour of this car: "midnight blue". The middle of the night was never blue; it was always pitch-black. When he looked through his telescope at the most glorious stars, an abyss gaped beyond them: the bottomless pit that knows no colour.

Demski and Bitterle were discussing the story of an Apulian olive farmer who the year before had decapitated his neighbour's sheep and entire family. The man had ended up in a high-security psychiatric institution, diagnosed with "paranoid schizophrenia".

"It wasn't him," Demski said.

"Why not?" asked Kovacs.

"Because an Apulian decapitator wouldn't even go as far as Rome – that's assuming he managed to escape from psychiatric incarceration."

"Do you know that many Apulian decapitators?"

"Do you know a single Apulian who's ever made it this far?"

Kovacs racked his brains. "The house red at Piccola Cucina," he said. Demski removed his black-framed glasses and rubbed his forehead.

Lipp arrived in the meeting room with a tray balancing a teapot and cups. "Where exactly is Apulia, anyway?" he said.

"For God's sake," Demski groaned. Kovacs thought of the young woman in the dark-red jumper with gold stars and her many limoncellos. He wondered how she had spent New Year.

"The stiletto," Bitterle said.

Lipp gave her a stupid look. "The what?"

Bitterle tore a piece of paper from her notebook, sketched a quick outline, and marked one place with a star. "The pencil heel of the Italian peninsula – that's Apulia," she said. Lipp blushed and murmured something about "not really liking it at school."

Kovacs looked at Bitterle. She was wearing a roll-neck jumper and trousers, as she always did at this time of year. Not particularly memorable clothes. Stilettos are just geography to her, he thought, nothing else. "Mrs Brain" would never wear a red jumper with gold stars. I'm not so sure about the limoncello, he thought – she might perhaps drink a limoncello with Demski. He was the one she had been closest to from the beginning, before her husband died. She could even get emotional in Demski's presence, although her conversation always retained an intellectual element. The two of them loved to engage in animated diatribes against the arrogance of certain self-professed authorities in criminal psychology, who gave themselves the pompous label of "profiler", and who wrote books with titles such as *Human Monster* or *What Geoffrey Dahmer Taught Me.* "This garbage is sold to people with repressed aggression and low intelligence quotients," Demski used to say, and Bitterle would nod back with glowing cheeks. He is clever and arrogant, and she is clever and modest, Kovacs thought; the bottom line is that each thinks the other is bright, and that produces an obvious trust.

When anybody asked Demski what he did for a living he usually replied, "student", which was correct in the sense that he had been doing a very irregular correspondence course at a Belgian university for years: sociology, ethnology and group dynamics. Nobody could judge whether he was making any progress. From time to time he talked of essays he had to write; the most recent one a meta-analysis of the literature on job satisfaction amongst female Turkish academics within certain EU countries. That sort of thing sounded plausible, in a way, although none of his colleagues had ever read a single line of his work. There's something dodgy, Kovacs sometimes thought; a sore point, a dark place – something that makes him hide away a part of himself.

Perhaps it was connected with his Christian name, George, which he pronounced with a French accent on account of his mother, who had been born Bequerel in a small hamlet near Grenoble; or perhaps it was just pretension on Demski's part. He lived with Monika Spängler, a very thin physiotherapist, and their six-year-old son in one of the rental flats that the diocese had built in the largest of the abandoned farm buildings. In spite of the staggering annual subscription he was a member of the fly fishing association, owned a dinghy which was moored in the municipal yacht club, and was a regular visitor to the opera or concerts in Vienna. He liked sitting in Café Peinhaupt on the Rathausplatz, where he would drink a coffee or Pernod. In summer he and his family were quite frequently to be found in the public pool by the lake, and every other winter the three of them would take a holiday by some tropical sea. These details were common knowledge, as was the fact that Demski smoked cigarillos, never carried a firearm, and was reliability personified.

"Have you found anything apart from Apulia?" Kovacs asked.

"A perverted Bavarian stable groom – he started by mutilating the genitals of Haflinger mares, and when he got bored of that he got stuck into little girls," Demski said.

"There's no direct connection with heads."

"No, but with animals."

"True. What happened to him?"

"Psychiatric institution, like the Italian."

Overall, Bitterle reported, their research of the accessible international databases confirmed and unfortunately repeated what they knew already from the literature on the subject: individuals who cut off heads and mutilated faces were almost always psychos, predominantly schizophrenics, sometimes people with what was known as "psychotic personality disorders".

"We're talking about those pallid boys who, when they realise that they're never going to get away from their mothers in this life, grab the cleaver or butcher's knife and separate her head from her shoulders."

"Sounds wonderful," said Wieck.

"It's not," Demski said.

"I mean 'separate her head from her shoulders'."

"Just the language, you mean?"

"Exactly, just the language."

I wasn't wrong about her, Kovacs thought. She pays attention to nerve-ridden beekeepers and to the minutiae which nobody else notices. He looked at her in profile. She's got a beautiful nose, he thought, large, the tip turned slightly downwards. She was wearing a wine-coloured fleece coat; the sleeves were ten centimetres too long. For some strange reason, that doesn't bother me, Kovacs thought.

Lipp put a cup in front of each of them and poured out the tea.

"Who's got the most legible writing?" Kovacs asked.

Demski groaned and stood up. "What do I put where?" he asked.

"In 'What have we got?', 'dead bees'; and just underneath it, 'a connection – tyre marks'."

Demski went over to the board, pushed it closer to the table and looked for a marker pen on the shelf below. Kovacs saw that in the meantime all sorts of stuff had been written on the board. In "What do we need?", for example, someone had scribbled "a motive" and "a murderer"; or in "Who's doing what?", "Demski's on holiday." The more people you've got working on a case, he thought, the more childish they become. But he kept quiet.

While he took his first sip of tea, scalding his tongue in the process, he could see that there was something else on the board: a name with a question mark after it – small, purple, written in those precise block letters. He read it and felt a minute triumph welling up inside him. Even Maestro Demski made the odd mistake.

"Daniel Gasselik is in prison," he said, blowing into his cup and eyeing the board above its rim.

Demski shook his head. "He's not."

Kovacs put the cup down. "What do you mean 'He's not'?"

"Our Herr President . . . ," Demski said.

Kovacs closed his eyes. He could see himself leaning there against the back wall of the courtroom, and could hear Nortegg, that powerful white-haired man who was also known to be very youth-friendly, saying without any hint of regret, "In view of the extraordinary brutality of the crime and the lack of remorse shown by the defendant, this court sentences him to nine months' imprisonment. The time spent on remand will be deducted from the overall sentence." He could still sense some of the relief he had felt back then, and he remembered how this feeling of relief had helped him forget the annual Christmas amnesty that was in place. I'm such an idiot! he thought.

"Why didn't anybody tell me?" he bellowed, crashing his fist on the table. The cups jumped and were now sitting in their own individual footbaths. Nobody moved. Kovacs got up, silently, fetched a cloth from the kitchen, and cleared up the mess. This sort of thing happened to him every few years.

"I did tell you." It was Lipp.

Kovacs pulled a doubtful frown. "When?"

"On that ramp up to the barn. I'd photographed everything and you were coming out of the house with the Maywald children and their father. Mauritz was there, too."

Nothing, thought Kovacs. It's all gone as if it's been deleted. And Lipp is still being nice and not telling everyone that I forgot the camera on that occasion. "Well, I must have missed it amidst all the chaos," he said. A whole week, he thought. For a whole week we've neglected to chase up Gasselik, just because I thought he was still in prison. He stared at the board. "Do you think he could have done it?" he asked after a while.

Demski raised his shoulders. "Of course I do," he said. "In theory I think he's capable of doing anything."

"What do you mean 'in theory'?"

"I think he still lacks the resources for a case like the Wilfert one."

"Resources?"

"Muscle power and driving licence, for example."

Kovacs could see a pale Demski following the lanky boy out of the interview room, a scarcely controllable anger in every movement he made. "If it had gone on any longer I'd have slammed my fist into his face," Demski had said, and nobody had doubted him. Gasselik had spent the first hour and a half lying to them, even though there was a mountain of evidence against him, then he did an instant U-turn and explained in a calm manner why he had jumped on the boy's arm: first, because the latter's behaviour had warranted it; and second, because that was the only suitable way of dealing with fucking wogs. The worst thing of all, Demski said, was this continual smirk on his face; Gasselik smirked throughout the interview, closing his eyes from time to time as if in a dream, like some birds do with their third eyelid. "As if in a dream," Demski said – Kovacs remembered the exact words. The atmosphere surrounding that case was also very peculiar. Bitterle had broken off her interview with Gasselik's mother after twenty minutes, saying that she could not deal with such a soulless individual any longer. The woman did not even know whether or not her son had passed his school exams. Of course he got the odd dose of corporal punishment, but for some time now that had been solely her husband's responsibility because he was a good deal stronger than she was. Under questioning, Daniel's father, Konrad Gasselik, told Strack he was quite sure his son was in the right, and that the little Turk had not just got in his way but had also provoked him, as Turks are wont to do. Then Herr Gasselik asked him what car he drove and invited Strack to pop in one afternoon for an extended test drive. He had a first-rate restored E-type Jaguar in the showroom, for example, which was perfect for a gentleman greying at the temples. Strack had responded with a quizzical laugh, and nobody ever found out whether he went to see old Gasselik or not. Anyway, not long afterwards this tin duck appeared on Demski's desk, with half of its right eye missing. Demski said that he wound it up at home sometimes, and then it would shoot through the flat at high speed and with such accuracy that you thought it might take off at any moment and fly away. He usually took it home at weekends, and Kovacs pictured it sitting on his bedside table, keeping watch while Demski slept.

"What do you suggest?" Kovacs said.

Demski thought for a moment and then shook his head. "It wasn't him."

"But he's the son of a car dealer – I bet he can drive."

"He hasn't yet got the right build for the Wilfert case."

Sometimes football players don't have the right build, Kovacs thought, for the national side, perhaps, or the Champions League. "What do you suggest?" he asked again.

"I'll call probation," Demski said.

"Why?"

"He must have been allocated a probation officer. Perhaps he's picked something up."

"Walter Grimm," Bitterle said.

"How do you know?" Kovacs asked.

"Because in our region there are three probation officers for young offenders – Jolanthe Beyer, Irmgard Schneeweiß and Walter Grimm – and there's no way a woman would be chosen to look after a psychopathic bone-crusher."

Kovacs felt a little uneasy. Grimm was a small, stocky man, notorious for never leaving home without an electroshocker weapon. Kovacs imagined him as someone who had been beaten up mercilessly at school, and who later needed three hundred hours of psychotherapy. The last time he had come into contact with Grimm was when one of the latter's clients raided a petrol station and shot the cashier in the upper arm. After the man was imprisoned, Grimm uttered a single sentence: "Never let him out." Kovacs still had the vivid recollection that, at that precise moment, he thought Grimm was finished, stone dead.

"O.K. You call Grimm and see if he knows anything," he said.

Demksi gave a satisfied nod and wrote "contact probation" on the board.

"And what about Gasselik himself?" Lipp said. "We'll leave him alone for the time being," Kovacs said. "He mustn't get nervous."

"It wasn't him," Bitterle said.

"Why not?" Kovacs asked.

"He's only sixteen."

Demski let out a loud laugh. "We've been there before," he said. The truth is, Kovacs thought, nobody can stomach the idea that a sixteen-year-old could slit the throat of an old man and then smash his face up. He could not stomach it either.

There was still a good hour-and-a-half until the funeral started. Kovacs had taken Lipp with him as well as Wieck, and Demski had merely mumbled something about "always doing everything on my own", but did not offer any further protest. The two of them looked surprised when Kovacs headed for the lake, but they said nothing. They went past the district authority headquarters and the finance office and, just before the road sloped down to the leisure centre, they turned into Eschenbachring. As he walked beside her, Kovacs observed Wieck's lissom gait and realised how good he had felt in her presence since the first time he had met her. It's different from being with Patrizia Fleurin, he thought, and completely different from being with Marlene, but it's good. Given her age she could have been his daughter; perhaps that was the thing, perhaps it was also because his own daughter was so different. She would never move with such agility and never come close to being as perceptive of the world around her as Wieck.

"You're not serious," Lipp said when Kovacs made for the 'Tin' terrace.

"I'm always serious about sitting in beer gardens," Kovacs replied. He asked Lipp to clear the snow from one of the tables. Kovacs himself went inside and said hello to Lefti, who was doing a Sudoku puzzle in the lounge. "Don't get up," he said. "I know my way round here." He fetched three stackable chairs with cushioned seats from the storeroom, carried them outside, and positioned them around the table. He sat and gestured to them to join him. "Perfect conditions, make yourselves comfortable." "Minus four degrees," Lipp said, pulling a sour face. Wieck adjusted her coat, pushed her scarf up to her chin, and sat down. Lipp growled.

"The sun's shining," Kovacs said.

They began discussing strategy by running through the people who could be expected to attend the funeral: the five Maywalds; Wilfert's son, who ran a drinks import firm in Munich, his ex-wife and their seventeen-year-old daughter; the two of Wilfert's siblings who were still alive – his sister, who lived with her second husband in Bruck an der Mur, and his brother, who might not come as he was in a wheelchair following a severe stroke which had left the right-hand side of his body paralysed; Wilfert's late wife's three siblings and their families; the neighbours, although the farm's location meant that these consisted of just two families; delegations from the hunting club and O.A.P. association; and perhaps a few close friends. That was it. In her last interview Luise Maywald had said it was a long time since her father had had any really good friends.

"Will the hunters do a rifle salute?" Lipp said.

At that very moment, Lefti opened the door to the terrace. On the table he placed a tray with a large, round clay pot, three light-blue glass bowls and cutlery. "*Bismillah*," he said.

"*Mahlzeit*," said Kovacs.

"What is it?" Lipp asked.

"Root vegetable tagine with couscous," Lefti said.

"No, I mean that '*Bisma*' thing."

"*Bismillah*. In God's name. That's what the host says in Morocco at the beginning of a meal."

Lipp did not reply. Kovacs lifted the lid and sniffed. "Star anise and coriander."

"To put the stomach back in order after the holidays," Lefti said. He's more serious than usual, Kovacs thought. Something's up.

"I don't think hunters let off their rifles at funerals," Kovacs said, and the other two agreed with him. Soldiers perform rifle salutes, maybe the Tyrolean riflemen do as well, but not hunters.

Lipp ate with gusto. Time and again he dipped a large chunk of flatbread into the sauce. He's never eaten anything like this, Kovacs thought. Try as he might he could not remember what Lipp's mother looked like.

They decided that Wieck should keep an eye on Wilfert's family, Lipp on the other funeral-goers, while Kovacs would watch the surrounding area. Lipp would also take pictures, just in case. The murderer who tries to get close to his victim even after the crime might be a cliché, but nobody could say with any certainty what murderers thought of clichés. Kovacs tried to picture the cemetery: the area with the tall, sculpture-laden gravestones just to the right of the entrance, where the town's nobles and some select grandees were buried; the neo-Gothic hall, where bodies lay in state, with its narrow arched windows and the shocking Resurrection fresco; the row of old cypresses inside the north boundary wall. It would be cold, and because of this the funeral-goers would not just protect their necks, but wrap themselves tightly with scarves and hats, which was only right. No clear faces, he thought – how appropriate in this case.

The door to the terrace opened. Lefti was talking to some-body. Kovacs turned around. A foreign-looking man in an orange-coloured winter coat came out. Tall, slim, perhaps thirty years old, no hood, no gloves. He placed two chairs a few metres apart against the sunny wall of the building.

Lefti walked around the table. Using a pair of silver tongs he put pieces of candied ginger into narrow glasses, and poured over peppermint tea. "Ginger warms you up," he said. With a brief sideways glance he added, "That's my cousin." Then he went and sat over with the man.

Step by step they discussed the expected funeral procedure, the ceremony, the location. "What are we expecting in fact?" Lipp said after a while. Kovacs looked at him in surprise.

"Somebody who likes to show himself," he said. All of a sudden he felt uneasy. It was a combination of Lefti's cousin and the fact that Wieck appeared less alert than usual. She kept on peering to the side and fiddling with the arm extensions of her fleece coat. She likes the man, he thought, and I'm jealous. He tried in vain to picture him with a few packs of Semtex attached to his body and an electronic detonator. The man had a conspicuous, rolling laugh and Lefti was almost boisterous in his company; that was odd. Where's Szarah, thought Kovacs, with her prudence and sobriety?

When they got up, the shadow of the Kammwand was projected onto the veil of mist across the lake like a hologram. The deterior-ation in the weather that had been forecast for the coming days was not yet apparent. Kovacs had the taste of parsnips and Hamburg parsley in his mouth. He thought of Marlene, and how he liked it when she cooked; then of Demski, about whom he still knew so little. Finally he thought of sixteen-year-olds who smirk and break other people's arms, and of men who throw children against metal bars.

SIXTEEN

My hand feels weird – like a block of ice on the outside, and inside like a fire which is getting bigger and smaller. I know that if I stand out here in the cold long enough, with just the cloak and my thoughts, everything will become normal again; and when that old man with the slit throat and mashed up head is lying deep in the ground and they fill the hole, it'll all be over. I imagine myself sitting in my starfighter, flying high over the ice planet, Hoth. Far below me a herd of tauntauns are galloping over the endless tundra, maybe fleeing from a wampa, the huge predator, or maybe not. Nothing can happen to me, and it doesn't hurt any more either, because a long time ago I got a mechno-hand like Anakin Skywalker.

It all began when Dad went through the house in the morning – five times, ten times, fifteen times – because he'd forgotten to sort out a few things like the floor sealant in the servicing area or the new garage door. Daniel stood by the microwave and said it wasn't the end of the world; Dad just made a small sign with his hand: to the office.

When Daniel comes back you can't see that much, only that his lower lip has a slight split, and when he walks he twists his body to the right. If he had his hooded jumper on you wouldn't notice anything funny about his face. He takes a sheet from the notepad by the phone, writes something on it, and thrusts it at me: Gerstmann's cat.

He goes out of the room, his body twisted to the right, and doesn't turn round. I realise straight away that it's not going to work. So what if Gerstmann is a stuck-up groundsman, with a stuck-up groundsman's wife and three stuck-up groundsman's children, and that he deserves every bit of it? It doesn't alter the fact that they all live in one of those enclosures in the north of town, on the fifth or sixth floor, with only a balcony – nowhere near any garden. This means that the tortoiseshell angora cat which he always talks about as if it were his fourth child – and which they say is just like you'd imagine Gerstmann's cat to be, i.e. an arrogant, stuck-up groundsman's cat – always stays in the flat, and nobody gets near its neck, let alone with a knife.

When I go into Daniel's room and tell him this he punches me, and then again, which is fair; after all, I did say no, and he's the Emperor now because he's putting the grey hooded jumper over his head. From here his face looks as if he's had a bad allergic reaction, with swollen, bright-red eyes and everything, but in the shadow of the hood it all disappears. He says that it doesn't matter about the cat; the ugly angora animal will come to our street one day, and then Gerstmann will show up with his stupid face. I'm happy about that and say, yes, he will turn up. Then I say – just because this comes into my head – a dog, the next thing I'll get will be a dog. He's satisfied with this and says that as a reward he'll tell me a story from his time inside, or maybe even show me something. Just so long as I've deserved it.

The fridge is empty. At New Year anything left in there is always chucked out. Lore has to do that, otherwise Mum has a fit. I'm just checking to make sure. She could have forgotten something. I throw the black cloak over me, put on the mask, and lie on the bed. I breathe and make the right sound. I am Darth Vader.

There's a Spar on the corner of Ettrichgasse and Linzer Straße. I know the thin lady with the red glasses at the meat counter. I know she's got a daughter who's training to be a hairdresser, and that she drives a dark-grey Citroën. She understands straight away when I ask for a salami with a bell, or star, or Christmas tree. She says that it's already been ten days since Christmas, and that there's normally not a demand for that type of salami at this time. She looks in the refrigerator room all the same, and finds the rest of one with a comet in it. A five-pointed star and curved tail. She asks me how much I need and I say a hundred grams, because everybody asks for a hundred grams when buying salami, and she lets me have it for half price because nobody else wants it.

A short way along Linzer Straße, first right, past a billboard, right again, and then it's the second house. There are several antique figures in the garden – gods, nymphs and that sort of thing – but all made of some nuclear-proof plastic. I go another fifty metres, to where Linzer Straße curves to the left, and straight ahead there's a really small pine wood. You could almost call it a park but it doesn't have any benches. I go into the middle of it, under the trees, so that nobody can see me. I look at my watch and I'm sure: in ten minutes.

The door opens and, although I can't see him, I know that Reithbauer is standing there on the steps in his bus-driver bulkiness and saying to the dog, "Off you go!" And the dog scurries down the steps, jumps up in the air, pushes the handle of the garden gate with its paws, and then it's out.

I keep my eyes on it as it zigzags its way along the road, back and forth, back and forth, from one lamppost to the next. While it does this I take off the rucksack, put the mask on, and take out the packet of Christmas salami. The dog is so fat that with each pace its belly swings a little to the side, to the left, then to the right. The thing's a salami itself, and salamis are there to be sliced. It's the sort of thing Daniel might say – you see, you can justify anything. I put the warhammer in the snow next to the rucksack, and push out the blade of the Stanley knife as far as it will go. A dog with a fat neck needs a long blade. When the dog reaches the edge of the wood, I call softly, "Cora!" The dog stops, pricks up its ears, and then comes over to me, its tail wagging behind. Dogs don't give a toss if you're wearing a Darth Vader mask; they always go by the smell of salami in your hand. "Cora, sit!" I say. The dog obeys, sits down a couple of metres or so away from me, and emits a stupid whimper. I take a double slice of comet salami in my left hand, the Stanley knife tight in my right, and slowly go over to it. I put out my left hand, say, "Good Cora," and at the very moment the dog extends its neck and carefully takes the salami with the tip of its muzzle, I stab it.

You don't think that a knife won't pierce a dog's skin as it does a human's; and you don't think that when the fully extended blade of a Stanley knife tries to pierce a dog's skin with a layer of fur, it will bow like a handsaw getting stuck in a piece of wood. So at the vital moment you hesitate, only for a split second, but that's enough. The dog yanks its head around just as I'm attempting my second thrust, the blade snaps, and when it bites my hand I can see half a slice of Christmas salami hanging from its right lower canine tooth. I hit and kick it until it leaves me alone and runs away howling. I grab my things and run away, too.

When I get to the boathouse of the wildlife observation centre – the place where the lake never freezes – my hand is hurting so much that it's unbearable, and it's still bleeding. The Stanley knife with what remains of the blade is in my left hand, and if any-body saw me they'd probably think I'd just tried to slit my wrists. I kneel down on the jetty, right next to the boathouse door, and when I see that it's too far down to the water I lie on my tummy. The moment I put my hand into the water I stop feeling the cold which is getting to my body through the snow.

I remember thinking what Wawrovsky, our bodywork tinsmith,

once told me: "If you burn your hand, like on the engine mount or exhaust muffler, the most important thing is to plunge it into ice-cold water until you can't feel it any more." Then I thought of skiing with my parents, which was a pretty unpleasant affair, as Dad kept on barking, "Upper body forwards!" or something like that, and if you didn't do it he'd clout you one, right in the middle of the piste. Finally I started thinking of the ice planet Hoth, and how everything's white there, and even Han Solo wears a white padded jacket while riding on a tauntaun through the tundra. I now had no feeling in my hand whatsoever. Just to be on the safe side I left it in for another minute, and when I took it out it was all white, too. No more pain and no more blood, just like Wawrovsky said, even though it wasn't a burn. I stroked my hand with the mitten and threw the Stanley knife into the lake. Nobody's going to find it in there.

Now I'm standing in the cemetery, in a spot where nobody can see me, and my hand's starting to hurt again. I don't think it's because I ought to have left it longer in the lake, but because I didn't carry out the job properly. Daniel will tell me that if such a thing happened inside they'd smash your hand to a pulp. Then he'll keep on pouring alcohol onto the bite until I say that it's really burning.

They'll be here in ten minutes, twenty at most, in a long, black procession. With all the snow the whole thing will look like a scene out of an old film. I can picture an altar server at the front carrying a crucifix on a long pole, and another one swinging a censer. I can also picture the priest making the mistake of asking whether there is anyone present who wants to see the dead man again, and someone actually standing up and saying yes, and someone else opening the coffin lid at the head before the others can shout "Stop!" I think that when they fill the hole with the dead old man, it will all be over and at some point later on I can ask Daniel how he did it.

SEVENTEEN

The aisle stands before him, crystal clear. Like a block of ice into which the cone of light from the rose window pours. The people are down below, scarcely any room to move at all.

Inside he is shuddering. It is cold beneath his breastbone. His breath is freezing inside his body. He can hardly exhale it.

May the Lord be with you.

And with your spirit.

Some people stand. Some kneel. A moment of uncertainty, as always.

May Almighty God bless you. The Father, the Son and the Holy Ghost. Amen.

At the end they sing the "Bless, O Holy Virgin". The tear-jerker. Anybody failing to howl during the third verse cannot have had any real connection with the deceased: *Bless, O Holy Virgin, our final hour here! / Whisper words of comfort, and remain very near. / Come close our eyes with your hand so soft and light. / Bless us both in life and throughout th'eternal night. / Bless us both in life and throughout th'eternal night.*

At the front of the aisle, the light-coloured oak coffin. On top, the wreath made out of fir twigs, holly and box, punctuated by hawthorn berries and a few dark roses. The ribbon is black with a narrow, golden trim. "A last goodbye. Luise, Ernst, Ursula, Georg, Katharina." Frank, the oldest of the altar servers, raises the processional cross. He is wearing woollen gloves with alternate grey and black fingers. The coffin is lifted onto a trolley and wheeled to the door.

He puts his hand inside his tunic, pulls up the zip of his quilted body warmer, and feels in the side pockets. iPod on the right, fingerless gloves on the left. For all eventualities.

The boot of the hearse is already open. The coffin is carried down the steps by the portal and pushed into the car. To the left and right, people standing around looking helpless. He hears the gentle noise of the car engine directly behind him. I'll go quickly. That is one of the few things that he can think with any clarity.

Perhaps they will not come. He will stand on the platform, open out his arms, and nobody will be there. They will be sitting in their small house in the small village by the River Salzach; they will not have come, and he will turn round and put the headphones in his ears.

You try so hard / But you don't understand / Just what you'll say / When you get home.

Through the courtyard at the front, out into the wide main driveway. Opposite the Rathausplatz. A few high piles of old snow under the chestnut trees. Left into Stiftsallee, along the south side of the monastery. For a while the smallest of the bells rings out.

He has Clemens to thank for all of this. An urgently arranged meeting for all the priors and abbots of the diocese, he said. Because of the problems with the new bishop. There was no way he could not go. Robert had commitments in his parish and Jeremiah was recovering from a hip operation. There was no alternative.

The young policeman directing the traffic at the junction with Abt-Karl-Straße salutes as he goes past. He salutes back.

Along Abt-Karl-Straße, into Weyrer Straße, dead straight to the cemetery. The wrought-iron gate is wide open.

One earphone. The left one.

Because something is happening here / But you don't know what it is / Do you, Mister Jones?

All the paths in the cemetery have been cleared to perfection; most have even been gritted. Weinstabel has done the whole thing himself. The gravedigger is standing in front of the tool shed, small and gaunt, in a dark-grey loden coat, fur cap in his hand, his head bowed.

The grave is at the eastern end of the cemetery, in the penultimate row. It is somewhat raised, so you get a good overview. A total of 311 people are inside the cemetery walls, twenty-seven of these at the graveside itself. A bit to the side are the bugle blowers, on the central path the representatives of the public institutions, including Steinböck, the Bürgermeister, and Jelusitz, the Bezirkshauptmann. Behind these, the delegation from the hunting club, and around a black and silver flag a group of ancient men, representatives from the friendship league.

The coffin is placed on the straps of the lowering apparatus. The name of the manufacturer is on the black lacquered frame: Lovrek. Perhaps all the coffin-sinkers in this world are called Lovrek, he thinks, and Herr Lovrek is rolling in it.

He knows that he has to say something but his brain seems to be void of any ideas.

Grace be unto you.

He gives a sign to the four men in the bugle band and they play a chorale. He worries that it is going to disrupt his music as well. He shelters his left ear with his hand.

When someone attacks your imagination.

The people are looking at him in astonishment, but he does not care.

Directly in front of him, the daughter and son-in-law of the deceased with their three children. Close to the mother's side, the younger of the two daughters in a green quilted jacket with a picture of a squirrel. She is the only one of the family without a small bunch of roses.

One of the buglers has a problem with the high notes. Perhaps it is because of the cold. Luise Maywald has tears in her eyes nonetheless. She stares into the distance, past the wall, past the treetops of the lakeside woods, too. Her left cheek has gone a purple colour.

He knows that he has to speak now. He thinks of the Book of Ecclesiastes. He knows it by heart. But still he motions over to one of the altar servers and pretends to read out of the book.

To every thing there is a season, and a time to every purpose under the heaven: a time to plant, and a time to pluck up that which is planted; a time to mourn, and a time to dance; a time to be born, and a time to die. A time for everything.

They all bow their heads. He knows he ought to say something about the life of the deceased, and he knows that he has left his notes in the liturgical book, but at the same time he is breaking up and flying off somewhere in several fragments.

He has counted three people from the police: just to the left of the door, Florian Lipp; by the path that leads to the grave, a young woman with dark-blonde hair and ear muffs, whose name he does not know; and by the eastern boundary wall, directly behind him – and thus out of his line of vision – Ludwig Kovacs. Lipp was one of the pupils in his very first mathematics class, a slim, dark-haired boy, always circumspect, kept his own counsel, no escapades. They say of Kovacs that he loves nothing better than the quickest way to a simple explanation. Once he had been in charge of interviewing all the teachers when it was rumoured that large amounts of cocaine were changing hands in the abbey school. Kovacs' behaviour in the interviews had been neutral and he remained impartial throughout – all in all, he was very proper in his approach.

You put your eyes in your pocket / And your nose on the ground.

A gust of wind sweeps across the cemetery, here and there sucking up the snow like mini tornadoes – a metre high, perhaps one and a half. He puts his arms around his body to prevent the tunic from flapping about.

You should be made / To wear earphones.

The Bürgermeister takes the pause as an invitation, works his way to the graveside, and pulls his notes out of his pocket. He looks around at the crowd, as if at the beginning of an election speech. "Father! Members of the Maywald family! Fellow mourners!" – authority needs official words. You can rely on politicians.

He looks around. If they were here he would have known by now. Sophie would be standing somewhere in the background, restraining the child, as it would not be right to embrace by an open grave.

In the right of his field of vision he notices something familiar. He tries to concentrate.

Something is happening here / But you don't know what it is / Do you, Mister Jones?

Set apart from the crowd, on a slightly wider path, is a woman in a wheelchair, wrapped up snugly in blankets. Franziska Zillinger from the old people's home in Waiern. She appears to be listening to the Bürgermeister's speech, and from time to time she shakes her head. She gives the occasional dreamy smile. A young man in a grey coat leans on the handles, no doubt someone doing community service. He moves from one foot to the other and hunches his shoulders.

The corner with the water fountain. The cypresses. Nineteen of them. Suddenly there is an extra person standing by the second one from the right, as if they had just emerged from the trunk of the tree. So 312 in total. Small, dark coat, blue headband, a rucksack on the ground in front of him. Björn.

He turns round. Kovacs is still in his place. He is leaning against the wall, right next to the grave of Engelbert Stransky, the former organist at the abbey, writing something in his notebook. He cannot say whether Kovacs has noticed everybody who is present.

Of Björn he thinks: a wanderer, who is passing by chance. Or a boy who steps forward in class and writes something on the board, a sentence which stops in the middle. Of Kovacs he thinks: "stately and plump", and he pictures him slowly climbing some stairs, something on his arms that he cannot recognise. A knife, perhaps.

Introibo ad altare Dei.

The Bürgermeister steps back. His whole speech has discussed the life of an unassuming man in the service of the community. Nothing but hot air.

Introibo ad altare Dei.

Ad Deum, qui laetificat iuventutem meam.

He steps over to the grave and begins to turn the crank handle. Lovrek, he reads again. One of the bearers nudges him and whispers something in his ear. He withdraws his hand and allows him to get on with it.

Earth, take that which is yours.

Outside the gate a dog is barking louder and louder.

The coffin is entering the abyss.

The point at which things begin to rhyme.

He pushes in the second earphone.

EIGHTEEN

There were days that began very early. Half asleep, you tried to tell yourself it had nothing to do with you, but that was no help. You looked around and there was nothing to make you happy. Apart from the fact that the cat was still alive.

Irene had not been able to sleep any longer. First she had tossed and turned in bed, then she had sat there, her back braced against the headrest, staring into the darkness. He had woken up and dozed off again, and when he awoke a second time she had gone. He put on a pair of jeans and a jumper, and went looking for her. She was sitting in the stables, in his armchair, listening to the Schumann concerto, the Jacqueline du Pré recording. "Are you sad?" he asked. She did not answer. He fetched her bentwood chair and sat down next to her.

"Is it good to confront yourself with the unattainable, if you're feeling bad anyway?"

She turned her head and threw him a brief glance. "She just plays that so beautifully." After a while he stood up quietly and went into the kitchen. What a psycho-jerk I am, he thought.

He had fed the cat and then started to make breakfast. Orange juice, toast, grilled bacon. She's missing Tobias and she hates Tchaikovsky, he thought. He looked at the clock. The Schumann concerto lasted half an hour. He went over to the stables again and interrupted her at the start of the second movement. "How many times is that now?" he asked. She raised four fingers.

He put his arms around her.

At ten past six, just as he was pouring the second cup of coffee, the telephone had rung. Clemens, the abbot. Bauer was in a weird state; it had been especially awkward at the funeral the day before. The Bürgermeister himself had rung; he was not angry, no, more concerned; after all they knew Bauer. Clemens was surprised as Bauer had given the impression of being quite stable of late. This is why he'd had no qualms about entrusting him with the delicate ceremony. What is more, term had started after the Christmas holidays without any problems, and there had been no complaints from the pupils or staffroom.

He hung up and watched Irene spoon out some pear jelly from the jar. "The hospital?" she asked. He shook his head. "No, Bauer. Clemens is bringing him over right away." A bonkers Benedictine father, he added. He's meant to be burying an old man whose skull has been beaten to a pulp, and yet it turns into something comic. Irene remained silent, and he wondered why it was only when talking to him, the psychiatrist, that the abbot called the friar "Bauer", whereas otherwise he used the title "Father Joseph". Irene continued stroking the cat for a while and then stood up. "Do you need the stables?" she asked. He shook his head. "No, I'll go to the office."

Bauer's movements were perhaps a little more awkward than usual. But apart from this Horn could not detect anything different. In the last week or so Bauer said he had increased the quetiapine dose to 250 milligrams per day, and he was gradually noticing the effect of this. That sensation that his body was full of blastholes was returning, and he felt it was just a matter of time before a huge explosion smashed it to smithereens. Yes, of course he had been running like the wind – day and night – and of course he had been listening to his music.

"Even during the funeral?"

"Yes, even during the funeral."

To be more precise, Bauer said, he had listened to "Ballad of a Thin Man". The reason why he had chosen this track – he assumed his explanation would be of particular interest to a psychiatrist – was that it was a song about out-and-out paranoia and it stopped him feeling so lonely. Just a smattering of residual tension, Horn thought, a slight projective causticity that makes the other responsible for his own misery. Otherwise there was nothing suspicious: no incoherence in his thought, no lapsing, not even the whiff of an associative relaxation, no hearing voices, no experiences of outside influence or external control, no assigning excessive significance to things, no ideas of greatness. If you were unaware just how quickly Bauer could go over the edge and how quickly he could also recover, you would think Clemens' description of the previous day's events pure invention.

Horn held Bauer's wrists and elbows and checked his passive flexion. "Quetiapine doesn't cause parkinsonoid syndrome," Bauer said.

"Can do, sometimes."

Anyway, it was part of the psychiatrist's procedure and was the only opportunity to touch the patient without making him suspicious. Horn kept quiet about this.

"Did you notice anything during the funeral?" he asked.

Bauer thought about it. "Yes," he said. "The company that manufactures the coffin-sinker is called Lovrek. I hadn't seen that before."

The excessively keen reality control of the psychotic patient, Horn thought, while reflecting that psychiatry must have begun with the observation of people in a very peculiar way. He also thought that "coffin-sinker" was a fabulous word.

Bauer spoke about how difficult it was to recall impressions from phases in his life when a prevailing inner certainty had sooner or later crumbled into bits. He also talked about how anxiety arrived in waves, and how fragmentary the process was of perceiving and ordering things. "Buglers," he said. "Four of them. The Bürgermeister, opening and closing his mouth, but none of his words reach your ear. A green jacket with a squirrel on it."

"Excellent," Horn said, and Bauer gave him a puzzled look.

"I mean, that you took so much in."

I'm not telling the truth, Horn thought, but he felt no trace of guilt, because he was just delighted that the little girl had been there and that nothing dreadful had happened. He pictured her standing at the graveside, staring down at her boots, one hand in that of her mother's, the other clenched at the bottom of her jacket pocket, three steps away from a priest who was talking gibberish and who had a white wire hanging down from his left ear. Suddenly he was convinced that she still not yet spoken.

"Are you in a fit state to work?" Horn said. A tiny grin crept over Bauer's face.

"That's Clemens' biggest worry – that people will go to mass and gossip about me afterwards; or that I'll say I'm able to teach and parents will start complaining that in class I've said something like: 'Nothing is certain, not even the commutative law of addition.'"

Nothing is certain, Horn thought, you even get used to that. When they had started hiking together he had not been able to keep up with Bauer's pace. Over time he had understood that a constant questioning of things did not reflect an urge for destruction, but the need to feel coherent in the world and at one with yourself, however fragmented you perceived your personality to be. He remembered the early sessions, Bauer's mistrust, his own efforts to find out what attracted him so much to this man, and Irene's words one evening: "If I were a psychoanalyst I would say it had something to do with homoeroticism – thank God I'm not one!"

"Do you think you're fit to work – yes or no?"

"I've worked before in a quite different state from this."

Horn tried to picture Tobias and his classmates, with Bauer standing at the front explaining the trigonometric function or the intersection of three planes in space, and coming out with the odd thing that was totally unrelated. He wondered whether he also told them about his wife and child, and how much of this they believed. To begin with, Horn had accepted everything that Bauer said: the names, the faces, the house with the garden which unfortunately was a bit shady, the wife's love of Scandinavian literature, the child's predisposition to neurodermitis and his ever more insistent demand for a small white dog. Then, doubts started to surface in Horn's mind. There was not a scrap of evidence of genuine contact between Bauer and these two other people. What is more, all the stories had been nothing but harmonious, even idyllic: no unhappiness, no ambivalence, no conflict. Bauer had just smiled when Horn first shared these observations with him; and even later, when Horn was quite forthright and said he thought the whole thing an elaborate, paranoid construct, Bauer did not contradict him. For the most part, the fantasy had remained resistant to the neuroleptic medication, probably because Bauer was unwilling to let go of it. This was the case with all intricately constructed delusions: people balked at losing them because they provided an immediate psychodynamic benefit.

"Go up to three hundred milligrams," Horn said. "At least for the next two weeks."

Bauer nodded. He does what he likes anyway, Horn thought, and part of him did not have a problem with that. Once, when he was still uncertain as to just how real these two mystery figures were, Horn asked him why he had entered a monastery if his wife and child were so important to him. Bauer answered, "That is for me and my God only. In other words: you don't understand." At the time they were still on relatively formal terms, and Bauer would behave in a self-assured and detached manner which vanished later on.

They sat there in silence for a while, both of them looking out of the window. By the birdhouse a bullfinch was trying to assert himself among a flock of great tits. "There's been the odd hoopoe there in the last few days," Horn said. "You don't get that often." Bauer did not seem to be listening. The cat came and rubbed up against his leg. She wants to go outside, he thought.

Outside in the hall Bauer turned to Horn. "There's something else I noticed," he said. "Franziska Zillinger from the old people's home in Waiern was at Wilfert's funeral, as was the younger Gasselik boy." Horn stopped for a second. Then he said, "I don't know a Franziska Zillinger," and shuddered in the wake of the cold shaft that had just passed through him.

Clemens was not in the kitchen, but with Irene in the stables. The Schumann concerto was playing again. Clemens was sitting on the bentwood chair, leafing through the C.D. booklet. He got up quickly and, for a brief moment, the hang of his habit revealed that he had an erection. Horn could understand. On the back page of the booklet was the pretty, long-haired girl in a sleeveless summer dress, smiling, her eyes closed and the instrument leaning gently against her body. "I was just following the music," the abbot said. "I thought at first it was your wife playing."

"I'm afraid not," Irene said. She stretched and stood up. She had never liked Clemens.

Horn talked about the multiple sclerosis which had ended Jacqueline du Pré's career before her thirtieth birthday, and no doubt created the myth that had sprung up about her person. "Precocious achievement," he said. "Someone who's able to do things at the age of twenty that others can't manage till they're fifty." Irene turned off the music. For a second she stood there quite still, as if she did not trust the silence. The sounds are absorbed by the walls and later they are slowly released to the room, like an acoustic stove. That was one of her favourite ideas. When she spoke about it she shook with excitement.

"Some people have only reached their thirties when they die, and yet they leave behind a work that changes the world," the abbot said.

"Like Schubert." In fact, Irene detested Clemens, especially when he tried discussing religion in the style of a Sunday sermon. Horn perceived him as an awkward and needy individual. Her view was rather different.

"Doesn't anything strike you?" Clemens asked when they were sitting in the car, driving into town. Horn was startled. He had been thinking about precocious achievement, about the phrase, "someone who's able to do things at the age of twenty that others can't manage till they're fifty". Presumably there were some people capable of certain things at the age of sixteen. For a moment he had considered asking Bauer's opinion on the matter, but he left it. Who knew which mental images Bauer's fragile psyche could tolerate and which not? With the palm of his hand Clemens caressed the steering wheel and dashboard. The car was new: a black Passat Variant with four-wheel drive. A gift from Seifert which was far more valuable than what he had given in return, the abbot said. Horn knew that the VW and Audi dealer's children were still too young for the abbey school. It must have been something else. He did not care.

He asked the abbot to let him out after the roundabout. He needed the few hundred metres of exercise and fresh air.

The water level of the river was low. A thin layer of frost covered the gravel banks. On the other side of the river, at the top of the concrete steps leading up to one of the houses in the old town, someone was looking towards the lake. The compact shape stood out clearly against the light-blue sky. He could not tell whether it was a man or woman.

About halfway to the hospital he bumped into Brigitte and Laszlo, who had done the night shift on I23. They looked happy and purposeful, as if they were on their way to have breakfast in one of the lakeside hotels such as the Bauriedl or Fernkorn. Gabriele Zehmann had passed away shortly after midnight, they said; nothing had occurred on the psychiatric side. Brunner had come in specially to administer the opiates herself to Frau Zehmann. The youngest of the three daughters was pretty hysterical – everybody was rather surprised by this, but you never could predict how relatives would react in the end, even after an illness that had dragged on for many years. Gabriele Zehmann had suffered from a rare, autoimmunologically mediated pulmonary fibrosis, and given her general condition an organ transplant was out of the question, even though she was barely sixty years old. She had been far more accepting of it than her family; she said to Horn while they watched television together, "I'm just running out of steam before the others."

Although Brunner was only thirty, he thought, she was somebody you could rely on when it came to death. She had a remarkable gift, so who cared if her assessment of day-to-day life – particularly where men were concerned – was a bit loopy? Perhaps I'll get multiple sclerosis too, he thought, a more accelerated version than Jacqueline du Pré's, and I'll soon need a hospice ward. He made a snowball and threw it at the "No Parking" sign in front of the entrance to the hospital. It hit the edge.

It was breakfast time on K1. Magdalena was standing by the food trolley in the middle of the corridor, spreading jam on bread, mixing muesli, and pouring hot chocolate. The children who were allowed out of bed came over, took what they wanted, and ate at the large table in the day room. All of them were still in their pyjamas, some were running around barefoot. The smaller ones were helped by two trainee nurses, neither of whom looked older than fifteen. Horn felt a momentary need to stand there and watch. It was similar to the desire he would sometimes feel to stop his sons from getting older.

The window in his room was open, and it was bloody cold. Bianca, the cleaning lady, had forgotten all about her work, and was no doubt enjoying a coffee somewhere with her colleagues. If he were to challenge her she would not show the slightest remorse. He turned the heater right up. Limnig, the senior consultant in radiology was said to be having an affair with one of the younger cleaning ladies. Limnig was an unremarkable looking man who, besides the possible uses of spiral C.T.s, liked talking about Anglo-American writers, such as Faulkner, Updike, or Alice Munro. Beatrix Frömmel, the head X-ray assistant, had hated him since the cleaning lady story surfaced; the others in the team could not care less about it. Horn was sure that none of them read Faulkner or Alice Munro. He considered how Irene might react if she found out he were having an affair with a cleaning lady, but a clear answer eluded him.

During the morning meeting there was a long discussion of the euthanasia law which had been passed the day before with the votes of the Business Party and the Nationalists. Brunner was absolutely appalled; she had tears in her eyes and stressed over and over again that she would refuse to become the tool of a commercial-fascistic utilitarian ideology.

"Come on, nothing like that is going to happen here," Leithner said, trying to pacify her.

"People will come to us and demand it," she said.

"So you'll just say, 'I'm sorry, we don't do that here.'"

"They'll say, 'What are you waiting for, come on and put an end to it!'"

"Then those people will have to go somewhere else."

"It all sounds very simple," she said. "But what are we supposed to do? Look after people and then, right at the end, send them off to die somewhere else?"

"Either, or," said Cejpek. It was clear he was getting cheesed off with the discussion.

"What's that supposed to mean?" Brunner said.

"Either we do it ourselves, or people go off to Switzerland, Hungary or the Netherlands."

"People don't go anywhere if you treat them properly."

They discussed the feasibility of a binding ethical code in medicine, relatives' right to object, and that form of assisted dying which was regular practice outside of the law. Horn noticed how little the subject interested him; he found himself thinking, I hope I don't fall asleep, and I hope I don't think aloud. Then his mind wandered.

He thought about his house, the covered terrace which was still not yet paved, his plan to change the heating fuel from oil to woodchips, and Irene's desire to pull down the larger of the two barns and build a pool in the smaller one. He used to tell other people he would never have an old house again; only a romantic and a clueless townie such as he could have allowed himself to end up with this one. Deep down, however, he knew that the strangely angled building suited him down to the ground – all that talk of being a clueless townie was pure affectation. He had been wondering of late which of his sons would end up taking the house over, but before he could come up with the mere hint of an answer he was so badly struck by the idea of being an old man that he was unable to think it through any further.

Brunner nudged him. Leithner was giving a lecture on the previous month's departmental workload, and outlining his serious concerns, especially regarding the psychiatric beds. "Christmas comes every year," Prinz said. Horn was astonished as Prinz never came to his aid. Nobody gets anywhere with cynicism, Leithner said. Prinz thought that was the main point of Christmas: a show of cynicism. Horn had rejoined the meeting. He said that at present he had ten beds occupied; more than 80 per cent capacity and close to the annual average. But Leithner was slow to be assuaged. In the past few weeks he had seen a serious dip – a hole even – and he, after all, was the one who bore the responsibility. Horn sighed. Your classic Austrian consultant, he thought: opportunistic and a coward through and through. Broschek sometimes said that her boss behaved like a true masochist because he revelled in the prospect of impending doom. Then Cejpek would sneer that doomsday must be pretty close, as the pestilence of the psychoanalytical world-view had already infected the departmental secretariat. I know nothing about Inge Broschek, Horn thought, examining the somewhat anorexic-looking, forty-year-old woman sitting next to Leithner with her pen and notepad. He bent over to Brunner.

"Has Inge Broschek got a husband?"

Brunner looked at him dumbfounded. "What do you want from her?" she asked.

He grinned. "Nothing," he said. She did not appear to believe him.

Linda had come back from her holiday and had ten times as many freckles as before. She was now wearing a T-shirt with Campbell's soup tins on it.

"Where's your Christmas jumper?" Horn asked.

"At the cleaner's," she said. "Because of the ketchup that came with the spare ribs."

He felt this sudden worry that the stains might not come out, and then thought this an absurd reaction. He tried to imagine Irene in the soup-tin T-shirt. The picture that came to mind was very nice, even though he knew she was not fan of pop art. The hollows of Linda's collarbones lay appetisingly in the neckline of the T-shirt, her small breasts sat in the two outer soup tins, and the sleeves went right down to knuckles.

"Is anything wrong?" Linda asked.

"Where did you get the T-shirt?"

"In London, in the museum shop, in that old power station."

"When were you in London?"

"Last autumn. For a long weekend."

The casualty sister flies to London for the weekend with her aggression-suppressing forester boyfriend, he thought, and I still haven't seen the new Tate Modern.

"Did you like London?" he asked.

The first thing you noticed, she said, was that everything was enormous and so far away from everything else. Even the distances from one bridge over the Thames to the other were immense, she thought, but her Rheinhard had wanted to take the tube as little as possible, despite the fact that the terrorist attack had been some time back. Another coward, Horn thought as he walked away. He looked back over his shoulder at Linda and wondered what it was she liked about someone who was afraid of everything but trees.

The floral arrangement on the table of the casualty room had completely dried up. He removed the candle and threw the twigs into the rubbish. He remembered how Irene had insisted on climbing up to the dome of St Paul's even though she was pregnant, and how at the top she had been totally out of breath, yet had beamed with delight. They had spoken of the future, about the child, about her chances of being accepted by various orchestras, and about his training as a specialist doctor. There had been no talk back then of Furth. For a moment he wondered what to do with the candle, then he put it in his pocket. Red with golden stars. Irene sometimes said that she had nothing against kitsch in small doses.

Elena Weitbrecht, the supermarket manager with the tics, had an extravagant shake in her right hand. After a short examination Horn was sure she was putting it on. I really don't want to know why she's doing it, he thought. He left her on the same medication, mentioned a period of observation, and instructed her to return in a week. She seemed half satisfied with that. He saw a twelve-year-old boy who had for some months been avoiding school by devising intricate compulsive rituals. He had driven his whole family to despair; Horn referred him for a psychological test. The retired builder with a hypochondriac somatisation disorder was prescribed a daily fluoxetine pill.

Horn still had two files in front of him when Ley made a sudden appearance in the doorway. Horn could see at once that he was seriously ataxic, even at rest. After he asked him to come over to the desk, Ley staggered in a wild zigzag across the room.

"I need to be readmitted, Dottore," he slurred, endeavouring to smile. His eyes were red, with pinpoints for pupils.

"What have you taken?" Horn asked.

"My mum also thinks that I need to be admitted."

Horn felt his anger rising. "Where is your mother?"

Ley pointed to the door.

"Fetch her in."

In vain, Ley tried to pull himself together. Horn waved his hand at the boy and went to the door himself.

The woman was sitting in the farthest corner of the waiting area. This time she was wearing an olive-green tweed suit which was two sizes too small for her. From the second-hand shop, Horn thought.

"What are you doing?" he asked in a loud voice. She looked at him with a worried expression. "What do you mean?"

"Why are you bringing him in?"

"He's been like that since New Year's Eve," she said. Then she fell silent.

Horn took her arm and pulled her into the room. Her son was still grinning. Horn forced her to look at his pupils and gave a short lecture about the effects and side-effects of opiates. "But Dottore, I didn't take any of that opiate shit," Ley protested. Horn tugged up the left sleeve of his sweatshirt. "You're scratching me, Dottore!" Ley tried to pull his arm away from Horn.

"In America I would sue you." The young man could scarcely keep his body movements under control. His mother stood there, ignored the needle pricks, and looked at the floor.

Horn could suddenly feel that he had crawled out of bed shortly after five o'clock, and since then he'd had to deal with the apprehensive greediness of an abbot and a senior consultant, a cleaning lady who did not care if he froze, and a casualty sister who had made him face the fact that for the last twenty years he had not once thought of just jumping on a flight to London. He stood up.

"Get off home, both of you!" he said. The woman lifted her head.

Ley said, "You can't do that."

"What do you mean I can't do that?"

"I need to be admitted to a ward."

"As urgently as you need an appendix operation," Horn said.

Ley shrugged, then opened his eyes wide and clung onto the edge of the desk.

"He's taken everything under the sun; he's in a complete state," the woman said.

"And all of it since he was last discharged?" She nodded. Horn made a gesture of resignation.

Meanwhile, Ley had managed to get up. As he was unable to fix his eyes on Horn, he looked somewhere at random. He began to yell. "You bastard! What do you plan to do with me?"

"I've told you already. I'm sending you home."

"You want to operate on me, you fucking pervert!"

"Nobody wants to operate on you. You're totally paranoid. You're going to go home now, you won't take any drugs for three days, and then you'll come back and see me again."

"Did you hear that? He wants to operate on me," Ley said to his mother. The woman took a small step towards Horn.

"His father will kill him."

"I don't believe you," Horn said. There are spiders, he thought, who inject their saliva into you, then they suck your insides out, and before you can do anything you're a pale, empty shell.

"He'll just beat him and beat him."

"And you?"

"He'll beat me, too."

"I don't believe you."

"I'm not going to let them do it to me!' Ley dragged his mother to the door. He's sucking her insides out and she's doing the same to him, and in truth there's not much left of either of them.

"By the way, where's your nose ring?" Horn called after him. Ley stopped just outside of the room, supported himself on his mother's arm with his left hand, and with the right felt his face to check. He seemed to think about it for a few seconds, then made a dismissive gesture with his hand, and the two of them disappeared.

Linda peeped over the reception counter. "Sorry. They just barged in."

"Don't worry about it," said Horn.

I spoke to him like an adult, he thought. Either I find it really important to keep my distance, or my unconscious is mixing him up with his mother and I'm addressing him like I do her, without thinking about it.

"You're to give your ward a call," Linda said.

I don't like junkies, Horn thought. That's the truth.

Liu Pjong's wailing cascaded down the stairwell as far as the ground floor. Sometimes misery was kind enough to announce itself before you met it face to face. Sebastien Stemm, the surgical head nurse, who bumped into him at the entrance to the operating wing, offered a sympathetic "Have fun." "Thanks," Horn said. Right from the start Stemm had been a great help when dealing with the resentment that existed towards psychiatric patients in the hospital. Some people said that it was because he had a schizophrenic half-brother; others said that was not true at all. Either way, Horn thought that Stemm was a decent human being.

When he opened the door to the ward the first person he saw was Ernst Maywald standing in the middle of the corridor. Next to him was Katharina, and right at the back on the left, Caroline Weber was sitting by the wall, closing her ears to her screaming baby. In the background, Frau Pjong's voice surged rhythmically back and forth. Madness forms clusters, Horn thought. "Please send them all out," he said to Christina, who had just come out of the sisters' room. She nodded and handed him the restraining belts. "Liu is in her room," she said.

Raimund and Hrachovec held Frau Pjong down on her bed. When she saw Horn arrive, her eyes flared and she screamed even louder.

"She wanted to have the baby," Hrachovec said. He was sweating and red in the face.

"Frau Weber didn't want her to," Raimund said. Horn could see a fresh bite mark on his right arm; in one place it was bleeding slightly.

"Have you had a tetanus jab?" Horn asked. Raimund grimaced and nodded.

The moment that the belts were fixed to the bed frame and fastened around Liu Pjong's wrists, she calmed down. Horn decided to put her to sleep anyway, and sent Raimund to prepare a Dormicum infusion. He discussed with Hrachovec what they would do afterwards. They had to notify the patient support service and the court, irrespective of whether a transfer to the clinic would be necessary or not, and they also had to inform Richard Jurowetz, the woman's partner, of what had happened. They agreed that he would find it most difficult of all. "He loves her," Hrachovec said, and for a second it sounded quite funny.

While they were attaching the intravenous tube and setting the flow speed of the infusion, Liu Pjong lay there with her eyes closed, silent. It was only when Horn got up and requested Hrachovec to remain by the bed for a little longer, that she said, "Well, it *is* my child, and she's called Liu like me. Anybody who says anything different is lying!" Hrachovec seemed to want to say something in reply, but Horn put a finger to his lips.

"When she's asleep, take the straps off," he whispered to him as he left the room.

Outside, Caroline Weber's husband had arrived with warm clothes for his wife and daughter, a brand-new baby carrier, and a chocolate cake for the ward team. He said goodbye to them all and thanked them profusely.

"He's scared," Christina said when the three of them had left.

"I'd be scared, too," said Raimund. This thing with Liu Pjong and the Webers and the baby reminded Horn of something, but he could not say what.

He thought of Irene and Michael as he walked out into the stairwell. Perhaps she's also been thinking that our son's a type of devil, he thought, and I've paid too little attention to him. Neither of us have ever asked ourselves what he's afraid of.

"It's not easy for you, either," said Ernst Maywald. Horn shrugged. He could not think of anything suitable to say. Katharina was looking out of the window. The screaming did not seem to have unsettled her much. Horn pictured her standing right by her grandfather's grave, in her coat with the friendly squirrel, a slight hint of defiance in her face, and he imagined her thinking of swords you could defend yourself with, and of helmets with visors which protect your head. He remembered now that Luise Maywald had called him and asked whether he did not have a spare slot any earlier. Unusually, Katharina only had three classes at school that day. Her husband could dash out from work, bring her to the session, and she herself would collect her afterwards. He remembered that he'd said yes almost at once, and he thought he had done that because the woman had got on his nerves. Mothers did that to him sometimes.

They walked through the administrative wing to get to K1. It was the quietest area of the entire hospital. An elderly lady with a patent leather bag was waiting outside the entrance to the accounts office, but otherwise they did not meet anybody. Ernst Maywald kept his gaze fixed straight ahead. Horn noticed that he took giant steps, which meant that Katharina had to walk pretty quickly next to him. When he had asked for Horn they had sent him to I22. The man apologised; he was unaware that psychotherapy took place elsewhere, and his daughter had not been able to tell him the right way. Katharina did not appear to detect any reproach in her father's words. She made her way determinedly to the ward door and only turned round when her father called to her that he was off now and that her mother would come to collect her. When he waved to her she just looked at him in silence.

Katharina came into the room and went straight to the book-shelves. She seemed very happy to find the princess doll exactly how she had left it the last time. She took it off the shelf, together with the book of heroic legends, and put both things on the floor in the middle of the room. Then she took off her boots and coat, circled the room in her tights, and got a medium-sized drawing pad and the tin of oil pastels from the art drawer. She squatted on her heels, took a pastel out of the tin, turned the pad round, and started to draw. Horn leaned back in his desk chair. There was a marked reduction in the girl's tension since their last session. The grandfather was finally in the ground; now she seemed able to calm down. Out of sight, out of mind: for the most part the psyche of a seven-year-old child still worked in concrete fashion – that, at least, one could bank on. It was obvious she had not seen the murderer; as far as she was concerned he did not exist.

The first thing that Katharina drew was a large rectangle a few centimetres in from the edges of the paper. She then drew a second rectangle, another centimetre or so inside the first. A frame that provides stability from the outside, he thought – something we'd all like. He thought of Ley and his mother; and of Bauer, who was forever going on runs around Furth and plugged in his earphones in the cemetery. He also concluded that the continual reworking of psychiatric theories was nothing more than the desperate attempt to construct a more or less sustainable framework around madness.

Beginning at the bottom left-hand corner, Katharina meticu-lously coloured in the space between the two lines. Only in the middle of the lower bar did she leave a space free. She stopped, appeared to think for a while, and then wrote something in the space in block capitals. "What are you writing there?" Horn said. She looked at him and said nothing. When he leaned over to take a look at the word she covered it with her hand and pulled the paper to her chest so that he could only see the reverse side.

After a while she slid away from him, looked around the room, and then pushed the book of legends to a spot on the floor where there was direct sunlight. She put the drawing on top of the book and then the doll inside the frame. A girl lying on her bed, Horn thought, and underneath there's a book with a hundred knights – a strange version of "the Princess and the Pea". "The princess is lying in the sun," he said. Katharina looked at the palm of her right hand and then stood up. She went to the desk, glanced into Horn's eyes, and took the small scissors out of the cylinder-shaped wooden box which contained the pens. She kneeled again, grabbed the doll, and carefully started cutting into the outer layer of the tulle dress from the lower rim. Horn was tempted to intervene, but he held himself back. The beginning of a reaction formation, he thought. The identification with the perceived aggressor. This is how her unconscious attempts to get to grips with fears of being killed.

Katharina cut out a square piece of tulle from the dress and put it on the puppet's face. Horn pictured the knights with their helmets, and Katharina's grandfather who had not had a visor in front of his face. She is the doll, he thought. She's protecting herself in his place, and she's also showing that she can defend herself.

Katharina remained kneeling on the floor and seemed to be thinking. At that moment the phone rang. Horn cursed to himself when he picked up the receiver. Katharina lifted the scissors and, with purposeful snips away from the seam at the waist, began cutting the dress off the princess.

It was Edith, one of the experienced sisters in casualty surgery. "Mike said I should ask you to come. The little Schmidinger girl has been crying and vomiting for an hour."

"Is Mike with her?"

"No, I am."

Katharina wrapped the two strips of tulle that she had cut off around the doll's head several times. Then she put the scissors to one side, sat down, pulled her knees up to her chest, and looked at her work.

"Can you get Mike for me?'

"I'm afraid I can't at the moment."

"Why not?"

"He's got to stay by the ward entrance."

With the tip of her index finger, Katharina stroked the tulle cocoon around the doll's head.

Then she said something, a single word.

Horn jumped. He instinctively reached out into the room with his left arm. Catch the word, he thought. Stop time and catch the word.

"Are you still there?" Edith asked.

Yes, I'm still here, Horn thought. I'm standing here like Moses parting the Red Sea, trying to catch a word.

"Yes, I'm still here," he said. "What's Mike doing at the ward entrance?"

"He's making sure that the father doesn't come back in."

"Which father?"

"Birgit's"

Horn hung up. For a second he felt all light-headed. Stop time, catch the word, put my arm down, he thought, and then: Schmidinger.

He got up carefully, as if he might break something, stepped over to the girl, and kneeled beside her. "I heard what you said just then. I made a note of it, you can be sure of that."

Katharina lifted her finger away from the doll's hood. Now Horn could see what she had written in the empty space in the black frame: LOVREK. It took him a while to grasp it. Bauer, this

215

morning, he thought. Impressions from the funeral, the coffin-sinker. Year one in primary school, he thought, she can write lots of letters already. Sometimes she gets them mixed up.

The phone rang again. As he got to his feet he felt himself getting annoyed. Two words, he thought: one spoken and one written. Two girls – one who needs urgent help and one who is still providing conundrums, plus a psychopath – and the telephone ringing all the time. "I'm coming," he barked into the receiver.

It was not casualty, but Irene. She spoke softly. "Please don't be angry that I'm disturbing you. I just wanted to tell you I've decided not to play the Tchaikovsky."

He suddenly felt helpless and empty, and did not know why. Although the girl was sitting next to him on the floor and could hear everything, he said, "Katharina has just spoken for the first time. She said a very peculiar word. Before that she wrapped some tulle around a doll's head." Irene said nothing. He listened to the silence.

NINETEEN

It was a sort of déjà-vu. Kovacs felt a childish pleasure when he realised it. Demski had rung him at home only once, three years earlier when late one evening he had tripped over the edge of the shower and smashed his face against the fittings. Demski had injured a cheekbone and with the best will in the world it was obvious that he would not be in a fit state to come to work the next day. He had still apologised a thousand times, for his "blunder", as he described it.

Now he was apologising again, and again a thousand times, *and* in the same tone. This time he did not call it a "blunder" but an "error". In fact he said, "It's possible that I've been taken in by an error." Kovacs felt a brief and childish pleasure for a second time, because Demski had never been taken in by an error before.

As agreed, he had called Grimm, the probation officer. Gasselik had indeed been allocated to him. Grimm said that he did not very much like young psychopaths, in part because their prognosis was so poor: all of them sooner or later got a long spell in the clink for serious violent offences. But, oh well, a job was a job. He had visited Gasselik twice in prison at the end of his sentence, to explain the function of probation, but he had hit a wall of utter disinterest. They had not developed anything approaching a relationship so, to be honest, he had not been surprised when the young man had neither turned up at their first scheduled meeting, nor phoned him. Prior to Gasselik's early release Grimm had spoken with two prison officers, to discuss any particular personality traits etc., and both had smiled in a curious way and said, "You'll see, that one's going to turn into something."

Kovacs was attempting to put a sock onto his foot with only his left hand. "Did Grimm undertake anything on his own initiative?"

"What do you mean by 'undertake'?"

"Did he ring him? Did he go and see him?"

"He didn't say anything to that effect."

To be paranoid and bone idle was a very disagreeable combination, Kovacs said. The first thing was that Grimm's electroshocker must be taken away, because he was just using it to defend his own passivity. The sock remained hanging from Kovacs' little toe and he could not shift it any further. Kovacs cursed.

"Anyway, he's not so important now," Demski said.

"Who? My sock?"

"What do you mean your sock?"

"Oh, just forget it! Get into the car and pick me up."

"Why? What's the plan?"

Kovacs tried to toss the sock away, hitting the table leg with his instep. He groaned. Demski was getting suspicious. "If Marlene's with you and you're in the middle of having sex then I could ring back later," he said.

I've just fucked my foot against the table leg, thought Kovacs, that's the sad truth of the matter. "We're going to pay Gasselik a visit," he said, after taking three deep breaths.

"What do you mean, 'we'?" Demski said.

"Us two, you and me."

"I'm not sure that's a good idea."

"Why not?"

"Well, you know he's got some previous experience of me."

"And you of him," Kovacs said. Demski almost belted him one during the interrogation, he thought. He's afraid of him and hates him, that's the point. "He despises you. Perhaps that'll cause him to make a mistake," said Kovacs.

"Why does he despise me?" He could hear that Demski was annoyed.

"He felt your fear. Psychopaths despise people who are afraid, and at the same time they need to feel power over them."

Demski said that he'd had far more pleasant jobs than to be the target of the sick inclinations of a psychopath, but he supposed he'd made his own bed. Made his own bed, taken in by an error: it's all just beating around the bush, Kovacs thought. Just like me he reckons Gasselik could have done it, and like me he's been thinking it from the beginning, so we don't need any of this violation of probation business or Grimm's outbursts.

"When can you get here?" he asked.

"In twenty minutes," Demksi said. Kovacs checked the time. He was satisfied. When they rang at the door the Gasseliks would be having breakfast.

He examined the red stripe across his instep. In reality it was not so bad, yet he felt miserable. Sometimes you just wanted someone who provided a bit of sympathy, it was as simple as that. He had to admit that Yvonne had not been bad at sympathy – You poor thing! Have you hurt yourself? Shall I bring you an ice pack? Do you need a schnapps? etc. Marlene was much more detached in this respect. But perhaps it all had to do with the moon.

Kovacs finished getting dressed. Sex with Marlene had not been that special: quick and incidental. Afterwards she had just shrugged her shoulders, said perhaps it had something to do with the moon and, a few seconds later, had fallen asleep. He slipped out of her flat and drove home. He had no desire to spend hours lying next to her in bed, staring at the ceiling and thinking how unlucky he had been in relationships throughout his life. He had treated himself to a couple of small grappas, climbed up to the roof, and focused the telescope on the Pleiades. While tilting the telescope over the lights of the town he again spotted the defect in the lens when it was very cold. This had been noticeable for about a year – a small, pale-yellow sickle in the upper right section of the lens, which disappeared as soon as the field of vision got darker. The horns of Taurus, the pale spot of the Crab Nebula approaching the zenith of Castor and Pollux. There had been a time when he could tell all these stories by heart, of Perseus and Andromeda, of Auriga with the little goat on his shoulders, or how Hercules strangled the Nemesian lion to death. His brother used to laugh at him for it; his parents had been indifferent.

The loud noise of youths arguing had risen up from the street. He had recognised, amongst others, the voices of "Sheriff" and his twelve-year-old cousin. Then he had decided to go back down to his flat.

"Do you believe in the moon?"

Demski was standing in the door and looking at him as if he were stupid. Of course he didn't believe in all that esoteric lunar nonsense, he said. On the other hand, you couldn't deny the influence of the moon on the tides, and if it was capable of making the sea come in and go out, then there was no reason to think it couldn't do the same with body fluids or the sap in plants. Why was he asking him such a bizarre question?

"I had a relationship problem, and perhaps it was the moon's fault. That's why," Kovacs said.

"So I was right," Demski said, giving him a look of triumph.

"What do you mean?"

"I was right about Marlene. And sex. Earlier, when you were waffling on about socks."

"O.K. You were right," Kovacs lied. He fetched an aluminium pot with fresh espresso from the stove. Demski accepted. He had never done that before.

On the drive to the town centre from the Walzwerk estate they were silent for a while. Then Demski said, "What have we actually got so far?"

"Nothing," Kovacs said. "Strictly speaking we've got nothing at all."

A group of schoolchildren was crossing from the Rathausplatz towards the abbey, so they stopped. "You're being too pessimistic," Demski said. "We've got a few things."

"And what are those, if you please?"

"A right-handed murderer, who acts rationally but is also full of anger. A place where the body was found which is certainly the crime scene as well. A definite tyre track."

"A green Lego brick. A few nails. A button. No fingerprints. No sign of any resistance. A face which, according the pattern of blood spatters, is most likely to have been smashed by a meteorite."

Demski cleared his throat. He's trying to cover up a stupid comment about meteorites with a cough, Kovacs thought. When Fleurin had shown him Wilfert's face, he had noticed how she beamed like a botanist announcing a new species of orchid. I know nothing about her, he thought. I don't know if she's got a husband at home, or an aquarium, or whether she presses flowers in heavy books.

"And what do you think about the stuff with the animals?" Demski said.

"Same as you," Kovacs said. "Young psychopaths start fires, piss their beds at night, and torture animals. That's what the textbook says."

"And if an old man gets in their way, it's him that's going to cop it and not the dog."

"Exactly." Kovacs failed to mention that he had secretly asked Mauritz to make a more detailed examination of the broken Stanley knife blade which was stuck in the neck of Reithbauer's fat dog, and that, besides tons of canine blood and hairs from a collie cross, Mauritz had found a single dark-green wool fibre. Nothing was official, as the killing of animals came under the banner of criminal damage; the criminal police were only brought in to deal with exceptional cases. Eyltz, the police chief, took such issues of demarcation very seriously on the whole.

They spoke a little more about Ernst Maywald, his body strength and his large hands, the strained relationship with his father-in-law, and about what role his function as employee representative and socialist union worker in the woodworking factory may have played in this. In interviews the family had never tried to hide the fact there had been conflict between the two; Georg, in particular, was quite willing to talk about how his father and his grandfather had rowed. They would argue, for example, about how the roof of the house should be retiled or about the right time for cutting trees. But it had never even got close to the point that he might be induced to murder the old man. "It's best to cut Christmas trees at full moon," Demski said. "That's when they stay fresh the longest."

"At least that's what the Christmas tree sellers say." Kovacs thought of the tiny fir tree with the three silver baubles and ten strands of lametta which had stood on Wilfert's chest of drawers, and he imagined that Yvonne and Charlotte had recently bought a plastic tree which they would take down on 6 January and pack away into a box to prevent it getting dusty.

There was black ice on Severin bridge. Demski took care to reduce his speed. "According to the weather forecast it should be getting warmer soon," he said.

"I can't feel anything yet," Kovacs said.

Konrad Gasselik's bronze-coloured Range Rover stood between other vehicles in the car park. A man in green overalls with neon-yellow stripes was chipping old snow from the asphalt surface. In most of the windows of the residential block the curtains were still closed. "They're saving electricity," Demski said, pointing to the street lamps. Only half of the halogen lights were on. The mental alertness which switches on automatically at the crucial moment. Kovacs took a sideways glance at Demski: a muddy-coloured raw leather jacket with fur collar, freshly ironed trousers, regulation haircut: short as always. In spite of everything Demski would succeed him one day.

"Why are you grinning like that?" Demski said.

"I was thinking about the tin duck you left in the back of the car," Kovacs said. Demski winked and said nothing. It was impossible to see whether he was blushing.

Manuela Gasselik opened the door. She was wearing a light-blue dressing gown, a fringed white cotton cloth was looped tightly around her neck, and her hair was tied in a loose bundle. A slight look of horror flickered across her face, then she relaxed again. "I know you," she said, smiling. Kovacs nodded and offered her his hand. "He's in his room," she said.

The hall smelled of cigarette smoke. A large heap of coats and winter jackets was hanging on the coat rack. Music floated in from the radio in the kitchen. Through the open door he could see a blond boy sitting at the table eating cornflakes. For a second he was confused. "Björn, his brother," Manuela Gasselik said. The boy raised his head for a moment and gazed into space.

They stopped in front of the third door along the long corridor. She grasped the door handle. Kovacs took her arm. "Where's your husband?" he asked softly. She looked up and shrugged.

"I don't know. He might be off with a customer. Do you need him?"

He hesitated for a second. "Perhaps later," he said, then thought, why do I have the feeling that I need the husband? He glanced at Demski. He looked as tense as a bowstring.

Daniel Gasselik was sitting at his desk with his back to the door. He lifted his fingers from the computer keyboard, reached for his neck, pulled the hood of his dark-grey sweatshirt over his head, and turned around slowly. He was grinning. Nobody said a word.

"How's your son, Herr Demski?" Even the voice was still clear and scratchy like that of a thirteen-year-old.

"Why are you missing your probation appointments?"

"He's starting school in autumn, isn't he?"

"I don't know what that's got to do with you."

"I'm just interested. I mean, you're interested in my probation."

"So?"

"Grimm's an incompetent arse."

"How could you know that?"

"Would you let Grimm look after you?"

Kovacs started feeling edgy. Demski's got to learn to avoid falling into these traps. "I'm sure you know these interrogation games," he said to Gasselik. "In real life they're just as you see on television: where were you on this occasion? Who's your witness? So, can you remember where you were late on the evening of 26 December?"

"Here."

"What does that mean?"

"Here, in this room."

"You were alone, I assume."

"No, my brother was with me."

"What were you doing?"

"Playing. As usual."

"So how can you be so sure that you were here?"

Gasselik closed his eyes and made the sign of someone's throat being slit. "That was the night the old man was killed, wasn't it?"

Kovacs said nothing. Lost in a dream, he thought. When Gasselik closed his eyes that was the phrase that came to mind. Demski folded his arms tightly, clenching his fists in his armpits. In the paper it had said that first the man's throat was slit, and then his skull was mashed to a pulp. Was that right? Kovacs stared past the grey hood and over to the computer. The screen saver had started up. Three heads from *Star Wars* which appeared and vanished one after another: Darth Maul, the Emperor and Darth Vader. As soon as he'd read it he'd wondered what it would feel like to mash a skull to a pulp, what it would feel like in your hands when you let the hammer go and the bones offered resistance for a split second before giving way. He'd imagined it again and again – it must be a hundred times now – looking down at the blood continuing to spurt out of the cut in the throat; the forehead or the right half of the face already dented. You'd then get the urge to have another crack, and then a third and fourth one, until there was nothing recognisable of the original face.

"The best thing is the noise," Gasselik said. "Do you know what it sounds like when a bone breaks? Do you know how it gets right inside you? You can't ever forget it."

Kovacs thought of the light sabre in the *Star Wars* films, of Yoda's mini light sabre and the scene in which Darth Maul, cut in two by a single stroke from Obi-Wan Kenobi, topples into that bottomless shaft.

"Are animal bones the same as human ones?" Demski asked. Gasselik looked shocked, then he laughed out loud.

"Geese, cats, dogs, hamsters – I'm afraid that wasn't me either," he said.

"Are you sure?"

"Absolutely."

"Who then?"

"Who's the police here, me or you? Anyway, all that comes

under criminal damage as far as you're concerned, even in the worst instances."

"Who, do you think, could do something like that?" Kovacs asked. Gasselik cracked his two middle fingers. Then he pushed his fingers under his thighs. "Some psycho," he said. "Someone who hears voices or acts on the instructions of a higher power."

Kovacs thought of the Apulian decapitator and his image of Lefti's cousin with a belt of explosives around his body. He felt pretty stupid. Which of us isn't a psycho? he thought, and turned to go. "Have you got any woollen gloves?" he asked from the doorway. Gasselik thought for a moment. "Yes, I have," he said.

"How many pairs?"

"One pair of mittens. One pair of gloves – the kind with removable fingertips."

"What colour?"

"The mittens are grey, the gloves reddish-brown."

"Excellent. Thank you."

There was a blank look on Demski's face. Kovacs pulled him out into the corridor and closed the door. "I'll tell you in the car," he said.

Manuela Gasselik was sitting in the kitchen, flicking through a magazine and smoking a cigarette. When she saw Kovacs and Demski coming, she stubbed it out, tied the white cloth around her neck, and stood up.

"Did he talk?" she asked.

"He did," Kovacs said. There was a glint in the woman's eyes. He felt sorry for her. "Can your son drive?" he asked.

She laughed. "That's the one thing my husband taught him. When he was ten."

"How often does he drive?"

"Haven't a clue. He takes a car out of the car park and drives around. Just like that. Nobody checks on him." She couldn't care

226

less, Kovacs thought. The further away he drives the happier she is.

The street lights were now switched off. The sky above the assembly hall was blue with a touch of orange. The man in the green overalls was shovelling lumps of ice onto a small lorry. He quietly cursed to himself and kicked the back wheel several times.

Kovacs sat in the car, reached behind, and got Demski's tin duck from the back seat. He put it on top of the dashboard and let it hop along the windscreen. Desmki was baffled.

"What are you doing?" he asked.

"I'm talking to it," Kovacs said.

"And what's it saying?"

Kovacs stared for a moment at its blind eye. Then he returned it to the back seat.

"It wasn't him," he said.

Wieck was shrieking as she stomped up and down the meeting room. Lipp stood by the wall looking at a loss, and Bitterle sat motionless at the table, her hands clasping a teacup. Kovacs unzipped his coat. "What happened?" he asked. As she passed the board, Wieck grabbed the sponge and hurled it across the room. "Now I *am* worried," Kovacs said. He stepped over to the desk, poured himself a coffee, and waited.

"We were in Bergheimstraße, as planned," Lipp said.

Wieck went over to Kovacs, leaned on the table, and shouted, "And then this sleazy sod is grinning at us, saying, 'Do you really believe I could do anything to my daughter?' And you say, 'Yes, I do.' And he keeps on grinning and says, 'But look at me – I'm mentally ill. Even if I were capable of it, there's nothing I can do about it!'" Kovacs' mind wandered as he stirred sugar into his coffee. He thought how nice it was to tramp through the snow with Wieck, and how wonderfully she fumed when she was angry.

"You were at the Schmidingers' then?" he asked.

Lipp nodded.

"If I remember rightly," Kovacs said, "that was not what we'd planned."

Lipp gave a swift reply. He said they'd thought it might well be useful to take the opportunity to speak to the girl's mother. He had phoned the woman beforehand and she said, yes, she was indeed alone; her husband was at the hospital with their daughter. Nobody could have known that he would be standing there at the door. Wieck sat down, reached for a napkin, and wiped her eyes.

"In fact it made no difference," she said.

"What made no difference?" Kovacs said.

"Whether he was there or not."

"I don't understand."

They had started with the neighbouring house on the left, Wieck explained, forcing out of bed a young railway official who had just gone to sleep after his night shift. So the man was in a pretty bad mood. Yes, he did have a wife, he said; and no, he certainly didn't have a dog. He could provide a four-year-old son who was at kindergarten at the moment, if that would help. He said he had never seen the letter she was holding in front of him, and he could not imagine that his wife would have written it, even though there was no doubt that Norbert Schmidinger was a mentally deranged individual. What did he mean by "mentally deranged"? they asked the man. He said, "He stands on the balcony with his binoculars, looks into every window he can see, and if he gets randy enough he whips out his cock and has a wank. That's what I mean by 'mentally deranged'." That is what the man had said, after which he apologised for having used that sort of language in front of a woman.

Bitterle raised her head. "Do you really believe he does that?" she asked. "I mean, so publicly."

"I've no idea what that arsehole gets up to," Wieck said.

Lipp tried to hide a smile by putting his cup in front of his face. Everybody looked at him.

"What is it?"

"Nothing."

"You're laughing?!"

"I was just trying to picture this endurance test – minus fifteen on the balcony . . . I'm sorry, it's very crude."

"Yes," Wieck said. "It *is* crude!"

If they want to stay in this job, Kovacs thought, they're going to have to keep on putting up with the crudeness of the erect male organ; and he thought that he would rather have a man who wanked publicly on his balcony than one who broke his child's legs, any day. Bitterle drew a penis on a piece of paper and then crossed it out. Wieck saw it and calmed down.

As soon as the door to the other neighbouring house opened, a small dog rushed at them through the front garden, she went on. It was yapping loudly; it must have been a dachshund cross. A woman, perhaps sixty, appeared at the door in a shocking flowery housecoat – Hannelore Iffenschmid, a former secondary-school teacher. "You saw her face, and the housecoat below it, and you knew at once that she'd deny everything," Lipp said.

Kovacs could remember how confused the woman had been, how shrill her voice had sounded, and how she had said she was calling from a phone box because she did not want to be identified. He thought that this specific combination of naivety and timidity was characteristic of the country as a whole, in particular of certain groups of people such as teachers, police chiefs or leading politicians.

No sooner had the woman let them into her hall, Wieck said, than she had indeed embarked on a comprehensive and consistent denial of everything: no telephone call, no letter, no girl's legs being battered against a metal pole. "She'd even have loved to deny she had a dog," said Lipp, but that would have been tricky, so instead she said that dachshund crosses were ten a penny, even in this town. At that point he had been unable to hold himself back. He said to her, "Perhaps not for much longer." This gave her one hell of a fright, and he asked her whether she read the papers. The dog, by the way, was called Augustus.

She's afraid that he'll stand on his balcony and look over at her through his binoculars, Kovacs thought. And she's afraid that he'll take out his thing which she probably doesn't even dare to give a name; but most of all she's afraid that he'll take her dog and batter him somewhere.

Bitterle asked whether the woman had made any comments about Schmidinger, and Wieck replied that she hadn't said anything apart from the fact that it was her principle not to poke her nose into how other people brought up their children. She had more important things to worry about, such as her garden, her dog and the house. The dog, meanwhile, had spent the whole time hopping against her lower leg – a quite asocial brute.

Wieck did not want to say anything more about Barbara Schmidinger; she found it so frustrating that this woman had just sat there with a vacant expression and, like the old cliché, repeated her husband's story: a dark-blue estate car, the bumper hitting a young pair of legs, driver vanishing, and in all the confusion nobody noting the registration number. But the eeriest thing of all, Wieck said, "was this appalling man suddenly standing there in the room. You could see from his demeanour, his tone of voice, and the expression on his face, just how certain he was that his wife had not given anything away."

Kovacs could picture the woman's straw-like hair, and how she spent the whole time cowering. Sometimes, he thought, the magnitude of a threat was the only significant benchmark in life. He felt miserable.

Wieck looked over at Lipp. "And then I made a mistake," she said. He could see the tears welling up in her eyes again. All of them were waiting. Demski scratched at the sugar at the bottom of his coffee cup. She said that she had persuaded Florian to drive to the hospital. She had gone to U14, the accident ward, presented her I.D., and said she had to ask Birgit Schmidinger something. The ward sister was hesitant, saying she did not know if that was a good idea. Her father had just been in, and that had caused her considerable anxiety. In the end, however, they had let Wieck in.

The little girl was lying in bed, and an older ward sister was reading to her from a book. Everything seemed very peaceful until she said that the two of them were from the police. The girl's eyes burst open wide and the whole of her body started to tremble. Wieck could not think of a sensible way to calm the situation. The sister motioned for her to leave, but for some idiotic reason she asked, "Does your mum have something in the garden that she hangs the washing on?" At this the child started howling pitifully, clawing into the blanket with her fingers, while repeating the same single sentence over and over again: "It was a blue car. I'm sure it was a blue car." Wieck stood there, feeling guilty and angry at the same time, and was clueless as to what to do until a tall, lean doctor arrived – the psychiatrist as she later found out – and sent her out.

"'A blue car,' she said. 'It was a blue car.' She's five years old. Five!" Wieck was sobbing.

Kovacs grabbed his coat and got up. "I've just got to pop out for a bit," he said. As the others gave him puzzled looks, he added, "To organise something."

As he was going down the stairs he thought of Marlene, who had recently said that this job was absolute hell and that it was irresponsible to let young people do it. He also thought of Gasselik with the ugly red and black face of Darth Maul right behind him, and of Norbert Schmidinger stepping onto the balcony with his binoculars. Finally he thought of "Sheriff" who knew people that would do anything you asked them to, given a small amount of cash and a few assurances.

Outside the main entrance Mauritz heaved himself out of his silver Renault and waved Kovacs over. "I've been out of town again, trying to bring this beehive disaster to a conclusion," he said. "And I talked to Christoph Moser, the young farmer who discovered it all. He claims to have seen someone in the wood that morning. It doesn't really fit with what we've got, but he insists he's right."

The picture appeared in Kovacs' mind of walking that day through the winter larch forest, along the tyre tracks, and how they had chatted in a relaxed way; and yet he also remembered the vivid impression that something was unresolved, but he could not tell what.

"Did Moser recognise the person he saw in the wood?"

Mauritz nodded. "Yes, but he didn't think very much of it, he said."

"And?"

Mauritz closed the car door behind him. He took off his right glove before starting to talk. It looked a bit funny.

TWENTY

There they are. They're crossing the car park. There are two of them, and maybe they'll take him with them. Just like before. It won't do them any good. At some point he will conquer them. Perhaps now, perhaps in the next star age, perhaps in the one after that. He is the Emperor. I know that he's got all the time in the world.

I don't eat my cornflakes any quicker than usual. They ask about my dad. He's gone somewhere, Mum says. Actually he's over in the office. They all go down to Daniel's room. Mum comes back and lights a cigarette. I hate it, but she doesn't care. She doesn't care about Daniel, either. Luke Skywalker and his sister, Leia, get adoptive parents when their mother dies. My mum hasn't got a clue who Luke Skywalker is.

Through the wall I can hear them talking quite calmly. The interrogations that start calmly are the most dangerous ones, Daniel says. At they end they do you in. I check my rucksack: the mask, the warhammer, the new Stanley knife – the big one from the set of three – the school things, the cloak. I reach under the mattress and pull out the thing that Daniel uses to show me what it's like inside. At the front it's made of silver and it's black at the back. It looks a little bit like Yoda's light sabre. Nobody must find it. I stuff it in with the other things.

The coat, the boots, the cap. When I put the mitten over my right hand it hurts, even though I smeared four different creams over the hole under the plaster. Had I been bitten by a pit bull rather than a collie cross, my hand wouldn't be there any more, Daniel says. It was a sign from the dark side of the Force, he says, and if I kill a pit bull next he'll make me his deputy. I don't know how long it'll be before I'm able to do a pit bull, but Daniel says that I've got time and that I should study him. Konrad Seihs, the fascist bastard, has got a pit bull, Daniel says. He lives in Linzer Straße, left at the second crossroads, fourth house. That's a task for later, he says.

Mum never hears us when we go out. She's either still lying in bed or she's sitting somewhere smoking a cigarette. Daniel says she's a good-for-nothing bitch. I'm not sure that's true. Sometimes I don't believe my mum thinks very much. That means it's not so tragic that she couldn't give a toss about us. At the moment she's got B.H. around her neck. I don't know how that happened. Daniel says it's nothing. Anakin Skywalker's mum dies in Episode II. He also gets by without her. Anakin doesn't have a dad. He's never missed him. Yet he became Darth Vader.

The bald bus driver. In winter he wears this woolly hat which fits the back of his head exactly, like a lid. He's alright. Sometimes you get people who you feel do their job and could never be unfriendly, like R2-D2. At some point they simply burn out, then it's too late. That's the disadvantage.

The bastard is sitting in the row just behind the driver; Markus is next to him. Markus isn't a problem, he never says anything. The bastard talks incessantly. Homework and *Who Wants to be a Millionaire?* and *Need for Speed Underground*, all the usual stuff. I tell him I got up late and look away. That doesn't change anything. He gives off bad vibes.

In the passage to the first courtyard a short corridor branches off to the right. Actually it's the back entrance to the abbey pharmacy. A few metres along is a recess with three blue dustbins.

I crouch behind them and wait. I think about the fact that on Hoth you can dig yourself snow holes anywhere. Nobody would find you in one of those, no wampa, no Jedi, not even Yoda. The church clock rings out four bright chimes and eight muted ones. I count up to one hundred, then I make a move. I've got a mission.

Leo always comes by bike. He lives nearby and the tyres of his B.M.X. are so wide that they also work on snow. The number of his chain lock is 1407, his birthday. That's stupid, but everybody does it. I open the quick release and put the saddle a little lower before I sit on the bike.

Daniel smacked me, then again, and said that I was to stick to my tasks. Then he pressed my face against the newspaper article, and I said I didn't do it. He said if I was lying he'd fuck me up the arse, exactly like they do inside, and then he said that there was a strange power at work.

From the time we were all there, the whole class, I can remember that the path begins by the road behind the ochre hall of the woodworking factory. All the primary school kids go there at some time, and you get a detailed explanation all about the pollen and the back legs and the queen, and at the end you get a small jar with a sample to try.

The surface has been cleared of snow up to just beyond the last house. After that it gets hard. There are two deep tyre tracks and I cycle in the right-hand one. I stand on the pedals and try to get a proper rhythm going, but it's so bumpy that every few metres I have to put a foot on the ground. After the first bend the path is covered in a whole pile of snow, perhaps from a small avalanche, or maybe it's been shovelled there. I lean the bike on the side. I don't lock it. Nobody comes here. I climb up the mound of snow. At the top I throw the cloak around me and put the mask on. I push it over my forehead to the top of my head. Then I continue on foot, in the right tyre track as before. I imagine I'm sitting on top of a tauntaun and just have to give it orders. It runs forward at high speed and it doesn't have any problems with even the steepest climbs. I wonder about various things, like how quickly the bees froze to death when their hives were destroyed, whether some of them flew on another five metres or even to the trees at the edge of the wood, and whether it was possible to do it all in the same way as the stuff with the ducks and cats – with a warhammer and a lot of force. And I also wonder whether in the meantime they've been badgering Daniel with a damp towel, or using various psycho-tricks, and whether they've threatened him with sleep deprivation or solitary confinement. All I know is that he won't have said anything, not a single word.

There are eleven bends in all, before it flattens out. Another thing I learned from Daniel was this: life is safer if you count. I put the mask over my face. I start breathing like Darth Vader. There's no more undergrowth, the trees are not as dense any more, and after two or three hillocks you've got an open view of the clearing.

I stand there and I know that something is very wrong. I can remember it all in much detail. We see a pair of great spotted woodpeckers spiralling up the trunk of a pine tree; Frau Zelsacher, our teacher, has bags of fruit gums; Dorothea Schaupp falls over and cuts her knee, and someone picks her up and carries her the last little bit to the place where the meadow is in summer. I can remember exactly the brightly coloured beehives, and even that the first hive in the bottom row is painted dark-red, and I also remember the old black barn behind on the right. Everything is exactly as it was before. But that's not right at all.

I noted that it said "a picture of destruction" in the newspaper, and it also said that sixteen beehives were demolished. Here there are twenty-two hives lined up: twelve in the bottom row and ten in the upper one. All of them are fine. I walk slowly past the wood-shed. Nothing has been destroyed, absolutely nothing. There's perhaps thirty centimetres of snow on top of the shed roof. At one end somebody wiped away the snow; who knows why?

I'm going to go straight home on Leo's bike. I'll go to Daniel's room and tell him, "There is no strange power, it was all a big mistake." Then I'll look at him and ask how he did it with the old man, what car he used, what tool, and when he did it, seeing that he spent the whole evening in his room with me.

I cross the open space to get back to the tyre tracks. They lead straight up to the black barn.

There is no lock on the barn door, just a wooden handle. I turn it and open the right door a tiny bit. At first I can't see anything, but then I can make out something.

TWENTY-ONE

There are twelve people in the staffroom. Now there are thirteen; Verena Steinmetz has just come in. She is carrying her red briefcase as if she were a lawyer in an American film. There is nothing on her desk. Brandhuber's place is next to hers. On his desk is a fourth form "textus", a copy of Virgil's *Aeneid*, Livy's *Ab urbe condita*, and twenty-seven exercise books from the sixth year. Brandhuber is not there yet. He does not start teaching until second period. The phosphorous tube to the right above the door is flickering. That is new. On Altmann's desk there is a copy of *Autorevue*, half an apple, an unopened chocolate bar and a trial copy of Mistlbacher's new mathematics book for juniors. Altmann is standing next to Krivanel and laughing.

A dense web of gridlines is hanging in the room. He has been here for two and a half hours, spinning these threads back and forth, back and forth, between objects and heads and tiny trivialities. Nobody else has noticed it yet. It is no longer remarkable that he is the first one. He is always the first one. He is going to throw himself into this web. It will hold him. Sylvia Ruthner looks at him. He looks away. She is a bad woman.

Call things by their names. Take them for what they are. An exercise book is an exercise book. A bad woman is a bad woman.

Right at the bottom of the pile on his desk, a laminated sheet of paper with the Rule, A3, printed in small type on the front and back. He has underlined three sentences with a marker pen:

The time has come to rise from sleep.
Run, so that the shadow of death does not vanquish you.
The talkative man is not stable on the earth.

On top of that, his papers. First period, maths with the seventh year; second period, maths with the first year; third period, religious education with the sixth year; fourth period, free; fifth period, religious education with the first year. Textbooks, exercise books, notepads. Four small piles next to each other. Sometimes life consists of threads and piles.

Freyler asks him how he is. He says fine, thank you. Freyler puts the model of a human eye on his desk. He is a nice man, but sometimes what he does creates a peculiar atmosphere.

The time has come to rise from sleep.

Earlier he had been thinking about the woman and the child, about how often she goes to the hairdresser, and whether she has a little colour put in her hair from time to time. Now he thinks that in a few years the child will be learning about the sensory organs, and that perhaps he will have a teacher who brings ox eyes into the classroom, and then he will raise his hand and say, yes, I'd like to cut one out, too.

He takes the pile on the left and waits. Around him people are heading for the door. Seventh year. The first discussions about curves. The astonishment of some pupils that it always works: you set the first derivative to zero and you get the high point and low point.

Out into the school hall with the others, into the stairwell, up to the second floor. He goes along the corridor.

Through the large arched window one can see the car park down in the first courtyard. Altmann's Espace, Steinmetz's turquoise-coloured Peugeot. Keindl is getting out of his old Mercedes. He often arrives late. Someone is coming over from the main entrance. The headband, the rucksack, the small figure.

Björn. He goes straight over to the bike racks and tampers around with something.

He can see him standing at the back of the church and between the cypresses in the cemetery. He can hear him saying, "Daniel's back."

The web is now getting tense. Here and there a thread snaps.

He puts the small pile on the floor by the window and turns around.

Run.

Back along the corridor, down the stairs, right to the gate. He sees the rucksack disappearing in the archway. He breathes in air through his nose. It has got a touch warmer. Right across the courtyard. He is running.

I'll walk to the depths of the deepest black forest.

Clemens has forbidden him from bringing his iPod into school. He has threatened to bar him from teaching if he refuses to obey. At the moment he is not really fussed by this. He still gets his music in his ears. All he has to do is to reduce his quetiapine dosage again. Otherwise everything goes quiet and empty.

A short way along Stiftsallee, then straight over the railway and left into Grafenaustraße. Björn seems to be in a hurry. He can see that it is not his own bike.

Something feels wrong. The trousers, the warm jumper, most of all the shoes.

I saw guns and sharp swords in the hands of young children.

The blocks on the estate, then the three halls of the woodworking factory, the smaller olive-green one, the larger olive-green one, the ochre one. On the extension of Grafenaustraße is a group of old peasant barns; behind them the forest begins.

Björn takes the right of the two tyre ruts. He stands on the pedals and looks like he is struggling. This is because the tracks are coarse. The snow is still hard and cold.

He is now running quite slowly. In some parts his soles still slip, however.

At a point where the path is laden with snow, Björn gets off the bike and puts it to the side. He climbs onto the mound of snow which is right across the path and continues on foot. He does not turn round. He looks hectic.

He can see Björn standing in the cemetery, between the second and third cypresses on the right. When the old man is under the ground and everybody has left the cemetery, he approaches the north wall. Björn does not run away. He asks him what's wrong and Björn replies that there's nothing wrong, apart from the fact that Daniel's back. He's the Emperor of all beings, and he talks about a number of things you can learn from. One of the things he says is that, inside, everything is relative. For example, it's much better to be fucked up the arse by a bit of metal or rubber than for them to do it with their own cocks. It's the sort of thing you don't know beforehand.

Where black is the color, where none is the number.

The bike belongs to Leo. He had it when they did their last school outing.

He climbs the heap of snow. Perhaps his son has also got a bike like that, spanking blue, or silver with a reddish-brown fox on it. Stabilisers – you still need them when you are five.

The tyre tracks continue on the other side.

There will come a time when he will take off the stabilisers for him, hold the back of his saddle, run a few steps alongside, and then he will let go and he will ride a short way on his own and be totally amazed.

Björn speedily climbs the snaking bends which make up this goods track. He has put something around his shoulders which from a distance looks like a black coat.

He leaves a distance of one and a half bends. He takes medium paces. Turning to the side he has a view over the whole town. A vertical column of smoke is still rising from the chimney of the woodworking factory. Sometimes he can know the exact moment when the weather is going to take a turn. On those occasions it is like looking at the clearest sky imaginable, and then, when one takes a second look, everything has a yellow tinge.

There are eleven bends in all. Afterwards the slope evens out, and the path runs in a flat arc to the south-west. The trunks of the larches and pine trees are separated. The sun sends shimmering triangles of light into the forest.

Björn leaves the tracks and goes over to the beehives in somebody else's old footprints. He paces out the row, as if he needs to check something. He stops at the end of the row and rests his hand on the shed roof for a second. He turns through ninety degrees, returns to the tracks, and approaches the barn slowly. He is wearing a Darth Vader costume; that is easy to see now.

Where black is the color, where none is the number.

The overhang of the barn roof is bowing substantially in the middle. At several points the layer shingle has recently been re-done.

Björn steps up to the barn door and examines it. After some time, he shifts the latch and pushes it up a little way with both hands.

He gets closer with definite, equal steps. Björn does not turn round, even though he must be able to hear him coming.

He stands next to him, and the two of them peer inside the barn. He cannot make it out properly. Something like the arm of a crane is looming towards them from the darkness. Right at the top something black and threatening is clinging there. Björn has the Darth Vader mask in front of his face and is snorting.

Oh, who did you meet, my blue-eyed son?

He opens the door the whole way. Now it all becomes clearer. In the barn there is an old tow truck. Spots of yellow paint here and there, worn tyres with a coarse tread. On the platform behind is a swivel arm, at the bottom of it a steel winch, at the top the pulley. Directly underneath this, about one and a half metres above their heads, a medium-sized anvil is hanging from a strong, welded loop. As if it had come straight from the blacksmith, he thinks.

It's going to get warmer soon, he thinks. The Föhn will blow for a few hours, and then we'll start sinking in the snow. Then the rain will arrive like a grey wall.

TWENTY-TWO

I killed him.

It's quite easy. You go a step behind him, grab his hair with your left hand, bend his head back and make the cut with the right. You need a sharp tool, like a Stanley knife. But not one with a snap-off blade, or the whole thing will go pear-shaped. If you get the carotid artery, he'll be unconscious a few seconds later. You put him down just as you want him, then drive the tow truck over him so that the length of his body is between the two rear tyres. You align the anvil – you might have to push it forward or back a bit – hoist the thing up to the pulley, and let go of the catch on the winch. The anvil falls three and a half metres onto his face. You've got what you wanted.

I realise that the vehicle will be found sooner or later, and also that the little girl might have recognised my voice, as most of the primary schoolchildren in the town have heard it. I hadn't planned on losing a button from my sleeve in the process, but there's nothing I could have done about it.

As I said, doing it was easy. The period before was the hard part.

Afterwards I felt tired, nothing else.

There are those phrases you unquestioningly use as a guide in life, which then turn out to be utter nonsense, such as "Time heals all wounds." Quite the opposite is true. Time heals nothing at all, and sometimes it's just a few seconds that determine your whole life. To the end.

Imagine, for example, that I've got a brother. Imagine we're pretty close in age, and for both of us the other one is a bit like our other half. On one occasion, when I'm livid, I clobber him over the head with the meat grinder, and on another he yanks the neighbour's aggressive Alsatian away from me with his bare hands, even though he's already got me by the throat. Imagine I repeat a year, or even two, so I can have him sitting next to me, and it's to stay like that till we finish school. We wear the same clothes, read the same books and we sleep side by side. We're never apart save for the two weeks I have to spend in hospital with appendicitis. Afterwards he reproaches me and says that if I hadn't eaten so many cherry stones it wouldn't have happened.

It doesn't really matter where or when it happens. It could have been yesterday, or four weeks ago, or sixty years ago. It might have taken place in Furth, in Salzburg, or on the edge of the Thüringer Wald, in a village between Eisenach and Meiningen, on a low hill above the Werra. A few are people there, including *him*, my brother and me, and someone else who's called something like Dorner or Strolz or Zillinger. Let's say *he* goes into the first house, yelling all over the place, banging the table and demanding board and lodging. Because there's nothing there *he* marches the entire family outside – husband, wife and two daughters – and then *he* asks whether there is anybody else in the house, and the woman says yes, their son, but he can't walk. *He* asks where he is, and the woman says upstairs, and *he* forces her to go up with us. We find the son in a small room. He sits tied with a sheet to an armchair, and the woman says the wheelchair is broken. On the table in front of him the son has an unruled exercised book, next to it a flat wooden box with coloured pencils. It looks like he's loosened the pages one by one out of the exercise book, and he's made them into flags: the German one, the British one, the Italian one, the

French one. He's in the middle of colouring the area around the stars of the American flag blue. *He* picks up the flag drawings and gives the order: everything downstairs. We untie the son and I carry him down the stairs; he's quite light. Downstairs *he* puts the flags on the kitchen table, asks how old the son is, and the mother says fifteen, even if he doesn't look it, but that's because he's disabled. Then *he* says quite calmly that there is an order from Mansteuffel stipulating that every male over the age of fourteen living in a house displaying a white flag is to be shot, without exception. As *he* finds the British, French and American flags much more abhorrent than the cowardly white one, then there's no question that order will have to be carried out. My brother says you can't do that, and *he* says just see if I can't, I've got an order, only we won't actually shoot them. There's a stable with places for two horses, and above that a small hayloft. At the front a beam runs right across the room. *He* himself kicks the stool from under the husband. He hardly writhes. The son is cowering on the ground, his head between his crippled knees. *He* goes up to my brother and says, you lift him up and put him in the noose, that's an order, and my brother asks, what happens if I refuse? I say to *him*, you can't do that, and *he* takes his pistol, aims it at me and says to my brother, I'll shoot him first and then you. My brother puts the son in the noose and he hardly writhes either. I'm staring into *his* face the whole time, and it takes just a few seconds to engrave itself on my memory like nothing else in the world.

Imagine my brother then shoots himself, perhaps straight away, perhaps a year later. For a long time I think of doing it, too. Now I'm only half.

I can see the face in my mind. I always know where it is. In the end I follow it. I'm going to obliterate it.

*

He doesn't recognise me any more. For him I'm a stranger with a black bag. That gives me all the time in the world.

Don't look for us. You won't find us. What for, anyway?

The only thing I'm sorry about is the beehive business. It was totally pointless, and I didn't mean it to hurt anybody but me. As the end approaches some people lash out a bit around them.

By the way, do you know how bees overwinter? They go right to the middle of the hive, pack themselves together very tight, and don't stop moving.

TWENTY-THREE

The triumphal march from *Aida*. A second, and then a third time. It took Kovacs a while before he cottoned on. He put the beer glass on the table and rummaged around in his jacket pocket. Finally he found the thing. He flipped it open. It was Horn.

"You mean she talked?"

"Just by the way?"

"A single word, you say?"

"A noun with the definite article?"

"Say it again, I don't understand."

"Are you quite sure?"

"Yes, I get what she said: 'The honeyman.'"

He hung up. After a while he reached for the glass and ran a fingertip along a trace of froth. It had not frozen.

The light over the lake had a yellow tinge to it. He sat there and waited for the wind.